WAIT FOR THE WAGON

WAIT FOR THE
WAGON

RICHARD NETTELL

UNITED WRITERS
Cornwall

UNITED WRITERS PUBLICATIONS LTD
Ailsa, Castle Gate, Penzance, Cornwall.
www.unitedwriters.co.uk

British Library Cataloguing in Publication Data:
A catalogue record for this book is
available from the British Library.

ISBN 9781852002206

First published in 1939.

Printed and bound in Great Britain by
United Writers Publications Ltd.,
Cornwall.

For
Todd and Barney Joel.

Chapter One

THREE seamen were coming up Chywoon Lane from the Helston turnpike. Their footsteps had reached the man working in the hayfield, warning him of the approach of strangers, and he was watching covertly as he gathered odd wisps on his prong. There was no love between coast men and the Navy.

"Get down, Joel son, 'mong the hay," he called over his shoulder to the boy on the wagon.

Most likely it was a runaway they were looking for, although if it was trouble they would find it among the tinners. Then he remembered that since the affair at Boscrege – when more than one member of the press-gang had been flung down Old Shaft and left to drown among the shrieking bats – it was said the Navy was trying new tactics, sending small parties to snatch a man here and there. For a crowd of angry miners could be ugly enough to make even the militia chary of interfering. He moved back a pace or two so as to put a tree between him and the lane, but the very movement seemed to draw the attention he wished to avoid; the footsteps ceased and he judged that they had seen him.

"Ahoy," a coarse voice shouted. "Ahoya, there."

Undisturbed, he gathered a bit of nearby hay on the prong; in doing so he moved out from the shelter of the tree and saw the apparent leader and one other were climbing the hedge while the third remained on the road. Their haste displaced several of the top stones, which fell with a clatter to the ground.

"Look now, what thee'st done. There's a hurdle in gap further up, if 'ee feel thee'st got to get into the field, use that. I reck'n we've more to do all day than mend hedges after 'ee."

"You're speaking to a bo'sun of the King's Navy, so keep a civil tongue in your head."

"No Andrewartha'll keep a civil tongue while your kind is treading his land."

The bo'sun crossed over the field and leaned, with his arms folded, against the tree trunk. "We're after a deserter, name of Thomas Trickett, and we've good reason to believe he's being sheltered in this neighbourhood."

"Most likely he is."

"You know where? You've seen him?"

Slowly Andrewartha gathered up the hay, then leaning again on the pitch-fork said, "And what if I have?"

"You'll tell us. Under King's Regulations it is a crime to help or harbour any deserter from the Navy and meets with heavy penalties, as you know very well."

He laughed. "King's Regulations or no, if a hungry dog were to beg food and shelter in these parts he'd get it; we've heard tell plenty of your stinking craft and rotten tack. If thee'st a mind to find your man you'll need to be about the job, for you'll have far to go and a pretty bit of searching to do, I reck'n."

The bo'sun winked knowingly at his fellow and straightened himself.

"Perhaps you're right, my cockerel; but d'you know this – so long as I take a man back with me I'm not caring whether his name is Trickett or not. And there's this, too; you'd make a better sailor than that other lubber. Now, how would you like to serve the King? Answer that?"

So they were out for trouble; then by St. Germoe, they'd get it if they bothered him. His eye, trained in his work to judge striking distance, was keeping mark of that between them, and he noticed too, out of the corner, that the seaman was shifting his position, working around to get behind him.

"Serve in the King's tubs? Not me. Why, there's none of 'em can sail within three points of a Porthleven lugger, nor a Cornish fisher, but couldn't spew something better than you tow-haired barnacles that call yourselves. . ."

The bo'sun was moving forward, threatening, "I'll press you, you Cornish cocky; and till I get you tied to the yard, shut your mouth."

Peeping through the hay up on the wagon, young Joel saw that his father was about to be attacked. But Andrewartha had been preparing for just such a situation; he sensed the man approaching from behind even while his attention was on the bo'sun.

"Meanwhile," he shouted as the fellow advanced on him, and, raising his prong, lunged forward aiming high. "This'll close yours."

The wad of hay caught the man full across the face and chest, and the two points, directed with the precision learned through pronging hundreds of loads up into outstretched hands, passed either side of his throat, and carried backwards with all the weight of the drive, pinned him fast to the tree, blind and stifled.

But the seaman was at him, on his back; indeed the force of his rush had lent thrust to the shaft and planted it deeper in the tree than Andrewartha's arms alone could have done, and that was no small depth. And worse still, the third was coming to his aid, was already halfway across the field. Leaving the ash shaft quivering in the air and the grasping, threshing hands of the pinned man clutching uselessly towards it around the truss of hay, Andrewartha lurched around with his arms held to his sides by a strong grip from behind, and rammed himself backwards with all his weight, catching his assailant between him and the tree. There was a gasp of pain as the fellow's shoulders crashed

9

on the bark; Joel saw the hold relax as he fell away and his father swung about, free to meet the third.

Just in time to dodge a vicious sweep from a drawn cutlass, he ran towards the wagon. The sailor followed, knowing well enough he had his man at a disadvantage, being unarmed as he was. But Andrewartha had his start, knew the ground and his objective, and in a second or two had reached it – the cart-whip. He snatched it up and turned with it already sweeping over his head. The long hissing lash snaked out, and jerked back as it found its mark; there was a yell of agony as a flaming red weal cut across the man's mouth. The whip flew out a second time; the lash curled tightly about the cutlass just above the hilt and was pulled up sharply. The weapon, slackly held for a moment in the face of such an unexpected and painful attack, dropped out of the man's grasp and fell away out of his reach. In a leap Andrewartha was between it and its owner, the whip circling.

But the seaman had taken all he wanted.

"Not that, mister," he whined. "We get enough o' that aboard. 'Ave a heart and know when to stop."

"Get across there," he roared, "and put up those stones on that hedge. Quick to it."

The lash curled out sharply and cracked under his buttock as the man hastened over to do as he was told. Joel's attention returned to the others; the bo'sun was still pinned to the tree, clutching handfuls of hay from his mouth, gasping for air through his seed-filled beard. The seaman was moaning on the ground, lying full on his face to take the weight of his body off his bruised shoulder blades. Andrewartha ignored him and grasped the prong shaft.

"If 'twasn't a brave prong and a shame to soil it, I'd pin your cowardly liver to tree and leave 'ee to rot. Let this lesson serve 'ee, and keep 'way from Breage and Germoe, and keep your mouth from insulting their men. Press me, would 'ee?"

He lifted his heavy nailed boot and placed it against the man's thigh. Bracing himself against it he pulled on the shaft, the boot taking all his weight and crushing the flesh under it against the hard tree trunk. His victim howled with the pain and as the withdrawn prong released him, fell forward and rolled on the ground nursing his bruised leg.

A glance around showed the third of his attackers almost out of sight; he had not stopped to mend the hedge but had made off while the man he had intended to carve was engaged with the others. Andrewartha turned on his heel and came over to the wagon, tested the ropes across the load, impaled the fork in the side where it would not fall out and led the horses off in the direction of home, with young Joel trotting beside him almost bursting with admiration and eagerness to tell his mother what had taken place.

Elizabeth was a Nancurvis, and Joel had often heard his father say that how she ever came to marry him, Richard Andrewartha, a farming miner, he never could make out. The truth was he was a fine-looking man, dark like all his family and handsome, and came from sound yeoman stock with a name as good as any in Cornwall. For Andrewartha is good old Cornish, the name of gentry in the strictest heraldic sense, as it is derived from the land possessed by the family; it signifies "the upper town" in Gwithian, which is now called Upton, and those living there carried the name. And he was a man to please any girl's heart, whether she was tinner's maid or daughter of landowners and mineral lords like her folk up at Tregonebris, Wendron way, with all their fine carriages and servants. Years ago, long before her time, they too owned a whole lot of land up Hayle way and in Gwithian, and often, when the wind blew from the south-west and the sea was trapped in Mount's Bay, she would tell the children of the terrible night when a storm swept the sea inland and covered all their fields in sand.

Although many of Elizabeth's tales dealt with storm and shipwreck, Joel was already old enough to realise that it was an ill wind that blew no good to the coast of Cornwall. Their hearth was kept warm with wreck-wood, and often when the tinners were out following a vessel that had been caught in the Bay, he would run with them down to that cruel shelving strip, the long foaming white line of Praa Sands. There, when she had struck and the tide had ebbed, they would swarm over her like ants, and pick her as clean. In that district of tin and copper it was another source of possible wealth; it was their benefit by shipwreck, an ancient right in their eyes, and had given rise to the couplets recalling the days when they had a local reputation for a heartless system of wrecking accompanied by a ferocity towards survivors unequalled on the coast.

> *God keep us from rocks and shelving sands,*
> *And save us from Breage and Germoe men's hands.*

In Church and Chapel ministers had even prayed, not for shipwrecks to happen, but for those that must happen to be brought to their coast, for the sake of the poor and needy. How often the prayers were answered:

"The Lord will provide," the minister would thunder from his pulpit. Joel remembered one time when he had been straining to make his sermon heard above the sound of the gale. " 'Take no thought for the morrow,' He says. 'What ye shall eat, what ye shall wear.' And how often has that come true for us, my friends. Not a year passes but He provides for us, his bountiful harvests and minerals from the land, fish and wreckage from the sea. This very gale will bring us beaches strewn with wood to warm us in the winter, the shore abounding in valuable timber for our building in the summer. 'Fear God, and all these shall be added to you.' "

As though to prove his word, the door had burst open and a drenched figure entered, snatched his cap from his head, and gasped breathlessly to a nearby member of the congregation.

"What's that? What's that you say?" the minister demanded, leaning forward out of his pulpit.

"The tinners are out following a barque down the coast, sir. Most like her'll be on Praa Sands by now. Joseph here says he can't see how her's held off for so long."

There was a rustling and scraping as the whole congregation rose to its feet, prepared to make a hurried but reverent exit in the race of this fresh evidence of the Lord's bounty. But the minister knew his authority, and when and where he could use it.

"Stop!"

He climbed down and passed between the ragged lines of people who had already left their seats. Right down to the porch, he hastened; standing there in his black cassock, he faced his flock.

"Now then. All start fair."

Away they went, out of chapel into the rough salt wind, down the path through the narrow stone gateway into the road, hurrying, scrambling, leaning in the face of the gale, staggering sideways against it, the children of the Bountiful Lord, led by His priest to:

Fetch hammer and saa,
And away to Praa.

Often, after a storm, Joel and his father would go with other men and dig graves in the sand-dunes above the tide mark, laying in them bodies that had come in from the sea. Andrewartha liked to line them with clean warm straw to keep the cold sand off their poor dead faces. Without any burial service read over them, the sand was filled in over those strangers in their last resting-place. Home from the sea, unmarked and unmourned save by the simple compassion of the men who had found them.

Joel had heard many tales of the past, when the wreckers had lent Providence a hand in bringing vessels to the coast. In his mind he connected the old, old sandstone cross in Breage Churchtown with that cruel past and it was always an object of awe to him. Sandstone he knew was soft, he could rub it away with his finger, and yet this

13

cross was hard. He was told by Matthew the shepherd exactly what had made it hard.

"Blood, Joel boy, blood. That's what's made un hard; they did take the stoan after it 'ad been shaped and holed, and soaked un in blood. Come it 'ad dried into stoan, 'twas hard; 'most as hard as granite."

"Was it men's blood, Matthew?"

"That I don't know, not just 'zactly. But maybe 'twas. Belike men's blood would be harder than poor dumb animals'. 'Es, I reck'n 'twas men's blood, Joel. Wrecked men's, sure 'nough."

The boy gasped in fearful, excited horror. "What a lot it must have taken."

The old man nodded. " 'Es, a tidy bit. There's been a lot of men wrecked in these parts, and in the old days blood spilled easier, so I've heard tell."

And each time he went to Breage Joel would gaze in fascination at the terrible cross hardened by such a fearful method, and once he even went so far as to enter the churchyard alone and suck the rough stone to find if it tasted of blood; but it was only sore on his lips and tongue and slightly briny from the flying spray carried inland by winter gales.

As Joel approached his tenth year, an argument rose more and more often between his parents; it was one of the very few rocks on which their joint opinion split.

"The Andrewarthas have been tinners for as long as I can mind," his father reiterated. "I'm a tinner myself and proud of it, and Joel'll be too."

"And what'll happen to him? The same as happens to you all," warned Elizabeth. "You start up at the mine at ten years old, and for the best years of life you're climbing ladders with your lungs bursting, so that at the top you spit blood; you're cramped sweating

14

in heat and bad air, then tramp home chilled to the marrow at ten o'clock on a winter's night. And if you aren't crushed or drowned, or haven't broken your neck down a shaft long afore, you leave work when you're barely thirty, a wreck of a man, and slowly die."

His father spat contemptuously. "That's only the worst side of it. If a man's lucky he'll make money; he may strike a rich lode any day and earn 'nough to keep him in ease and comfort all his life."

"You were at it a long time and did not even strike a middling kindly lode, leave alone a rich one, my dear. He's going to be a farmer."

"All right, he'll be a farmer; but he'll be a tinner first. Why, Elizabeth, 'tis a trade half as old as Cornwall."

"And what good has it brought her?" she asked. "There's no peace of mind where there's tin."

"No? Well see, for three thousand year the tinner's been waiting to strike a rich lode, and now's the time when he's 'bout to do it. Maybe tomorrow, maybe next week; any day it may happen. And young Joe's a-going to be one of the lucky tinners. Why, Solomon's temple was lined with tin from Ding-Dong and Levant; maybe the new Jerusalem'll be taking it from Great Work and Wheal Vor!"

Elizabeth sighed resignedly. "Take 'n' have your way, Richard."

In the early days of her married life she had soon grown to hate the mines. To have her own man going down those dark, black holes, sweating and toiling for long hours in extremes of discomfort, and often danger, by the feeble light of a guttering candle, was all so different from being the daughter of the mineral lord, enriched by that means. The mere thought of him down there had appalled her, a human mole drilling and blasting the rock, robbing nature's treasure house while depending on her for his safety; a morsel of flesh and bone and a drop of blood, and above it immeasurable weight of rock threatening to crush it into pulp. Neither did these fears pass with time, for she was not a tinner's daughter and so had not the training for a tinner's wife; she was without that queer fatalistic trust in God which carried them through, or stayed them when disaster came.

That was why, when her lawyer cousin, Duke Marrack, had at last persuaded her family to part with a dowry, she had insisted on her young husband using it all to set himself up with the whim teams of horses, contracting to haul up the barrels of tin-stuff to the surface instead of continuing to work at the lode. At six years old, Joel, their first born, had gone up to the mine with his father and started on his job. It was bedding clay up for the tinners' candles, each man needing a lump on the front of his hardened felt hat to act as holder for these, his only light below ground. A proper job it was, he thought, as good as playing at home with making pies. Later he had been set to fetch and carry the borers between the mine and the smithy where they were re-sharpened.

Work had strengthened and built up his young arms, so now at ten years old he was handed to Owen Kendell, who had in his time worked as a boy in the team made up between their fathers, and for the first time went down the shaft. Owen went first and made Joel descend rung by rung just above him, so that if he should lose his nerve it would be easy to press him against the ladder until he regained it. They had to keep eyes and ears alert for the barrel when it came bumping and banging on its way up or down the shaft, and often flatten themselves against the side as it passed. The descent to their level took about twenty minutes, but if going down was bad it was nothing to the climb up to grass at the end of the day's work; the pull on the arms and legs was terrible and the changing pressure of air strained the lungs. Although it was a point of honour among the younger miners never to give way to one another, Joel found at first it was often necessary to step aside on the staging at different levels to get a breath, so the climb took twice as long as the descent. They got out the tin ore by driving steel borers into the granite rock and blasting with gunpowder, and it was his work to take the blunted tools back to the shaft and send them up to grass on top of the ore to go to Goldsithney smithy, and bring back a supply of sharpened ones that had come down. Sometimes, in the deeper workings, he was told to turn a small fan to force cooler air in towards the men; for the air was so hot that without this the candles would not burn, or else melt away.

"Come on, Joel, time for grub," Owen would call.

"Put out your candle, boy, thee cust eat in dark; a candle do burn up as much air as a man breathes," the other partner, Kit Watson, ordered.

Their pitch had followed the lode up a sharp incline from the level, just where it had dipped slightly; further along others were working and the sound of their hammers on the borers echoed through the adits. A man was singing slowly in time with his blows:

> *"My little, winsome Maggie,*
> *Singing all the day,*
> *How much I love her none can tell,*
> *My little Maggie May."*

"Hark to that," said Owen. "Ringle, ringle, now that's a grand sound. 'Tis like a band when there's a few chaps beating."

" 'Twould be more sense if they did listen to them borers; there's house of water down there somewhere, I reck'n, and they'd best go careful."

"How do it get there?" asked Joel.

"Well see, boy, we're not the first to go after tin and copper, and the old men didn't leave a plan of their workings. When their pitches got too wet they just left them to look after themselves, so over a while the water did collect down there and pile up and up, fathoms deep. When her's been gathering for a hundred year or more there's a mighty great houseful, and along come one of us and knocks a borer through into it. 'Tain't difficult to see what happens then."

17

" 'Es, and 'twill happen down there afore long," Kit prophesied. "They'd best beat a five-foot borer in front of them all time."

The harder work that followed after the boy had teamed up with Owen and Kit came easier to him than it might have done had the family not been living on a small farm and producing food for themselves, and, well cared for by Elizabeth, he was growing fast, developing a strength far beyond most boys of his age. Of necessity his arms and legs acquired the strength to take him up the many fathoms of ladder each day, and to push the loaded barrows through the level, and his eye was getting accurate through his occasional spells with hammer and borer at the lode.

While eating their food the men had taken a few extra minutes to touch off a pipe of tobacco.

"Now, boys, finished grub? Right, we'll light they candles and get on with it. Take 'n' hold that borer, Joel, and give un a turn now 'n' then, and see her don't get jammed up again this time."

Stripped to the waist, the flickering candle light glistening on their sweating backs, unbelievably dirty from the clay, powder smoke and red dust, they worked at the lode, Joel on errands for his partners, trundling the ore back to the shaft. Owen would usually give him a hand up the incline to get the barrow out of the first dip in the level, and it was while they were doing this one shift that a terrified cry came echoing from the working, followed by a mighty roar.

A hot wind blew past Joel's whitened cheek. Owen left him with the barrow at the top of the incline and ran back, shouting.

"Kit, Kit, what' a-happened?"

In a few seconds he came racing back, scrambling over the floor as fast as he could.

" 'Tis water, boy; 'tis a-coming like a wave. Get up on that there barrow, and God help us all. 'Tis house of water been struck."

The boy scrambled up on the barrow to bring his head near the ceiling, in the candlelight he saw Owen's white face against a black wall of water tearing down the level, already purling about his flying feet. Ceiling high it looked where he could see down in the hollow, rushing on at them with all its force, a great black wave. The tinner jumped up beside him, kneeling on the load to bring his head touching the roof, and he pressed his hands against it to wedge himself in.

"Hold to my back, boy; keep your head as high as 'ee can. We're done for, I'm feared, but we'll try as long as we can to live."

The water swirled over the floor beneath them where they were set firmly on the ore; Joel had obeyed in a cold terror, clinging to Owen's back and bracing his legs against the rush of water. Their candles had gone out in the draught of air blowing down towards the shaft, where they could hear the water already racing like a mill stream. In the darkness he heard it rising around them, he heard Owen trying to control his heavy breathing after he had raced the flood. It touched his foot, he felt it running into his boots, around his ankles, creeping up his legs.

"I reck'n we're done, as good as drowned already," he sobbed.

"Bunkum, my dear, we're still alive. A tinner's not so easy killed."

The water, although not rushing quite so fiercely now at the top of the rise, so that Owen with his hands flat and gripping what he could of the roof could steady himself against it, was all the time rising up and up. It circled Joel about the waist, touched his shoulder blades and slowly crawled up his back. He thought of his father up at the top, perhaps at this moment learning of the disaster below and wondering frantically what was happening to him. He'd be sad tonight to think his boy was drowned, like a rat washed out of his burrow. All of them would be sad at supper that night; and his mother had promised them herby pie, one of his favourites. Joel began to wish he had not watched the kittens drown; now, in a few minutes, he himself would know what it felt like to be drowned, shut in and held down by the rock, drowned without a chance.

"Does it take long to drown?"

"What a question! I've never drowned yet, and I've no mind to start till I must. Keep your chin up, boy, and keep your mouth shut."

The water reached his chin and at that height flowed past for a long time, until his neck felt like red hot iron, bent back as far as he could put it. The air was hot and foul, but they were thankful for what there was.

"My neck's a-breaking."

"Now, don't 'ee let it do that," Owen encouraged him. "For a tinner's never broke till his neck's broke. Put it straight a bit, I reck'n water bain't running so hard as 'twas."

A few minutes later he called back again to him. "Her's a-falling, Joel; I reck'n her's fallen a good couple inches. Seems us bain't done for yet, boy."

But he got no answer, and swinging round as the grip on his shoulders relaxed, he was just in time to grab at the boy's hair with his own cramped fingers and snatch him out of the flood. When Joel came round he was sitting on the barrow, his head tucked between his knees while his face was being smacked in no tender manner.

"Come, wake up, boy. Her's a-fallen. Her's a-finding her level."

"Am I dead?" he faltered.

"Dead? Why, thee'st cat's lives left yet. Water's down by a shovel hilt, a few hours now and the level'll be dry. What did I tell 'ee?"

Both knew that although the water had fallen to a couple of feet or so up where they were, it was on the top of a rise with a dip on either side and a further rise between them and the shaft. That hollow would most certainly be roof high with water still, cutting them off and preventing ventilation, leaving only a very limited amount of air between the two wells of water. In it they dared not light a candle, with the two of them breathing it would be gone soon enough.

"I reck'n we'll be the only ones alive by now, Joel. Whoever 'twas struck the house of water must have been swept up like a cork, though maybe if Kit were up at the pitch there'd be a pocket of air up there to save him. But the others down below, working away underhand, would be caught, poor chaps. Drowned, sure 'nough."

"Then I reck'n we'd best get back and see what happened to Kit."

" 'Es, I reck'n we had. Maybe if we can get through the dip where the water'll still be deep, he'll be safe up the pitch. But I'll go by 'self; 'tisn't fit for 'ee, for 'twill be too deep."

"I can swim; I bain't staying here alone in the dark. 'Twould give me the jitters."

"Well then, if we've got to swim 'twould be best to take off trousers and boots, and I reck'n to keep together 'ee'd best fix your belt around under your arms and I'll pass mine through it and catch hold of it."

This they did, and with the end of his belt in his hand Owen Kendall started off down the level, the water rising as the floor dipped. Before very long Joel had to swim as he was getting out of his depth, so that any hole he trod in sent his mouth under water, but by wading slowly along, his companion was able to keep his chin out of water and so gain an idea of its depth.

"Her's falling away, boy. Thee'st through it now. Pray God Kit's safe up the pitch."

A little further on Joel was able to touch the floor and wade breast deep, but below that the water did not fall, until by running their hands along the wall they found the entrance leading up to their workings.

They were so engrossed in making the passage that they had forgotten to shout, now Owen let out a bellowing inquiry after his partner. There was no reply, only a mocking echo. After pushing on for a few more feet, Joel stopped.

"There's water a-coming down from the lode," he said quietly. It could only mean one thing.

"Then 'twas hisself struck the house of water. Strange, when he took such fear of it. Poor Kit, he'll have had no chance at all, neither

21

will t'other boys down the lower workings. Drowned like rats, there's no doubt."

In the full realisation of their fellows' end both were still and silent for a few moments.

"Well, 'tis no good grieving for them now, we'd best be saving ourselves, seeing we're the lucky ones. Maybe our luck'll hold. And best be double quick about it, for there bain't too much air left in these parts."

They went back slowly the way they had come and eventually reached the higher part where the barrow had saved them from being washed away. Going on, it did not take them long to find the dip was still roof high in water, their retreat to the shaft being cut off by the lowest part being filled right up. They returned to the starting-place.

"There'll be 'bout seven fathoms of water lying through there, roof high, and after that 'twill get lower as the level rises. If we could get through we'll be safe."

"But 'tis too far. And if we stay here the air'll soon be done. I reck'n we're done for after all. Only now 'tis a matter of dying slowly."

"Hold your tongue, boy. I do tell 'ee, a tinner's never broke till his neck's broke. I'll get through, and so shall 'ee; I do love my wife, so there bain't nothing else to do."

On his instructions, Joel helped him to cut and tear their canvas trousers into strips and tie them together to form a rope of fair strength. He slipped his belt out of Joel's and fastened it around his own waist.

"Now, boy, see this here end's kidged in middle of my back. Tight – 'sthat it? Sure 'tis good and safe?"

" 'Es, that'll hold a church."

"Well see, I'm a-going to swim under that dip of roof and with luck I'll get through to air on t'other side. Let the rope run free so it don't hinder, but take 'n' keep the end of it safe so that I can pull 'ee through when all's well. If I want 'ee to pull back I'll give two sharp pulls, and then again. And when you're ready for me to pull 'ee give two at a time, and then take a deep breath and dive in as near to limit as 'ee can. I'll feel the rope go slack and I'll pull 'ee through as right as tuppence."

He coiled the rope over Joel's forearm as carefully as he could in the dark, so it would not get tangled but would pay out easily. They advanced into the flood on this desperate effort to get through to safety. At the limit of Joel's depth they paused.

"Good luck, partner; take a big breath after you've swum in as far as 'ee can, and leave the rest of it to me. We'll be through sure 'nough, Joel boy, don't take fear."

"Good luck," Joel tried to conceal the tremble in his voice.

In the darkness he heard Owen swimming away and then a wash of water lapped against him as he must have dived. The canvas rope went off his arm in jerks, fast at first and then more slowly. He had taken a deep breath and was holding it to judge how the swimmer was faring; with him it would not last so long and already he felt himself to be at bursting point. The line almost stopped its progress and then, after he had felt compelled to gasp for breath it began to jerk about madly. There was only one interpretation, Owen had not made his way through, he was trapped in the water under the rock, fighting for the breath which was impossible to get. An awful despair and worry filled the boy's mind – should he pull him back? Was he responsible now for his safety and what ought he to do?

Suddenly the canvas line was nearly wrenched from his fingers and paid out so rapidly he was fearful lest it should not be long enough. Could it mean that he had got through, or was he being swept away on a rush of water? Then the run ceased and for some time after the line lay inert in his hand. A great loneliness filled the solid dark packed about him. He thought of the others further back, drowned and floating somewhere in the waters, dead, and Heaven alone knew just where they were at the moment. He felt frightened; the suspense of waiting seemed awful, the time endless.

Two jerks shook his hand holding the line. At first he thought he had imagined them, that it was just a mocking dream; but two more came, and then a third pair. It was the signal to draw back. So Owen was returning? He had failed after all to get through. He drew in as fast as he could, there was little resistance and the knots passed through his hands one by one until he grasped a different line, thin and firm in his hand – a light, strong rope.

With joy shaking his fingers he knotted it firmly in front of his belt, and worked it well up under the arms. He gave the pre-arranged signal and swam to the limit of the air, then plunged and struck out under water. A nightmare followed in the next moments, each passing like a full minute or more. His lungs were bursting, his arms struck out wildly in the terror of the passage; the rock continuously bumped him down and held him under water, no breath, no light. His head seemed to swell, to be on the point of bursting. It seemed as though it were a useless struggle; easier far to give in quietly, to let the water have its victory.

"Thee'st not broke till thy neck's broke!" The words leaped out in red hot sounds across his brain.

He fought on, he had to, if it was only to follow Owen's example. The water was rushing towards him now and he was swimming against it, the rope pulled strongly on his chest, his head hit the rock above a hard crack, and he passed out in a blaze of light.

At last he had to swallow; the water was trickling down his throat, burning all the way – but it had a grand taste. It was brandy. Men were talking excitedly all around him; he opened his eyes and saw Owen sitting on the floor nearby, a bottle to his mouth and a grin on his wet strained face. The bal cap'n himself was kneeling beside him, rubbing his wrists to restore the circulation in his body. They helped them both towards the shaft, put them in the barrel and up it went. Joel pictured his father urging on the team; never before would he have raised a load up to grass that he would be half so thankful to see emerge from the black mouth of the shaft as this the whim was drawing now.

He heard later how men along with the foreman had gone up the level with hosepipes connected to pumps to start clearing up the water cutting them off from the workings. They had little reason to hope anyone remained alive, but the work had to be done and the bodies brought out; the pitches were good and if tinners had lost their lives there were others ready to bid for the lode as soon as it was accessible. It had not taken long to get the pumps drawing and the water, once helped over the rise, found its own way to the mine's adit. A man had stripped and had waded down the dip as far as possible, waiting to give word to the others when the water fell sufficiently to allow them through to the next stage. Peering into the black water by the light of his candle he saw a man's body drifting towards him and, clutching the hair of its head, was surprised to find he had drawn out Owen Kendell, half-drowned but alive and soon restored. As soon as he was able to speak they learned who was at the other end of his canvas line and had given Joel the signal after fixing a strong cord to its end.

His father gave him his jacket to wear around him on his way to the "dry" and as he was without boots one of the men offered him a pick-a-back. There was no demonstration of the emotion he must have felt over his son's safety; others were waiting around for their men to come up, but knowing well by this time that, when they did, it would be to have other men carry them away to the carpenter's shop, feet first.

"Thank God you're alive, my son," was all he said, his hand gripping the boy's shoulder.

Joel, twitching his thumb towards Owen, remarked, " 'Twas him mostly."

"There's for 'ee! Well, Joel'll make a pretty tinner, so he will. See 'ee first core tomorrow, partner."

That night Elizabeth put her foot down, hard. From his bed Joel heard her, and lay awake as long as he could to listen.

"I tell you he shall not go back down."

b

"But that bain't sense, my dear. Of course he'll go back down the bal. What's going to become of him, a miner, if he don't go back down?"

"That's easy answered if only you'd do what I've been talking about for so long now, and take a larger farm. Then there'd be no need for him to be a tinner, nor for Charles and Ralph; there'd be plenty and to spare for them all to work at, even the girls, if we had that parcel of ground more. Now, Rich, take 'n' get that settled up and no more talk about it. Get it done."

Andrewartha gave it his very careful consideration for a long while, sitting in by the wreck-wood fire, sucking his clay and occasionally spitting with great precision into the hottest part of the hearth.

"Well now, Elizabeth, if that's what thee west do, we'll do it. And we'll do it as soon as ever it can be done. Now you've won your way, but this much I do stick to – Joel must go back to his work just same as though nothing had gone wrong down there. 'Twould be asking for trouble to pet him up and spoil him; he's man's work to do and he must take same chances as all of us do take in our time. If he stays up now he'll never get the better of his fright, and'll go 'bout all his life feared of the bal. No son of mine's a-going to be made into a softie by his mother spoiling him."

In her heart Elizabeth knew the sound wisdom of this theory, that Joel should go back down as usual lest he took fear of being underground and became a coward.

"Very well then, as you say; but if you love me you'll let him get to the land for good and all as soon as you can, and t'others too. Take 'n' rest now, Rich, for 'tis been a long, anxious day for you."

The next day the boy went back down the shaft, along to the water-filled passage that had witnessed his terror, a terror none the less real for being controlled and subdued in the face of danger. With the others, boys no older than himself although he was by far the biggest and strongest, he took turns at the pumps, following the water back, gradually mopping up section by section of the flooded workings. In the damp heat the sweat rolled off their backs, leaks in the pump sent little squirts of water around them at every stroke, so that they were never dry. Their hands blistered and rubbed raw, and passed through a very painful time before they healed and hardened to a toughened, calloused state, but in spite of it all, or because of it, his muscles developed; he continued to grow and find more and more pride in his strength.

The pumping took him into many places in that strange honeycomb of workings where he had never been before. There were long, low adits scarcely big enough to let one man through at a time, the old men's work; openings as big as caves in the black granite, shelves and long sloping chimneys running up to some higher level. It was in the deeper sections the boys found the water collecting; down there in the receding depths they came across men's bodies, drifting into the wretched light of their candles, days, even weeks after the house of water had been struck. Kit's in one recess by itself, where it had been swept by the rush of water following the ill-fated blow on his borer which had brought the disaster about; he who had always dreaded the stored water and yet who had so tragically miscalculated at the last, when it should have been carefully tapped and led off.

The finding of the victims impressed itself deeply on Joel. He could not help seeing in each of them the fate he had escaped, and the condition of his own body had he been less fortunate. Down in the heat they were not good to look at, they had none of the calmness and whiteness of men drowned in the sea and washed ashore in the coves or up on Praa Sands. They had seemed empty and spiritless, but as natural as the shells cast up by the same storms, while these poor things had grown into nightmare horridness.

Often, tired as he was, even to the point of exhaustion by the end of the day, his night's sleep was disturbed by reliving the terror of the flooded mine, made worse now by knowing what fate lay waiting those who were trapped. Elizabeth, awake as often as not planning how the change over of her boys from miners to farmers could best be accomplished, would hear him shriek out in his sleep as he had been overtaken by his nightmare.

"House of water! 'Tis a-coming like a wave. I can't breathe, the rock's holding me down. Run, her's a-coming, her's a-coming. Oh, Mother, 'tis hard on me."

And she would run through to him and waken him from where he lay sobbing in the realness of his terror, putting her arms around him to comfort him against her breast.

"Have no fear, Joel; your mother'll not let it harm you. Take 'n' sleep now, my son, and God'll watch over you."

She would turn him over gently on his side, and kiss him; her firstborn, and perhaps for that reason she held greater affection for him than for the others, and her heart ached when he cried out in such terror. Awake he could laugh at his fears of the water, but the dread of it remained, deep down, mostly forgotten and yet always waiting to be revived, right to the end. His father never made any comment on the nightmares; he knew what it was to be underground, he had himself experienced the dangers of the life and seen plenty of death. Already, though only about thirty-four years old, his hair had turned grey and physically he was past the working life of a tinner below ground; and yet he was sound compared with most of his generation in the mines, for they were broken men going slowly to their graves and reaching them within fifteen years.

The recent years had added another daughter, Polly, to his family, and with the birth of a baby girl on Tuesday, January 16th, 1816, it became obvious that he could no longer hold off Elizabeth's constant requests for a larger place, and they would find one with his ready agreement. They would have to move, for with the sixth child Chywoon would not be so roomy as they had found it in the smaller family's day. And so the question came up for immediate decision. Now that Joel and Charles knew something of farm work as well as mining, and Betsy was growing into a useful little girl, if they were to carry out their hopes of keeping them all together it would be necessary to take a farm offering more scope.

It was rumoured locally that Higher Kenneggy was likely to become vacant soon, and being very handy between Rosudgeon Common and Prussia Cove, and of about one hundred and sixty acres, it seemed just what they wanted. On all sides it was bounded by mines, with Wheal Georgia up on the common, Speedwell on the cliff, St. Aubyn and Grylls on the west and Great Western up by the Helston turnpike; while on the farm itself was Wheal Speed.

"I want 'ee to say what's in your mind," Richard insisted. " 'Tis with your help we are where we are, and with your help we'll get beyond it. Now you say just 'zactly what you've a mind to do, and I'll bide by it."

For a few moments Elizabeth considered the problem. Actually, she had turned it over in her mind often enough before, and although her husband thought it was his project, it was she who had carefully planted its seeds, but she wanted him to continue to believe her opinion was no more than a deciding factor.

"I reckon you're right, my dear, and I'd like the children to grow up at Kenneggy. 'Tis bigger and smarter for them, and as you say the mine is very handy for the teams and would be a great help to us. I've heard tell it is good ground. And there's the sands down there, which would be fine for them to bathe from in the summer; it would be grand to have our own beach. Yes, if Kenneggy is coming free, we'll take it over."

Her father had taken care to carry the new baby up on to a chair and a chest before taking her downstairs, so she would go up in the world; Elizabeth decided to call her Salome, for it was a name that pleased her. At forty-two she did not look the seven years she was older than her husband, because of the hard life that always made a miner prematurely grey, while her early days had been comparatively easy. Since her marriage she had very rarely gone to her home, neither had her folk shown much interest in the children, except in

29

Joel, who had failed to appreciate it, but now they would often press her to bring the baby up to Tregonebris.

About that time Betsy took the small-pox and as it was very mild Elizabeth followed the usual practice of carrying the lymph from the sick child on a clean darning-needle and infecting the others so they should take it mildly too. This delayed the christening and it was not until nearly a year after her birth that she was taken to St. Germoe's Church and the ceremony performed by Curate Edward Rogers. That December Sunday afternoon was the last time the family attended at Germoe, for soon after they moved into Higher Kenneggy, and as the farm was just over the boundary, it brought them into Breage Parish, although the former village was nearer.

Joel was well pleased with the plan and had looked forward to the farm taking the bigger part of his time instead of the mine, and to the extra stock they would be able to carry; for he had a great way with animals and they responded well to his care. At Chywoon the nature of the land and its acreage had kept them in narrow limits.

" 'Twill be good to get away from these everlasting sheep. At Kenneggy there'll be plenty of high ground for the creatures, while there's meadows too down towards the cliffs and on Rosudgeon side where we can have the cows. That'll mean a bigger dairy and more cream and butter. There'll be the orchard too down there, 'twill be good to have fruit as well."

Richard was glad he took so much interest in the new place; it would help get his back into the work. And it showed promise to be a good broad back, for there was no doubt at all young Joel was becoming a fine enough boy.

30

Chapter Two

MOST Sunday afternoons found young Joel in a restless mood. Faced with a little free time of his own once in the week, there was so much to be done that it was difficult to decide what was best to do to get the most satisfaction out of it. When the two steam stamps began work up at Wheal Vor he had often ridden over to see the wonderful sight of dozens of heads thundering up and down on the ore with a sound that could be heard from Kenneggy, even above that of the water stamps at Sydney Godolphin. After a while they lost their attraction for him, and now he usually ended up with wandering off towards Kenneggy Sand or the cliffs, and dawdling along the footpaths beyond Sydney Cove copper mine, in a discontented, vaguely unhappy mood brought on by a feeling that he was not doing what he wanted. Mainly because he did not know exactly what that was. To pass the time and give himself some activity he would pick up boulders and, balancing them on the palm of his hand, see how far he could hurl them; he would walk on his hands along a strip of grass, or even along the top of a hedge.

One such afternoon he had reached a point away towards Porthleven, and finding there a low hedge with a patch of smooth springy turf below it, he tried a series of somersaults over it, trying to land on his feet without losing balance. After much perseverance he succeeded; to his astonishment handclaps applauded his success.

"That was a good one. But what's the idea of it all?" a girl's voice asked.

Confused and disconcerted to realise there was a spectator of his antics, Joel glanced about. Sitting on the stone stile at the end of the field, not twenty yards from him, was a girl of about seventeen or eighteen; as he stood leaning against the hedge in awkward silence, she climbed over the upright stones leading from the wall and came towards him. He felt shy and oafish, for he saw at once she was older than him, was slender and pretty in her walking dress; soft honey-brown corkscrew curls framed her face.

"Why are you so rough with yourself?"

Joel kicked the back of his heel against the wall; he was wondering why girls should always want to interfere. Why not leave a fellow alone?

"I hope you're not minding because I was watching?" Perhaps she sensed his adolescent antagonism, for she added, "I reckon 'ee did that last one well enough; 'twas grand."

" 'Es, 'twas not too bad. I was practising to take falls easy."

"Wrestling?"

She hoisted herself up on the hedge to sit quite near him. Easy as kiss she did it too, he thought, and then felt shy at the very thought of kissing. She was a pretty little sight.

" 'Es, 'tis what I most want to be, a good wrestler. I reck'n I want that more'n anything else I know of." He could have kicked himself in the next moment for being so confidential towards this interfering girl.

"Then you're lucky to be born a boy, for I did want the same when I was younger, but 'twas no good wishing for it. 'Twouldn't change me. But you're a fine strong boy, so there's nothing to stop 'ee from being a wrestler."

" 'Es, there's Father. He doesn't set much store on that sort of thing. It seems there's nothing counts with him save hard work. He calls it innplay, and time wasted."

She glanced sideways at him and smiled. He liked her better for smiling; indeed, she had so sweet a smile he found himself hoping she would give him another.

"My father was just t'other way 'bout. He was mighty disappointed I wasn't a boy, for he would have made me a wrestler; but seeing I was only a girl he just made the best he could out of me. He used to teach me chips and holds, and when Mother did say 'twasn't fit stuff for a girl to pick up he always said 'twas better for a girl to know how to defend herself than a boy, in some ways."

"Then you do know something of wrestling?" He was liking her better for it; by now he had forgiven her intrusion on his play.

She dropped off the hedge, shook her dress in place and came to stand in front of him.

"Push me over," she commanded.

"What?"

"I did ask 'ee to push me over. Go on, see if 'ee can."

He hesitated. It was not his habit to push at girls, and he did not know quite where to push. All the places where he would have lunged at a fellow seemed, when transplanted to a girl, too personal to touch. Perhaps she read his thoughts, for she laughed at him.

"Why do 'ee not try? I'm flesh and bone, the same as you; 'twill not hurt me to be touched. Or thee'st took fear?"

The taunt succeeded where the unexpected invitation had failed. He lunged out squarely, not roughly but with a steady force behind the flat of his hand where it touched her chest. She made a swift movement with her hands across the back of his fingers, at the same time leaning forward; he could not withdraw his hand in time and, before he knew quite how, he was forced down on one knee by the backbending of his wrist. Surprised, he reached up instinctively with his left hand to break her hold, but she anticipated his intention and stepped back, her small hands gripping his fingers to her palms, her thumbs over their tips, and he was held down quite out of reach for retaliation.

He laughed up at her, for a moment so interested in the skill she had shown that he overlooked the fact that he, a big fifteen-year-old lad, was held down on one knee by a slip of a girl.

"Bless me, that was pretty smart. Show me how 'twas done."

She released his hand and showed him exactly how the grip was made.

"Well see, although you're heavier and far stronger than me, I could hold 'ee down 'cause my weight and what strength I have in my arms was all 'gainst your wrist, and making it do something 'twasn't made to do. Now try again."

Joel feinted and lunged out lower, still mindful not to hurt her. At once she brought her hands down and gripped his wrist with a crossed over hold and twisted; in a second he was forced to the ground, where she could have held him had she wished by continuing the twist. He regained his feet and grinned sheepishly at her.

"Who did teach 'ee to do that?" he asked, wriggling his shoulder.

"Father. He was good at that kind of thing; he picked it up somewhere in the East, and he taught me. It amused him to make a tomboy of me."

Interest got the better of any feeling of shame at being worsted by a girl; and a curiosity to learn more about these tricks of hers that went so strangely with her gentle appearance.

"Then he did teach 'ee mighty well. Will 'ee show me some more?"

For an hour or more his interest was absorbed by a variety of grips and holds and tricks for releasing oneself from an opponent which she showed to him. Their novelty appealed to him so much that he willingly subjected himself to all manner of positions for the demonstration.

"Of course, you do let me show 'ee these while you stand quiet," she said almost apologetically; there was not a trace of superiority in her voice or attitude towards him. "If you were to set your mind to it I'm sure I'd not be really quick enough with them to be able to hold 'ee, 'cause you're so strong. But I wish 'ee could have seen Father, he was so fond of all these things he'd have loved to show 'ee how to do them properly. Maybe you'll find out for yourself now I've given you an idea how to do them."

" 'Tis something I never heard tell of afore. Is your father dead?'

"Yes, Father's been dead a long while. I do live with Mother's sister – Mother's dead too, you see."

"I do wish he were 'live now and able to teach me what he has taught 'ee. If 'twere fine next Sunday maybe thee west come along and show me more? I'd dearly love to get handy at it, and I reckon 'tis all a matter of getting hold in 'zactly the right place. Would 'ee?"

He looked at her earnestly, and suddenly noticed again what he had forgotten all the time he had been so intent on the art she had revealed; that she was a prettily dressed young lady, and he was an awkward lad floundering somewhere in that nondescript mire between boy and man. How could he dare to expect her to take more than a passing interest in him, a mere fancy that had come over her at the moment in order to while away a dull afternoon? And yet, instead of laughing at his suggestion, she gave him another of her friendly smiles, just as though they had known each other all their lives.

"It's been good fun this afternoon, and I'd love to come next Sunday. You see, 'tis so grand to play with a boy who can forget I'm only a girl, or at least forgive me for it. What's your name?"

"Joel Andrewartha; I'm from up Kenneggy."

"Mine's Caroline; isn't it a dreadful name? Caroline Rowe. But I do like yours. Joel," she repeated it as though to herself. "Joel; Joel. There's a strong, fair sound 'bout that. Joel Andrewartha, 'tis a fine Cornish name."

" 'Es? But I do like yours too. Caroline, why it's the Queen of England's name." He was not going to be outdone in polite friendliness.

"Is that much to recommend it?"

Neither was he to be led into a controversial subject, especially one he was not too sure about, so he hedged the query.

"Well, 'tis as fair a name as any, I reck'n," he asserted stoutly.

"And I reckon I'd better be getting on home, or Aunt'll be blackening it. Till next week, good-bye, Joel."

"Till Sunday; good-bye, Caroline."

Each went off in their home direction. At the end of the field Joel turned and glanced back. She had done the same and he felt a blush tinge his face to be caught so looking back at her, and hoped fervently she could not see it. But with a gesture seeming the most natural on earth she waved to him as she climbed the stile; he waved back and she disappeared from sight.

All the way home he tried to analyse his feelings, to find out why he had been able to take what amounted to a worsting from a girl, and one so slender looking in her Sunday dress and pretty bonnet. He, the fine boy who wanted to be a wrestler, had been put where she wanted him by a twist or a bend of her little wrists; it was true he had made no real attempt to resist her, yet he knew in his heart the touches she had used had a power behind them which it might have been awkward to come up against, even had he pitted his full strength against them. To have tested them thoroughly would have meant deliberate roughness, and that would have been unpardonable. The whole pleasantness and enjoyment of this strange afternoon had been in neither attempting to thrust any sort of superiority on the other; they had found a common interest, and kept it on a level between them.

How could he explain to the family what they had done together, without seeming ridiculous in their eyes? Or else giving an impression of her which would be grossly unfair? His father could and would be scathing enough if he knew he had been pandering to his interest in anything relating to wrestling, but if he heard it was with a girl he had been learning grips. . . He did not dare to think of the derisive hoots and taunts the picture would bring on him. It would be far better to say nothing at all; just to wander home as he always did and give no account of the afternoon, how he had spent it and whether alone or not.

All the hard-working week he thought of the coming Sunday, and the arranged meeting seemed exciting and grotesque. Suppose he could learn something of what her father had evidently possessed, how much would it be worth to him from the wrestler's viewpoint? Not much in actual contests, perhaps now and again at rare opportunities it might come in; but in the art he saw a glimmering of a higher value, for if he got a mastery of all she could teach him, what a superiority he would have over others in any rush and tumble, everyday scrap. And in the fancied possession of that superiority he realised he was gaining another thing, a confidence of being a better man than the next, of being able to hold his own against greater weight and strength beyond his years. On the other hand, there was the slight but terrifying risk of being seen tussling with a girl. It was small, the cliff region being deserted at most times, and on a Sunday afternoon particularly; the farm folk were indoors or about the town-place, the miners not working a core would be resting. There was only the chance some restless lad like himself might see him, but that would be worse than anything. If it got about that he, Joel Andrewartha, wrestled with girls, could he ever show his face in a ring all his life?

At one time this bogey of derision had him stifled and sweating; at another he was drawn irresistibly by the thread of Caroline's friendliness and desire to help him all she could in his pet ambition. He remembered how she herself had apologised for being a girl; it was not her fault she could not enjoy equal strength and freedom with him, and it seemed too unfair to let the chancey share-out of sexes spoil the friendship promising to grow between them. When at last Sunday came he did what he had known all along he would do: he went to meet her.

Joel reached the fields beyond Rinsey first, and perched himself on the hedge, already wondering if she would come or if she had changed her mind about him. He was still trying to discount every reason why she should stay away when to his disgust he saw a youth in dark blue trousers, fisherman's guernsey and woollen cap coming across the next field, from the very direction he had expected Caroline. This wretched intruder swung along towards him at a fine easy pace, as though he had a purpose, and, counting on this to get him away before she appeared, Joel was doubly dismayed to see him raise an arm and wave a greeting. He looked all around but could see no soul in sight, and yet he waved a second time, then paused on the stile and, after looking at him for a moment, swaggered right up.

Joel glowered up angrily at the lad and was astonished to see him snatch off his cap and allow a curly mop of hair to fall around no other than Caroline's face. His unbelieving eyes looked hard at her, at the coarse guernsey and the rough loose-fitting trousers, at the slim figure of her standing there straddle-legged, hand in pocket, swinging the cap jauntily.

"How do I look? Do I make a pretty boy?" she asked.

"Why, bless you, I did reck'n 'twas a boy. And how sick I did feel, thinking he was a-going to be in the way."

She swung herself up on the hedge beside him, wriggled on to a softer spot and began stuffing her curls back under the cap. Her sleeves were rolled up above her elbows, showing arms of light golden brown, lean but not skinny. She flexed them, and fingered what biceps she could achieve.

"There's for 'ee! No, it looks more through the wool, that's why I roll it up so high."

He tried the little bulge with his fingers, and smiled.

"There's not so much there, 'tis true, but 'tis good and firm; all muscle."

"That'll be the butter-making; it puts strength into your arms and wrists."

" 'Es, I reck'n it does, same as swinging a scythe brings up the muscles on your shoulders and back."

"I do like scything. My uncle would have me go chopping away with a sickle, but I told him I'd swing a scythe or nothing. When he did see I could do it he let me have my way."

Joel looked at her and grinned; he was beginning to understand her better, and his liking was growing all the while.

"You'll get that most all the while, eh?"

She laughed at the touch of shrewdness and seemed pleased at the compliment. "Maybe I do with uncle, and with John – he's my cousin, you know – but with Aunt I'm always told what to do."

She dropped down on to the turf and, reaching up, pulled him off the hedge.

"Come on with 'ee now, Joel, and get to work. I figured out all the best throws and counters I do know to show 'ee, and I've put on these clothes so that we can have a rare tussle."

That afternoon, and for several others in the following weeks, Joel proved to be an apt pupil, and she had a rare gift for teaching everything her father had passed on to her. More than anything she taught him how to fall, how to twist his body in the air so that, on striking the ground, the shock was taken up by the pads of muscle on hands and feet and buttock, instead of the vulnerable points of shoulder and hip. This to a Cornish wrestler would be an important acquisition, because a throw that would otherwise be a fair back could be changed by a clever landing into a mere hitch.

They enjoyed each other's companionship more than ever; it had fallen into an easy friendliness which enveloped the time they were together and made it pass happily without a trace of shyness. From being an awkward, girl-scared boy she was changing him into a self-reliant, easy-minded fellow and the rough hewn effect of his growing body was giving way to a balanced suppleness that showed off his fine young strength and promised to develop it towards a fine figure in manhood. She was getting proud of him, for as she said, to knock a great lump of boyhood into a presentable shape was much more gratifying than patting up the most perfect roll of butter. So each found in the other something undefinable which had been missing before and which, coming at the time when it was most needed, stilled that miserable discontent of adolescence.

As far as he knew he had kept his secret from the family; each Sunday he had wandered off and returned in much the same aimless way as he had always done. He had tried not to let any purpose show in this assumed aimlessness, and so far apparently he had succeeded. He was annoyed therefore when Charles suddenly took an interest in his programme for the afternoon.

"Where are you going this afternoon, Joel? I reck'n I'll come 'long with 'ee."

"I'll not be going anywhere particular; just wandering about, doing nothing."

"I'll come 'long with 'ee then; 'tis kind of dull always being by thyself."

Joel looked at his brother; he felt so much older than him, a kid just thirteen.

"Don't vex thyself, I do like to be dull once a week, if 'tis only to get 'way from you kids. I've a-gone by 'self often 'nough and now I reck'n I've got to like it best. I can't be bothered to look after 'ee."

The thought came to him that Charles was not so much rebuffed as pleased to be put off. Did he expect him to be away by himself to meet someone, and had the declined offer confirmed vague suspicions? After the midday meal he dawdled across to Wheal Speed and from there took the rough stone path down the cliff just above Pestreath Cove.

Just before the path dipped by Lesceave Cliff he chanced to look back and was dismayed to get a glimpse of Charles running to cover some length in his wake. It was the merest flash he had caught but it told him at once he was being followed by his inquisitive brother, and above his anger rose a great thankfulness that he had been granted this saving glimpse. He topped the rise and as soon as he was screened ran down the dip; getting to the shore side of the path he hid in the first secure spot. It was not long before he heard Charles running down the path, and as the sound of his feet died away, he looked out to see him climbing up towards the quarry and take the Rinsey path. As it was low tide Joel went down to the shore as soon as he was out of sight and made off in the opposite direction.

His mood was as dark as the granite rocks about him. Why couldn't Charles leave him alone and not come shoving his nose in where he was not wanted? Caroline would wait up there and he couldn't dare be seen so much as talking with her. She would wonder why he failed to appear, and what would she think of him? But it was wiser to leave her waiting this once and kill Charles's curiosity than risk his discovering where he had been each Sunday afternoon. With an eye on the future he decided it would not be wise to get home much earlier than usual.

The wretched afternoon passed slowly away as he dawdled home along the shore. The only streak of comfort in the greyness of his disappointment was the thought that Caroline would understand. That had been one of her many attractions for him – she always understood; she had done so right from the first time they had ever met. With her there never seemed to be the necessity of difficult explanations, or vain attempts to get his point of view expressed; she knew and she understood everything he had ever wanted her to, grasping it at once, no matter how fumbling had been his speech. And this time surely she would not fail him.

He did not see Charles until the family were gathered for supper; the boy looked horribly pleased about something, and before long it came out.

"Someone I met over Rinsey way this afternoon seemed to know me. I reck'ned 'twas a boy at first, but she was a girl dressed like a fisher-boy. Her'd a girl's face, and I reck'n I must have been looking mighty hard at her, for she says, 'Maybe you'll know me the next time you see me'. And her'd a girl's voice, so I said, 'Are you a girl or a boy?' She looked at me as though I were a whisht little thing and snapped pert-like, 'Why do 'ee ask? Has your mother not told 'ee the difference?' "

In spite of his embarrassment at hearing Charles talk of Caroline, for it must have been she, Joel was forced to grin at the retort she had given to his inquisitive tongue.

"Then she looked at me again, as though she knew who I was, and said, 'You're Joel's brother?' And I said, 'What do 'ee know of Joel?' 'Mind your own business,' she said at once and I thought for a moment she was about to clip my ear. Do 'ee know who 'twas, Joel?"

Joel stopped eating; he felt the eyes of all the family on him. He looked first at his mother, then his father; they were waiting for him to speak. Was he to deny all knowledge of her, the easiest course? His natural honesty forbade it, and on to that was his liking for Caroline. She was his friend, and a good friend; he had been glad enough of her companionship when all went smoothly.

"Do 'ee know the girl, Joel?" his father demanded.

"We're friends," he answered simply.

There was a fearful silence.

"Friends are you? And how long have 'ee been friends with a maid?"

"Some while now, Father."

"What's the girl's name? Who is she?" asked Elizabeth.

He kept quiet.

"Do 'ee hear what your Mother said? Answer her, boy."

"I can't mind her name. No, I'll not tell 'ee who she is. She's a friend of mine. What's the harm in me having a friend?"

"There's no harm in having a friend, but no son of mine's a-going to hang round the fields Sundays with girls, that I do tell 'ee straight. And if 'ee don't mind who 'tis, I'll tickle your memory." His father's voice was cold and threatening. "There's work here to be done and no maid's a-going to get hold of 'ee to put ideas in your silly young head. I'll not have 'ee out keeping company with 'em, as you very well do know. Get off your shirt and catch hold that door."

As he obeyed, watching his father undo the thick leather belt, Joel felt a wave of bitter resentment rising up against the injustice of it all. But he wouldn't explain, he would rather have had the skin leathered from his back than share the secret joy of that friendship, with the interpretation they might put on it, and of which, at his age, he was over-conscious. To tell them about their shared hopes of his developing into a fine wrestler and the part she had taken in forwarding them was quite impossible. No, he would rather take what his father considered was punishment in front of all the children than part with the happiness of those few hours spent with Caroline. He gripped the edge of the open door and hid his face in his arms, waiting for the snapping sting of the leather across his bare skin.

Even prepared as he was, a start escaped him as the first blow raised an angry red weal; his fingers tightened on the door above his head until the blood drained from them and they showed white against the dark wood. The leather snapped back and in a second fell on him again. He bit on his lip and pressed his eyes into his arms to keep back the tears of pain as his flesh became a sheet of fierce agony under the curling lashes which seemed to his tortured nerves to be cutting in to the very bone. Ten times the belt whipped out at him, and through it all he neither stirred nor moved his head, only by a scarcely audible catch of his breath and the ugly marks over his skin were the effects registered; but for these it might have been the wooden door that had taken the blows.

"Hold your hand now, Rich," Elizabeth cried. "You've given the boy enough."

With an abrupt gesture his father bade him put on his shirt. The children had fled from the room; the sight of their big brother taking such a flogging had been too much for them. As he pulled his shirt over his head he tried not to wince at the touch of it on his back. Cautiously he tucked it in around his belt, gazing straight at his parents.

"Now, Joel my son, do 'ee listen to me. Maybe I should have talked afore I leathered your back, but I reck'n now you'll be in a better frame of mind to heed what I say. We left Chywoon 'cause we reck'ned we'd want a bigger 'n' better place for you boys to grow into, with room for us all and work in plenty. I did tell 'ee that 'twas for you I was doing it, and 'twas agreed 'tween us that we'd stick into it and make it the best place in the parish. Now as soon as 'ee get 'long a bit and old 'nough to take 'n' share the work, what do 'ee get up to? Scuttling 'way to keep company with some good-for-nothing girl; a-getting ideas put in your head which 'tisn't old 'nough yet to hold."

Joel was listening with bowed head; he knew what his father had said about taking over Kenneggy was true. He tried to see how he had gone against the agreement between them, tried to see in what way he had harmed his work.

"There's only one thing to be in your head at your age, and that's the proper working of Kenneggy. I can't do it without 'ee – and your brothers as they get older – and 'tis to your own good that we work hard right now. And mark this, my son, as soon as a boy goes sweethearting his work do suffer. There bain't going to be any work suffering here, so sweethearting got to stop. Do I make that plain?"

In his own mind Joel was none too sure whether he had been sweethearting. Caroline was older than him, and probably had a beau – her cousin perhaps; he had never dared to ask her lest it should spoil the easiness of their friendship. He had not wanted a sweetheart; Caroline as she was had been a good companion. He resented his father's dictatorship, and fought against the injustice of forbidding a friendship outright because it was shared with a girl.

"And suppose it doesn't stop?"

"We'll not suppose that, my son." His father's voice was stern and hard. "While you live at Kenneggy, 'tis Kenneggy you've to think of. If the place doesn't please 'ee, there's no one keeping 'ee here 'gainst your will, as you very well do know. Thee cust go out and work for a master as a hired man, go back down the bal, or do what 'ee likes; 'twould be no affair of mine. But while you're here, then the working of the place will be sweetheart enough for 'ee for many years to come, and there's to be no girls taking your mind from the good of Kenneggy. Get 'long with 'ee now, down to sheep and get them tended for the night; and give your mind to what I do tell 'ee."

At the folds he leaned over a hurdle and gazed at all the upturned faces eagerly waiting for him to provide for them. He knew them all, each one was different in his eye and he knew every lamb and its mother; those that had had twins, and those that had given trouble when lambing. He tried to imagine how it would be if this were the last time he would tend them, to think that tomorrow they would be at the mercy of a strange hired hand, while he was away on poorer alien ground, slaving perhaps for stock another had neglected and spoiled. The picture was one he could not face; he knew already there was no choice for him to make. He was of Kenneggy now, as much a part of it as the sheep that trod and fertilised it for the benefit of following years; as the small fields hugged close by the low stone hedges protecting them from the salt, wind-carried spray; as the tin ore so grudgingly yielded up after the labour at Wheal Speed.

He could no more get away from Kenneggy than he could walk out of his own body.

Through all that week the dread of Sunday afternoon empty and without Caroline was with him. What was he to do? Allow her to expect him, to leave last Sunday unexplained, not tell her that from now on he was to have no other friend but Work? Obviously the easiest thing to do would have been to slip over one evening and tell her all that had fallen on him, but this he could not bring himself to do. There would have been the ordeal of walking up to a strange house to ask for her, and to answer the searching and most probably antagonistic questions of her aunt. Certainly there would be jeering hoots and shouts from children, perhaps the humiliation of finding Caroline did not really mind his absence. On top of all this was the painful result of disobeying his father, should he be found out.

As it happened he was spared the decision, for Sunday was a pouring wet day. Not just damp, with a half-withheld promise of a clearing to follow, but driving heavy rain which would, and did, last all day. Under the most amiable home conditions it would have been impossible to have met Caroline, and the crisis was shelved for another week. And then again it was taken out of his hands.

"I reck'n we'll take a stroll round," announced his father as soon as the midday meal was over. "Sec how things are getting on."

Together they set out on a quiet tour of the farm, studying each crop, each fold of sheep, every animal in the fields and stables. As they went his father's stick poked and prodded at everything that caught his eye, a stopped drain, a stone loose or fallen in a hedge, something that cried out for immediate attention or altered treatment. Only the mine they left alone, where there was activity even on a Sunday, but as though the shadow of Tin never left him the stick was for ever scratching at the surface, searching always for some clue to fresh wealth that might lie hidden in the folds of the granite below.

All the time Joel followed, his thoughts were with Caroline. Had she come to meet him, and what would she think of him thus twice to have failed to appear? This would surely be the end of everything between them, for even if she forgave his absence on the fateful day when Charles had spoken to her, she could never be expected to think of him again now he had failed a second time.

The Sunday afternoon excursion became a rule for them both. Sometimes Elizabeth or Charles would join them, but more often they went alone. Joel's presence was compulsory. It was the only chance in the week of seeing what had been done, or was growing round and about the farm-place. Every day was so complete in itself and so crowded with work that only on this one day a week was it possible to take time to consult the land or the condition of the stock, to plan out the work for the coming six days. It was a part of his education in farming, for he learned on that day what was the result of his work in the past, and how much better or worse it could have been done.

In time the young heart, which he believed to have been broken, healed up, leaving only a scar. The hold taken on him by Kenneggy gradually tightened, and there was never any thought now of leaving it for the sake of independence. He could never leave it of his own free will, not now he had worked out on it the pain and disappointment of his sacrifice. The healing had come in return; the land taking so much had given something back, and its salve had done its work all unknown, and his heart, then too young to break, had healed over the chips taken out of it by the rough passage through adolescence.

Chapter Three

BY the time Joel reached seventeen he was stronger than most men in the prime of their strength; tall and broad, he was a fine-looking youth with his dark thick hair, dark laughing eyes and smiling face. He was full of the untiring strength and energy of very young manhood; he could work for long stretches without showing any effect beyond a healthy capacity for sleep. In the mowing season he rose from his bed soon after three in the morning, took his scythe and whetstone from the stable and went out to the hayfield. With the early cockcrows came the sweet sound of sharpening steel, a careful rhythmic slur of the stone, for he loved a keen edge and would let no one else use his blade. With the edge to his satisfaction he would glance over the meadow and measure up just how much should be down before breakfast, then balancing the tool truly he bent his back and swung the scythe shortly to clear the first swath away.

Once started and the way forward clear, his scythe swished through the grass in a steady, unhurried stroke which cleared the swath and cut low into the thick bottom where lay the best feeding value for the hay. The fragrant smell of the dewy grass pleased him and with this glorious scent in his nostrils he never tired of seeing the thick swath fall as the hidden blade swung through it, and the idea of his relentless advance through the meadow gave him a happy satisfaction.

Kenneggy grew a lot of hay and oats to provide winter feed for its teams of whim horses, and Richard liked it cut and carted as soon as it was safe, from fear of overheating in the rick. As these were important crops he liked to have his labourers as independent as possible of neighbouring farmers' doings, and although, when they were free at Kenneggy, he would lend his men and wagon in order to rush in a threatened harvest, he never relied on similar aid, but occasionally there came times when it had saved him. For this reason he took on extra hands from the villages, and if a good man or girl offered from as far as Helston or Marazion he boarded them so as to get the full benefit of their time and strength without losing some on long journeying. Elizabeth liked him to take a strong girl, for then she got help in the house and dairy when field work was not taking her out, and as her health had been poor during the past winter he brought back Mary from Helston early in the season.

Elizabeth looked with approval at her on the day she arrived. A strong, well developed girl, nineteen and mature for her age, with dark hair that curled, heavy but well outlined brows over deep brown eyes that had been set in her pleasant face with sooty fingers. A ready smile showed good strong teeth and completed Elizabeth's satisfaction, for she liked people about her who were easy to look at and whose presence living with the family was not a misery to them after the first week. She had taken the girl at once to the wash-house, bade her strip to the pelt as she filled the wide tub with hot water, and then stood by to supervise a very thorough washing from the top of her head to the soles of her feet, with particular attention to both these extremities. Her liking for the girl increased on finding she was clean and good humouredly willing to show she was well acquainted with soap and hot water. Satisfied that she was pure, bodily at least, the next thing was the clothes she had taken off; after

49

providing temporary garments she saw the girl put every article of her own in the washtub and deal with them to her equal satisfaction. This over, she felt she had done all she could to make sure there was nothing to offend the family's notion of cleanliness.

When Joel returned from the field the girl was hanging out her things on the line to dry. As he passed towards the door he looked curiously at her, dressed as she was in an old frock and apron of his mother's, and she allowed herself a quick glance at him over her shoulder. Their eyes met and they both smiled cautiously.

"Did Father bring 'ee from Helston?"

" 'Es, and Mrs. Andrewartha has seen I washed behind my ears," she answered, without stopping what she was doing.

"Ha, Mother'll have done that right enough. That's the christening; it makes 'ee one of the family."

He passed on into the house, thinking his father could have brought back something worse without looking far. He was shy of girls and embittered against them since he had been forced to break with Caroline, who by her easy friendliness had spoiled him for their company, yet the idea of seeing this one at every meal did not put him off his appetite.

The meal went through with the usual restraint felt when a stranger was with them, but Mary was unobtrusive in her manner and quick to see what was needed by any of them, and ready to rise unbidden to fetch or carry when necessary. As soon as he had eaten, Joel left the table and returned to the meadow, determined to make an effort to finish it before dark; for with him it was a rule, if it was in any way possible, to finish a job or a particular portion of it so there was no hang-over waiting to take a part of the following day from new work. The finishing of a field always gave him pleasure; he loved to see the uncut grass becoming smaller and smaller until eventually the moment of reward when one thin line of grass stood up until, stroke by stroke, it was mown down, leaving the meadow an open expanse of neat swaths.

Wait for the Wagon

The last blade razed, he stooped and taking a handful of the mow used it to clean the fragments of grass adhering with the evening dampness to his scythe, worn bright and polished along the edge and with its stiff back dark and shining like ebony. This done, he drew a rag from his hip pocket and most carefully wiped the steel clean and dry. He straightened his back, flexed his arms and leaned for a few minutes on the snathe to enjoy the full pleasure of the end of the day. Slowly he strode across the swaths to where his coat lay on the hedge, pulled it across his shoulders and turned off home, carrying his scythe over his shoulder.

While Joel and Matthew were mowing the second meadow, Mary and the children were set on to turning the previous day's cut. At noon they returned to the house and Mary came back with the dinners for the men, pasties wrapped in a clean napkin. For drink there was the pitcher of herb beer, home brewed, which she brought to replace the one they had emptied during the morning. They sat in a row under the hedge, trying to get what shade it cast, while she unwrapped the meal and handed it out.

"Mrs. Andrewartha told me to ask 'ee if there was enough onion in it for 'ee, Joel; we're getting short and we're to try 'n' make them last out."

Joel munched critically for a moment, giving the matter his careful judgment.

"I reck'n 'tis to my liking, just 'zactly. We'll need to put in more this year, Matthew; with the kids growing and eating more, what we did won't be 'nough."

"I did tell the Master but he did say 'twere best to be a tiddly bit short than to have them go bad on us. I do like a bit o' onion in a pasty meself," Matthew added, and gazed into the one he was eating as though in search of it.

Mary laughed at him, and looked across to Joel and smiled; he caught her eye and realised that she and his mother were parties in giving him the best of the pasties; not only were the contents of his better flavoured and juicier, but the others probably had no meat in them at all. His mother, he knew, was given to doing little things like that for him, saying he had so big a frame or he worked so hard, any excuse served to carry it off before the others. It gave him a little thrill of pleasure to find Mary was aiding her.

"How's hay-making, Mary?" he asked.

"Oh, 'tis a-going well enough; we've been wasting no time and 'twill be turned afore long and drying."

"I see thee'st quick at it," remarked Matthew. "I do hope you're not a-scattering it?"

"No. 'Tis a good mow and well cut, very near ground. Are we on carting tomorrow? Will 'ee want me to pitch or load?"

"I heard Father say we'd be on carting if weather holds. He'll tell 'ee what he wants 'ee to do, 'tisn't for me to say, but I 'spect he'll put 'ee on pitching, for he usually loads hisself. He says I can pitch faster'n him and this year he reck'ns I'll be pitching faster'n ever."

"I reck'n 'ee will too, if 'ee comes on same way as 'ee have with mowing," said Matthew. "And I shouldn't be surprised if he don't have me up with him, for thicky girl looks as though her could toss it up pretty quick herself."

They all laughed, and when the children joined them they outlined pictures of their father buried up on the wagon, and a conspiracy was set afoot for that purpose. And the next day, when loading began, it soon became apparent that this was what was going to happen. The hay had been cocked in lines down the field and the wagon moved up and down between them, the team of horses starting off every time Joel called, "Hold fast," to warn the loaders. As Matthew had predicted, Richard had him up beside him, for Joel could pitch up a heaped prong with an ease and speed which took a smart bit of handling to get it built well on; and Mary too could throw up a prongful at a steady pace. The children had the wooden rakes and it was their work to collect the tailings.

Outdoors and in Mary proved herself a good worker and this,

combined with her pleasant manner and good looks, made her liked by all the family. Joel liked her chiefly because she left him alone, never trying to make him talk or notice her, for although she looked after them both very well, of the two it was the Master she strove to please; and this satisfied Elizabeth. At first she had some fears lest the girl should make eyes at her handsome son; so had Joel himself, in the conceit of youth, and he was very well pleased with the way things had settled, and soon lost the shyness he had felt at first.

Before very long, however, without being able to give a reason for his supposition, Joel found himself convinced that his father did not like Mary. Certainly he was a quiet man and did not talk to any of them very much, but it was rarely, if ever, he addressed an unnecessary word to her in these days. It could not be on account of the work in the fields, although he nearly always dropped into this manner if he was becoming dissatisfied with a worker or if something was going wrong outside, for in Joel's opinion she was a dexterous girl, with a neat quick hand. If he was in the living-room and she was busy there, or coming in and out with things, he seemed unusually absorbed in his account books, his notebook or even bills and papers from his pockets; sorting out the stack he always carried and never seemed to lessen, humming the same two or three bars out of nothing at all, over and over again. If Elizabeth was in the room the girl did not seem to annoy him, it was only when he was with Joel or the children.

To be a stranger in folk's houses and to have no real home of one's own, seemed to Joel to be a poor life for any girl, and because of this he was always kind to her; he talked when they were out working, when they were creeping with bent backs hoeing under the hot sun, to make the toil less irksome. He liked her too because, although she was the elder, she managed to give the impression that she regarded him as rather a fine fellow, and had an admiring glance for him when he was making use of his young strength about the place.

When harvesting came along, he put a keen edge on his scythe again and went out into the cornfields as soon as the dew was off the ears. Mary and Betsy followed him as he reaped, to bind the sheaves, and it was his delight to see if he could leave them behind; but it was soon apparent that she could gather up the straw, twist a bond and bind the sheaf as fast as he could swing the scythe. Harvesting gave a great deal of work. There was the reaping and binding to start, hot and tiring; until their backs grew used to bending under the sun they ached considerably. The sheaves had to be set up, and if it rained they had to be pulled down and rebuilt after drying.

One Saturday night his father pushed his chair back from the table and looked across at Joel.

"How's corn, Joel my son, is there much to set up?"

He had been expecting the question and knew how his father liked to get out for a glass or two at the end of the week to yarn with the others at the 'Falmouth Packet'. He also knew the corn must be set up before night.

"There's a tidy bit yet, Father, but don't stop back, 'cause of that. I've nothing particular to do, so I'll just stroll out and set it up quietly. I'll not rush myself and I reck'n I can manage all right."

"Very well, as you say, Joel," – the tone he used implied that if he really was not necessary he would not help as he was sure the boy would get on quicker alone – "then maybe I'll get along to the 'Packet' and take a glass, and see what's doing up there."

He took down his jacket from its hook behind the door and threw it over his arm as he went out. Joel rose and was about to leave too when Mary paused on her way out with the dishes to the back kitchen.

"Maybe your mother'll let me help 'ee when I've these done. 'Twill be easier to have someone setting up with 'ee."

"Are you not too tired after the day?"

"No; no more'n you. Over a while 'twill be cool, and the best of the day. I'll be out to help afore long."

So Joel went out to the field to start. As Mary had said, it was a great deal quicker to have a helper, for if four sheaves were set together they stood so much better than the two alone with which he had to start each stook.

It was not long before Mary joined him, and between them, working at a steady pace, the sheaves were set up right over the field by the time dusk had fallen. As they set the last in place, they both seemed to realise what a warm quiet night had stolen on them, so still that they could hear the friendly sound of the tin stamps from Wheal Vor. It was the soft summer dusk which brought everything close and intimate, and Mary's eyes wandered towards the cliffs from where came the sound of a very gentle surf breaking on the sand at lazy intervals.

"I do like the sea when 'tis quiet," she said. "Let's go 'cross and have a look at it."

The field was on the slope below Old Shaft and just above Kenneggy Sand, which the family always regarded as their own property. They climbed down the rough path to the beach below and watched the tiny waves curling in from a sleepy sea. They strolled along the beach, both enjoying the peace and soft gloaming after the work and glare of the day.

"The water do look warm and tempting, Joel. I'm a-going to bathe."

"Bathe? At this time o' night?"

"Why not? What other time have I got? 'Twill be fine and fresh, and make me sleep. Well, I'm a-going to, and thee cust sit here and wait for me."

She moved away a few yards and Joel sat down on a rock to wait while she carried out her mad impulse. He felt no embarrassment, for the life in the farmhouse was naturally a cramped one and they were all thrown so much together that the fact of having her undress so near to him was not disturbing. In the dusk he could see her body gleaming white as she ran the yard or two to the water; as she entered and it rose around her, the gentle purling splash of the cool water sounded sweet to the tired boy.

" 'Tis warm as a bath. Thee'st missed something. Come on, thee'st took shy! Would 'ee come in if I did swim round to the next cove," she taunted.

This was too much, and in a second he had off his boots and clothes and was down the beach, striking out into deep water. A little way off he could see her face white against the water, surrounded by dark ripples as she moved.

"I'll give 'ee that much start and race 'ee to the rock," he called and struck out powerfully.

She was off in a flash and, to his surprise, made swift progress ahead of him. With a spurt, he just managed to touch the rock a second after she had got there, and they turned, laughing, treading water to recover their breath.

"Can 'ee float? I never can do that," she confessed.

"Easy, just look at this."

He allowed his feet to rise in the water and by wriggling his hands paddled around in a circle. Mary tried to copy him but immediately sank, and rose up spluttering and shaking water from her eyes. Joel came up behind her.

"See, I'll show 'ee. Let your feet come up now." His hands gripped her gently under the armpits and pulled her backwards; she let her body go up and in a moment she was floating. Joel suddenly went very quiet; the touch of her bare skin under his fingers, the firmness of her breasts seen over her white gleaming shoulder, all were queerly disturbing. He felt his throat contract and something press on his heart, making it pound violently. Impulsively he bent forward and kissed her cheek.

"Joel!"

Already he was away; overcome by his shyness he was swimming as fast as he could for the beach. She followed slowly and went to her clothes, took up an undergarment and, using it as a

56

towel, began to dry herself. She slipped on her frock and walked over to where he sat, trousered and with his jacket across his shoulders drying the sand out of his toes with his shirt. She dropped down on her knees beside him, ruffling her hair with the improvised towel.

"Joel, thee'st vexed with me?"

"Of course not; 'tis with myself."

After a moment's silence. "Why did 'ee kiss me, Joel?"

" 'Twas just how you looked; I couldn't help it."

"Then why did 'ee go 'way? Wasn't I pleasing 'ee?' '

"Thee'st too pleasing, as you very well do know. And I thought maybe you'd not like it."

She laughed softly as she sank down in the sand close beside him.

"Why, Joel, my handsome! As if I couldn't give 'ee just one little kiss."

He looked sideways at her, with the thin frock clinging around her strong young figure, and before his mind swam again the sight of her white body blurred and lovely through the water. His fingers tingled again as they had done when they had touched her cool skin. Before he knew quite what he was doing, his arm was around her and he lowered his head to kiss her full on the lips. It was the first kiss he had ever taken, with all the yearning of his growing desire.

"So you thought I'd not give 'ee a kiss, Joel my dear. Why I'd give 'ee anything . . . anything . . . you wanted."

Gently his strong arms drew her towards him; the feel of her under his hands, yielding and tempting, was a glamorous new sensation, disturbing him in a strange, choking-sweet way as nothing in life had ever done before.

Late that night, as he lay awake on his bed, he felt bitterly disappointed with himself. He felt as though he had been cheated in some way, as if life had promised so much, and in the end given such a very small thing. What he missed now was beyond his power to name, but perhaps it was his youth, for now he had said goodbye to it and was right over the threshold into manhood.

Like most boys just through the growing pains of manhood, he resolved to have nothing further to do with girls and honestly intended to keep the resolution. He began to revive his interest in the local wrestling, getting about among the young tinners and farmers' sons who shared his growing love of the sport, and attending every match so as to learn as much as he could from the best exponents in the district. Gradually that Saturday evening drifted further into the past and became like a previous chapter in his life, read and passed but still having a direct bearing on further events. At first he had feared Mary might appropriate him as her own possession but he misjudged her. Her manner towards him, outwardly at least, remained unchanged; she was still kind, friendly and very willing to do any small service for him. She saw his clothes were clean, dry and mended, and was ready always to abet Elizabeth in giving him favourite dishes and seeing they were served to his liking.

Another fear then began to trouble him; he worried lest he had risked his freedom and given himself into the girl's hand. This was not a pang of conscience, for he was sufficiently honest with himself to realise that if time could be put back he would have taken again what he was lucky enough to be offered. He had not forgotten how his father had beaten him and forbidden his friendship with Caroline; it had made him willing to snatch at just those few stolen moments of tenderness that Mary had given him, but it had also made him associate girls with pain and punishment.

Had he taken a bait and was Mary's calmness due to his being played? The thought was always with him; it was the last conscious effort as he fell asleep, in the morning on wakening it returned as fresh as ever. The more he pondered over the chances, the dearer his fancy-free heart became to him. He was not in love with Mary; he was conscious of a hope of one day falling in love, perhaps with a girl like Caroline, and he wanted to be free to fall. Added to all this was the great store he was setting on the wrestling, and for this alone he wished to remain single so that he could go to matches when and where he liked.

As the weeks slipped by rapidly – for no sooner did a week's work start than it seemed he was making haste to get it finished before Saturday night – the time for Mary's return to town came very near, which found Joel with strangely mixed feelings. He knew the house would neither be so comfortable for him nor so agreeable without her, he would miss too her admiration and the pleasant feeling of temptation surrounding her, but all this was balanced, weighed down even, by a sense of the relief that must surge in him after she had gone.

The weather had broken and he turned to jobs for the days when he must work under a roof. In the loft above the stable there was a pile of sacks to be sorted and repaired where the mice had nibbled. He collected needle and thread and looked out his leather sailmaker's palm for using on the stiffer seams – or more correctly, Mary had found it in the end, after much searching where he had left it in a safe place – and climbed up to the loft. He padded a box and wiped some of the cobwebs from the glazed slit that served for light and began to look over the sacks. Those he found needing repair he flung in a heap, the rest he folded up and laid aside ready for immediate use.

He had not been working very long before he heard someone enter the stable below; he took no notice, thinking it was one of the children, Polly maybe, coming to help. Steps mounted the ladder and, looking up, he saw Mary enter the loft. She smiled and brushed the dust from her hands, wiped away a cobweb that had caught in her dark hair.

"Your mother did send me with this hank of thread I found on top of the dresser."

She sank down on the pile of sacks and held out the thread to him. He took it and thanked her.

"I had disremembered her," he added, continuing to work.

She picked up a bag he had darned and examined it, somehow by the way she looked at it managing to convey that it was neat work.

"Joel. I'm a-going back to Helston the end of the week, as you do know."

He nodded. "We'll be missing 'ee. Maybe next year you'll come 'long to us again."

"Maybe," she sighed. "Though I don't reck'n Mrs Andrewartha'll have me 'gain."

" 'Course she will. Mother likes 'ee, same as we all do."

" 'Es, but. . . I do hate having to tell 'ee, Joel, but maybe you'll help me. I reck'n I'm a-going to have a baby."

He gasped as he stared at her anxious face in the miserable light that filtered through the dirty glass. In his throat he could almost feel the hook embedding itself.

"Do 'ee mind that night on the beach, Joel? I reck'n I must have been caught. Don't 'ee be too vexed with me, 'twasn't all my fault," she pleaded. "Can 'ee help me, for 'twill be kind of hard to get work soon."

It was true it was not all her fault, and because of that he supposed he would have to help her. The blow had fallen after all. Instead of the fleck of cloud on the horizon passing away, it had suddenly grown to overshadowing proportions and threatened now to break in a storm over him.

"How can I tell Mother and Father? He'll kill me, and I can't blame him if he do. Who could have thought so much trouble could have come from such a little bit of fun?"

Mary smiled and patted his knee. "Don't 'ee fret, Joel, 'twill be all right. 'Tisn't as though such a thing had never happened afore. It happens to a good few couples, only they do forget it when they get older. Your father can't say much to 'ee, for thee'st a man now, and a fine strong one, too."

Joel groaned, his pride and his spirit were sorely bruised by it all. To think such a thing could happen to him. In his self-pity, however, he did not forget the girl; he had a responsibility there and already he knew he would shoulder it. There was no decision to be made, only adjustment to the idea.

"I don't love 'ee, Mary, and I don't want to have to marry 'ee; but if you're in trouble and I'm to blame for it I'll not let 'ee be hurt. I'll speak to Mother and Father – I reck'n there's nothing else to do."

After the children had gone to bed he knew he must confess the trouble to his parents and take what scorn and shame they chose to pour on him. His face had flamed scarlet at different times during the afternoon when he felt he was about to state the truth; now the time was right on him all the colour drained away from it.

"Father and Mother, I reck'n there's something I ought to tell 'ee. Mary did tell me she's a-going to have a baby."

The effect on each of them was in its way astonishing. Elizabeth looked far more surprised and horrified than, with a handsome son and a good-looking young woman in her house, she had any right to be. But Richard hardly raised his head; if it had been, Mary did say the copper's leaking, he could have taken it with more annoyance, so little did he seem to grasp the calamity.

"Joel!" she gasped. And then, "Is it true what he says, Mary?"

" 'Es, Mrs Andrewartha," breathed the girl. 'I'm certain of it."

"And are you the father, Joel?" Elizabeth asked, her anger now getting the mastery of her first inclination to faint.

"I suppose so," he answered.

"But surely you know without supposing?"

"Well, then I am."

His father turned towards him slowly. Then he looked at Mary and met her eyes. Joel saw the glance each gave the other, and knew that Mary had nothing to fear from him; nor did she fear him, only his mother. He knew that in spite of that undefined hostility towards

Mary Richard would not do her injustice, would even protect her from his wife's tongue. His father's steady gaze returned to him.

"What makes 'ee so sure, Joel?"

He looked at him in embarrassment. "How do 'ee mean, Father?" But he was looking at Mary now.

"Have there been other men with 'ee, Mary?"

"No, only Joel. That I do swear to 'ee," she answered definitely.

"Mary," he said earnestly, and with surprising kindness in his voice, "I don't reck'n thee'st been very fair to Joel. He's young and not wise to women's tricks, as you very well do know, and thee'st given him no chance. You saw Joel was a good boy and fair minded, so 'ee ran after him till 'ee got what you'd a mind for, and then reck'ned you had him fixed. Well see, I'm not letting 'ee tie him down like that, bain't fair on him, and I'm not standing by and seeing it done. So I do tell 'ee straight."

"But, Father, I can't let 'ee give her all the blame, when 'twere my fault. I got to get her out of trouble, same as I got her into it."

Elizabeth gripped the sides of her chair and leaned forward, white and very determined. She foresaw what he was going to suggest, and because the plan had already crossed her own mind and been immediately rejected, she was resolved at all costs that he was not going through with it.

"No, Joel; what your father says is right. Mary should have known better than to have got you into this fix. She's more experienced than you, I've no doubt, and had all her wits about her. She's just set out to catch you, and I'm not going to allow it."

By this time the girl had dropped into a chair and was dabbing quietly at her eyes with a corner of her apron. So obviously had she fallen from grace in the family's eyes, and in such a short while. The sight of her tears touched Joel's heart, for a weeping woman always made him feel he must do, give, anything in his power to make her tears cease.

"But I don't see there's anything else for it, Mother. To save her name I'd better. . . "

"Hold your tongue, boy; you'll do nothing," roared his father. "I'll not have 'ee marry her, that I do tell 'ee once and for all."

The apron dropped back into Mary's lap. In a flash her tears were forgotten and her eyes blazed a challenge at him; she was on her feet in a second, fighting not only for the one means of saving her respectability but for the man of her fancy.

"And for why, Mr Andrewartha? Why shouldn't Joel marry me when I've got his child? Maybe you'll tell me that?"

He half-turned his shoulder to her, thrust his hands deep in his trouser pockets and sprawled out in his chair. His foot stirred up the wood on the fire and sent out a little shower of sparks. For a moment a smile flickered wryly at the corners of his mouth.

"And I will, girl. I'll tell 'ee one very good reason. If there's a child a-coming, 'tain't Joel who's father, as you do know."

They all looked at him in puzzled astonishment. The challenge had faded right out of Mary's eyes.

"Did you say he's not the father? Then who is?" breathed Elizabeth anxiously.

He shifted in his chair uneasily, and then looked in mild defiance at her.

"Maybe I am," he suggested quietly.

This supposition took his wife and son completely by surprise; they could only stare unbelievingly at him, while Mary gave way to uncontrolled sobbing, burying her face in her hands.

"You, Rich, to be the father of this girl's baby?" Elizabeth gasped. "Why, 'tis impossible. 'Tis no time for such a silly joke. Or are you just trying to save Joel from marrying a loose girl?"

"Not only possible, Elizabeth, but if Mary's right, 'twill be most probable. And I'm saving Joel, just 'cause he bain't a-going to be snared 'gainst his will by any girl. But mark 'ee, Elizabeth, say what you please 'bout me, and Joel here if 'ee want to, but don't 'ee call

63

Mary a loose girl. I reck'n there bain't a great deal of bad in her, no more'n in any other girl, and maybe there's a lot more good. I'll not have 'ee call her that, just 'cause being a natural woman, her's having a child."

Elizabeth sank back in her chair and bit her lip; the knuckles were white where her hands gripped the hard arms.

"I can't say what I've a mind to before my son and the girl, but later I'll talk to you. If this is all true, why has Joel been brought into it?"

Mary tried to control her sobs and speak distinctly between those that persisted in shaking her.

"I was fond of him. I reck'n from the very first day I did see him, and over a while, when I found how 'twas a-going to be with me, I thought if only I could get him to like me a little, maybe he'd think he was to blame and try to put things right. I've got no folk, and no friends who'll have me like this, and if you do turn me out, Mrs Andrewartha, I'll have to go to workhouse. There's no other place for me."

Richard made impatient noises with his tongue. "Turn 'ee out! Who said a word 'bout turning 'ee out? I did say you're not to marry Joel, 'cause you did trick him into making a young fool of hisself, same as his father's made an old fool of hisself, but I never did say one word 'bout turning 'ee to workhouse. No, I reck'n the child'll be Andrewartha same as me, and as Andrewartha he'll be reared. When he's born you'll be free to go where you've a mind to, leaving him with us, and over a while there's none will mind a thing 'bout 'ee."

"Well, upon my word! First you admit being unfaithful, and now you calmly suggest that I should rear your little bastard for you." Elizabeth gave a study of righteous indignation.

"Unfaithful my foot," he spat scornfully into the fire. "I'm not unfaithful to 'ee. My heart's as faithful to 'ee as the day we were wed, nearly twenty years agone. 'Twas just a moment of foolishness, temptation did get the better of me. And I bain't ashamed to say so; but I would be 'shamed if I didn't try to set things right for the girl. And you, Elizabeth, for all you pretend to have a sharp tongue, thee'st always first to help when help's wanted. The poor little child bain't a-going to suffer just 'cause I was in the mind to misbehave myself, and was too lazy to fight the notion; and you'll be helping me. And Joel, my son, do 'ee let this be a lesson to 'ee, and learn from your father's bad 'zample to keep clear o' women, and have no truck with 'em, for they do take away all peace of body and soul. There's only one woman's good for each man, and he can never be sure her's right one till he be safely dead and out t'others' way. Let it be a lesson to 'ee, Joel."

The result of the discussion had been so different from anything he had anticipated that it left Joel with a tangle of impressions and emotions promising to take a mighty effort to sort out. The discovery of an intimacy between Mary and his father disturbed the very foundations of his developing mind, it brought the image of his father down from the pedestal in pieces at his feet; while at the same time it made him very human and more closely in touch with his own life than he had ever been before. He had never imagined his father to be possessing the same disturbing impulses and desires as had affected himself. It seemed that because he had already begotten six children of his marriage no one expected him to have a roving eye on a girl. His lapse, followed by his blunt honesty in refusing to let Joel be blamed for falling where he himself had fallen, brought the two nearer to friendship than they had ever been since the day of the flogging. From being simply father and son they had risen, through a better knowledge of each other's weaknesses, to learn of certain strengths and become companions.

Mixed with the relief of finding he was not in honour bound to marry her, who had indeed merely hoped to make use of him, was a dash of regret that it had not been he alone who had received Mary's favours. Physically she had certainly attracted him and it would have pleased his pride to have felt she had found him attractive beyond others, but it seemed she had been willing to lend her favours higher first. It must have been after this his father found her presence a restraint upon him and was made so uncomfortable by it.

Joel knew now that he had been tricked into spending his young passion and felt a vague resentment against her for shattering his youthful illusions concerning her sex. Girls, all so young and fresh and innocent they seemed to adolescents, when actually they were born experienced, and knew before they had the chance to learn. For the first time he began to understand the reason for his disappointment over what he had unconsciously believed should have been rapture, over ecstasy withheld.

Through the winter life at Kenneggy was much as it had always been, and Mary stayed on with them. The long, dark evenings gave them more time to be together than the crowded, strenuous days of summer; although work occupied much of their time as they sat about in the candlelight, with a good furze blaze or a fire of peat from the lonely moors glowing in the hearth and filling the room with its pleasant tang, there was a sociality and warmth in being out of the rough weather that the summer gave no chance to find. Christmas brought the only time when they could allow themselves the luxury of doing nothing, just sitting about the fire and enjoying its heat on outstretched hands idle for a little while.

Elizabeth, contrary to what her tongue had promised but true to her husband's knowledge of her, was kindness itself to Mary, and never by word or action cast up to her what the four of them knew. She was not called upon to leave the farm-place or meet outsiders, so few knew she was with child or thought much about it. It was nobody's business but the Andrewarthas'. When, in the last days of winter, she was delivered of a son, Elizabeth herself, experienced enough in childbirth through her own and her neighbours' efforts, attended her. They called him Chris, and from that day Richard had him marked down to become what none of Elizabeth's had, a tinner, who working in Wheal Speed would one day beat his borer into a wealth of new metal.

Summer stole round again, with the wrestling matches, which, held on Midsummer Day, Lammas Day and other special occasions, had always drawn Joel. As he grew older and taller, the fact that he himself could throw any of his fellows who would play him was a reward for the study he had made of the methods of attack and defence practised by all the best local men. After he had turned nineteen, he began to come into his full strength, and the fine physical development which very soon was to be the envy of every man in the parishes was already taking the place of coltish youth. One day, up at Angove's smithy, he astonished even that strong man by lifting his mandrel clean off the ground without undue effort.

"By St. Michael! Joel boy, that there mandrel do weigh half-ton if it do a pound. I've seen three men hard put to shift un. 'Twould be a sin to keep such a boy as you out of the ring, and if you've a mind to I'll take 'ee in hand and turn 'ee into best wrestler this side of Penzance. How 'bout getting into shape for Lammas Day matches?"

"Would 'ee now? That'd be mighty good of 'ee, and I'd be proud to learn off a wrestler like you."

" 'Es, Joel, I was all right in my day, but that was long while agone; us must give way to the boys, no mistake. But I do know chips and ringcraft, and I'd learn 'ee all I know to see those arms of yours cast a man full back on grass."

" 'Twill be a proud day, come I do that. But if you'll teach me, I reckon I've strength enough and more to do it."

Angove took him in hand, and in a field off Millpool Lane, where it joined the turnpike at the back of the smithy, he taught him the finesse of the art, the importance of balance and how to preserve it by the correct placing of the feet both in attack and defence. He impressed on him never to loosen his hold unless it was to improve it, not even when he was actually being cast was he to let go, for many a bout had been snatched out of defeat by an opponent's tenacity and quickness to return to attack. Part of his training was at the same time a help in the smithy, for he was set to some useful sledging to develop his arms and steady his eye. To gain further insight of ring tactics, he sent the boy to a match which was being held at Penzance between local men.

Crowded about the ring roped out in the field, thirty clear yards in diameter, people were gathered four or five deep. Joel edged his way in until he could get an unrestricted view and watched the competitors and their sidesmen, the methods of obtaining and avoiding a clutch, the pet holds and those they tried hardest to avoid. Three pairs in turn faced each other in the ring, stooping, feinting and dodging in their efforts to get a good hold – strong well-built fellows clad in loose untearable canvas jackets on which all the holds were taken. Beneath this, stripped to the waist, their chests were seen broad and muscular through the collar rolled away from their powerful necks. Their stout breeches were belted at the waist and below the knee, fitting snugly over the rolling muscles of their loins and quarters; thin stockings covered their feet and came well up over the knee.

Quite often this preliminary took a considerable time and became monotonous to all but the keenest students of the sport, but once a hold was obtained it was grand to see the strong active men straining, the one to break it, the other to throw him to the ground to touch it with two shoulders and one hip, or both hips and a shoulder. The sticklers followed them closely, leaping about and flinging themselves on the ground to see and claim a fair back. Very often, so difficult was it to judge indisputably, that a second wrangling would spring up in the ring and take in outsiders either to strengthen or to stop it. It happened that the seventh man was left without an opponent and the promoters were calling for someone to fill the part.

"Come on, someone to try a hitch with John Trevise. For the sport of it; 'twould be no shame to be worsted by John, and 'twould be a grand thing to throw 'un. Come, who'll try on? A guinea for the man who can wrestle with John and worst him."

Someone standing near evidently knew Joel to be a promising wrestler, for he felt a push in the back and several men started to call on him.

"How about young Andrewartha here? Come, Joel, into ring with 'ee and show us what 'ee can do."

" 'Es, go 'long, my dear, try a hitch with 'un; 'twill not kill 'ee."

"Hi, Mister, Joel here'll wrestle with 'ee. He's prettiest youngster in the parish."

Joel found himself, not unwilling, thrust into the ring and was handed jacket and stockings. His opponent, older than he was, and somewhat heavier, looked at him with friendly interest; obviously he was confident there was nothing to fear in a raw boy, even though he looked a finely built, strong fellow. Someone appointed himself as Joel's sidesman and the bout started.

Already Joel had decided that he had better cut down the preliminary weaving and dodging as much as possible and force his man into action if he could rush a hold. This he managed within a few seconds and strove to cramp his opponent by crowding him, and for a minute or two they strove without much advantage to either. Then the heavier man shifted his position and, by an adroit movement, had Joel halfway across his hip, his feet scarcely touching the ground.

A roar went up from the spectators as they saw him about to be thrown sideways to the ground. But he was quick, too quick for the over-confident John, and in a flash he had the back of his heel over the front of his man's shin, and drove the upper part of his body forward with all his strength. For a moment there was a deadlock, muscles bulged and stood out like rocks under their skin. Joel summoned every ounce of his strength to gain an advantage; gradually he forced him back and off balance until they crashed on the grass together. Another roar from the crowd; it was the first time in his life Joel had heard applause given for him and it filled him with redoubled strength. As they had fallen on their sides and it took a fair back only, three points to the ground, to constitute a fall, they had to regain their feet, shake hands and try for another hold.

"Them's clutched!"

Again the feinting had been shortened by Joel taking a hold on the cloth between his man's neck and shoulder. At the same time John took a similar hold with his right hand, leaving their lefts poised in the air as, step for step, they moved about the ring, each watching for the other's move. Trevise made his first, and Joel found himself in a hug which would have cracked lighter-built ribs and crushed the breath from most bodies. He had his right arm over his man's left, he worked it further round and secured a hold behind the neck, then he waited, standing firm while Trevise made a great effort to lift him bodily. Skilful footwork had secured his balance however, and as the strain, proving unsuccessful, slackened a shade, Joel edged his right side in until they were both facing the same way. His arm went further about the neck, his left took a grip on the sleeve around his man and close to the side; his right leg locked from the outside about John's right and with this purchase lifted his foot from the ground and, by leaning well forward, dragged him over too, off his balance and, firm on his left foot, Joel continued the turn until he came down on top of him, heavily.

The strain relaxed, they separated and regained their feet. Joel was flushed and excited, yet more shy now, with the onlookers cheering him, than he had been when he entered the ring. For a moment John Trevise had an incredulous look on his face, but, good sportsman as he was, it soon changed to humorous appreciation of his own defeat, and he was first to clap a hand on the boy's shoulder and congratulate him.

Wait for the Wagon

" 'Pon my word, Joel Andrewartha, there's a pretty strength in your arm. Do 'ee wrestle much, 'cause you ought to? If 'ee set your mind to it, there's not a man in these parts could worst 'ee. Keep to it, boy, and if 'ee can take a fall sometimes you'll be a mighty fine wrestler."

"Thank 'ee," he answered, delighted at the praise. "I reck'n 'twas just a fluke I gave 'ee a fall. I've not played much, only with boys about the farm-place, and 'tis first time I've been 'gainst a wrestler. But I do like it; I do like it more'n anything I know of."

"Then you'll be a wrestler, and there'll be few to worst 'ee when thee'st grown to full strength. Do 'ee mark my words."

Joel hardly knew whether he was more pleased over these words of encouragement or over the golden guinea presented to him as prize money. He retired to the edge of the ring to watch the next pair in their bout, and many people gave him a hand and a praising word as he went. It did not matter very much to him that his next opponent was a more experienced man than Trevise, and strength alone was not of much avail against him. In science Joel was lacking badly compared with him, but in the struggling minutes that elapsed before his stubborn resistance was overcome and he took his fall, he learned more of wrestling than he had picked up in a hundred victories over other boys. The defeat was timely also in preventing him from becoming over-confident, and it stimulated his ambition to reach a height of skill like that possessed by this man, and the other who later faced him in the final bout for the best of three falls. It taught him he had much to learn, and made him eager to learn it.

When the gathering broke up and Joel drifted away among the crowd, he found his steps taking him towards Penzance market. In his pocket was the golden coin; it was grand to have money, and his very own, but money meant nothing to him for its own sake. It was simply a means of purchasing things he wanted, and it was going to be broken for that purpose very soon. He never thought for a moment of taking the coin home; for him, a triumphal return would have to consist of carrying some treat bought for the family, something they liked but could too rarely enjoy.

He wandered about the stalls looking at all the good things offered there; he looked too at the girls, some pretty and some just naughty. An intriguing few were both pretty and naughty, but he left them alone. Apart from the countryman's natural distrust of the town girls he knew many horrid tales of the crimps in these seaports. Penzance was not so bad as Falmouth, where he had heard men were enticed to their dens with women decoys, drugged and sold unconscious to some ship master whose craft was going out on the tide.

At one stall he found a pile of tasty-looking gingerbreads, a favourite sweetmeat among the family, and knowing well they would enjoy it for weeks, he bought a couple of pounds. Passing on he came to a brave heap of big red oranges; a rare treat they would be, and after enjoying a sensation of reckless extravagance he bought four. They were scarce and expensive and it was not often they were on the stall where one could even look at them, let alone buy. With his purchases he went down to the "Star" where he had left his horse, and set off home. It was dark long before he reached there; after stabling and tending the horse he went indoors with his parcels.

"Where's Salome? Has she gone to her bed? 'Cause I've brought her something from market."

"Of course she's in bed, 'tis late," answered Elizabeth. "What have you been doing, Joel? What have you got there?"

With a patter of small feet Salome came running into the living-room in her nightgown, her hair done up tightly in curling rags.

"I did hear you come back, Joel. Did 'ee say you'd brought something for me? Oh, Joel, what is it? No, no, Mother, I'll go back to bed; yes, I'll go at once, but just let me see what Joel did bring me."

From his pocket he pulled one of the bright oranges, and held it out to her. The little girl's eyes popped with amazed pleasure as she took it in both hands and held it as though it were the orb of the realm, of priceless value.

"Oh, Joel, thank 'ee; thank 'ee, Joel."

"And, Mother, this one is for you and Father, and these two are for the rest of us to share. Here are some gingerbreads, I did see them in the market, too."

They all looked at him in astonishment, which increased considerably when he pulled coins from his pocket and tossed them casually in the air before dropping them back.

"Where did 'ee get all that money, boy?" asked his father.

"I did win it."

"Not at cards, Joel?" Elizabeth's anxiety showed itself in her shocked expression and voice.

"No, wrestling. I was at the match and they wanted someone to play John Trevise; a fellow pushed me out in the ring, and as no one else did offer I tried a fall with him for the sport. I did throw him, too. They'd offered a guinea if he were thrown, 'cause they wanted someone to play. He was a pretty man, and did say I'd make a good wrestler."

"Oh, Joel, did 'ee really throw John Trevise? He's a good man I've heard tell." Charles's admiration was apparent.

"I'm glad you won, Joel; but be careful you don't strain yourself struggling with those big fellows," said Elizabeth.

" 'Es. I'm glad 'ee won, my son," his father's praise was sincere if not so enthusiastic. "But I don't hold with all that wrestling. A man's strength is given him to do his daily work, not to squander at inn-play. However, I reck'n 'twill not do 'ee any harm once in a way, but don't 'ee get wasting too much time on 't. So often with youngsters they do get to thinking on sport, nothing but sport all the day. When I was a boy of your age I'd 'nough work to keep me busy, and was tired 'nough at end of day to rest, and glad of it too, without all this sport."

" 'Es, Father, and you do work as hard as any man still, none harder, but it brings us mighty few oranges; and my sport did bring us a rare treat, eh, Mother?"

73

d

"Whist, Joel, don't answer your father pertly, 'tisn't proper."

"But 'tis true. Anyway, 'twasn't meant pert. I do get tired of hearing how hard Father did work in his day; I reck'n I work hard 'nough and if there's a bit of pleasure to be had now 'n' then it freshens 'ee up and thee oust get back to the job all the better. And I like a bit of wrestling for my fun. There'd be more cause for 'ee to grumble if I was drinking or wenching."

During this outburst his father was watching him with an enigmatic look on his face; impossible to say whether he was sympathising or growing angry. Elizabeth saw it and interpreted the latter, rashly, for she should have known her man better.

"Joel, now you're annoying your father. Say no more lest you spoil the pleasure in the things you've brought us."

"Ah, leave the boy alone. Maybe he's right. I reck'n I'm a-getting old-fashioned in my opinions." He looked at her and seeing the sting his reproof had left, softened his voice as he continued. "I do feel glad my boys have their mother's good sense. As you say, Joel, there's worse ways of spending all the leisure you get today."

An affectionate grin stole across Joel's face as he glanced at his father.

"Do 'ee wait till the boys are bigger; with three sons to help 'ee outside, and three daughters to keep the house to rights there'll be nothing for 'ee to do save one thing, and that's to keep us busy."

"Maybe you're right, Joel; there'll surely be something to keep me at it, if 'tis only that. Now 'way to bed with 'ee, for 'tis getting mighty late."

The next time he went up to the smithy he found Angove was not pleased with what he had learned about that evening.

"I did send 'ee to watch, not to go into ring thyself. But as you took a fall in second bout maybe 'twill not matter so much. For 'tis like this here, see, if folks up Penzance get to know 'bout 'ee, 'twon't be much good for us to put money on 'ee; us won't get no odds. And mark what I do tell 'ee, Joel Andrewartha, there'll be a packet of money on 'ee from hereabouts, Lammas Day. And by telling 'ee that I've no mind to make 'ee teazey, 'zactly, but just careful; for if you've a mind to you'll stand as firm as Great Iddy's Rock, and no danger."

His training continued in the weeks remaining before Harvest Home and all the best wrestlers in the parish came up Millpool Lane to the field to lend a hand with practice bouts for young Andrewartha, who was, according to Angove, to bring the belt again to the stannary. He made a good pupil, always ready to learn and to act on experienced advice, quick on his feet, and getting to the science of each throw and applying it with all his tremendous young strength. The mere strong man, the weight-lifting type, rarely makes much of a wrestler, for his movements are naturally slow and heavy, but Joel's nimble brain provided the swiftness of attack which was so essential to a good striker. These clicks were made with the side of the foot or heel, sharp, whippy strokes to trip an opponent or strike his supporting leg from beneath him.

On the day of the great match the crowd about the ring was hundreds strong, noisy and full of enthusiasm for its favourites among the competitors.

As each district had supporters for its own man a certain amount of argument and wrangling was going on, but during the bouts all followed and cheered every good move, even if the result was disappointing to local hopes. It was arranged so that no man played another from his own parish unless in the final.

Joel had lost all nervousness the instant he felt his opponent take a hold on his jacket, and had thrown his men in a style which delighted the majority of the crowd almost as much as it had Angove himself. An unknown man, he had met with opposition more than once from a sidesman and an opposing section of the onlookers, and in one bout his throw, counted by most as a fair back, was claimed as a hitch – meaning some part of either of the men's bodies had touched grass before the three points – and he was asked to play again. Perhaps because of a slight feeling of resentment, he had recklessly repeated the same throw but with such precision and force that this time there was no argument possible over the result. Being fortunate enough to draw a bye in the semifinals he was placed in the final to decide the champion of the day, opposed to one of the Kittos, a fine man from Camborne.

The final was to be decided by the best of three falls, with fifteen minutes' rest after a fall. They shook hands in the centre, retired to the edges, faced about and approached each other with every caution. Joel was out to win, both for his own glory and to justify Angove's patience over him; Kitto was older and more experienced, equally determined. Both had a great respect for the other after seeing how he had dealt with earlier opponents. Eye following eye, arms loose with hands ready and elbows safely to their sides they circled each other, just waiting to catch a good hold. Feet in line and always placed so as to have a secure balance, they followed each other's movements, ready to counter every attack.

Suddenly they closed. A shout went out from the crowd, as it always did when play really commenced. It had not time to die before it swelled to a roar. Joel had been thrown with what appeared absurd ease; a lightning stroke of the foot and inexperience had gone down before tried knowledge. As he offered his hand there was a wry smile on his face.

Angove would have none of his apologies as they chatted between bouts.

" 'Tis the very thing to make 'ee win, Joel boy. If 'ee had won a fall this bout your head would have been too big for your body, and belike he'd have 'ee on grass in no time at all. Now you'll be watching out, and 'twill be Kitto'll be over-pleased with hisself."

The stickler waved them into the ring again. Kitto closed almost at once: he needed one fall to win and was going for it. He had Joel's right wrist in his grasp and leaning forward inserted his own right arm under the boy's jacket, and up over his shoulder to grasp the opposite side of the rolled collar. It was a tricky hold, on the borderline, and owing to the tightening of the cloth one which could be retained against all attack. He strove against Joel and began to lean forward, attempting to force him down with his upraised arm and the pull across his shoulder. Always previously this attack had succeeded, but now something was going wrong – Joel could not be bent nor shifted by a fraction of an inch.

The crowd's yell of excitement faded into a dead silence. In amazement they saw the muscles on Kitto's legs knotting and rolling, they saw his great loins putting out all their strength, his neck cording with the effort. He might as well have been pushing at an oak-tree, so firmly Joel seemed to have rooted himself in the ground. Beyond a gathering of his muscles and a whitening of his upheld hand he was almost undisturbed, his great frame never gave for one moment beneath the effort that was draining the strength of his man. Kitto knew, and realised that Joel knew it too, that he had a hold which might bring him victory, but if it did not then no other could be taken from it. A fall had to be won now or the bout was lost.

Slowly Joel began to advance his body against the pull on his collar, taking the holding hand over with him. His right hand too was moving, over and down, bearing Kitto past the position where his advantage held to one where he lost all his purchase. His hand trapped in the jacket, his body bent now by Joel's weight and grip from behind, before he could bring himself to release the wrist he held, Kitto was caught on the shifting balance with a neat ankle stroke and fell with Joel on top of him, heavily on the grass. As he staggered to his feet green marks showed beyond dispute that it was a fair back.

One fall each, and the crowd was in a frenzy of excitement. Kitto evidently decided that youth would cause Joel to be nervous of the deciding fall, and played up to it, circling, feinting, dodging to wear out his guard, and then suddenly rushing in on him. Joel saw a right hand thrusting out towards him; had he prayed and all his prayers been answered he could not have had it more to his liking. In that fleeting second he took the wrist in a sweeping clip, drawing on the extended arm with his left hand, and with a jumping turn pulled it across his right shoulder as he hugged it to his breast. As his back was presented to his man he caught the same arm with his right hand above the elbow and thrusting up combined all his forces with Kitto's own rush to send him in that moment flying over his shoulder to land as flat as any pancake on his back.

"Flying Mare! Boys, what a throw!" Appreciation sounded all around, and Kitto, rubbing his shoulder ruefully, was the first to shake Joel's hand.

"I should have known. Only 'tis a throw needs a good man to make, and till now I didn't reckon on 'ee being just that good. But I do now."

That night the first championship leather was hung up in the long room of Kenneggy, and Joel went to sleep knowing he was at last what he had always longed to be, a wrestler, and one as good as any in West Cornwall.

Chapter Four

THE horses were the pride of the Andrewarthas' hearts; father and son, they had the teams ever in their minds and the welfare of the farm was wrapped up in them. Early and late it was the comfort and health of the horses that took first call on their time, and when his father asked if things were all right outside, Joel knew the degree of rightness was controlled mainly by their condition.

One winter's Sunday afternoon the two men were taking the usual walk around to study the land and stock. As they approached Four Acres, the sound of galloping hooves reached them.

"What's took 'em, Joel? Something's a-frigthening them, eh? 'Tisn't just good spirits making him gallop that way."

They quickened their pace a shade, and when they reached the field leaned on the gate to see what was happening there. Davy, the big chestnut, was pounding around as hard as he could go, and judging from the lather on his pelt had been at it for some time.

"Hi, Davy; whoa, boy, whoa," shouted his master. "Whoa there, whoa."

He thundered on past them, foam flecking his jaws, the sweat blackening his coat, and his eyes glassy and bloodshot.

"Best see if we can't stop him, hadn't we, Father? Can't let him go on like this. Whatever can have set him off that way?"

They entered the field and waited for him to come round, prepared to check him from either side as he came towards them.

"Watch out for his hooves, Joel. Mind what I tell 'ee now, and keep clear, for it seems he can't help what he's at."

"Don't 'ee worry 'bout me, Father, I'll watch out. Take 'n' care for thyself though."

But Davy bore down on them as unheeding as a wave on the shore and would have swept them over if they had not jumped aside to let him pass between. All their shouts and arm waving were of no avail; it was as though he had no instinct other than to outrun something that was behind him.

"How'd it be if I was to try to jump on him as he passes?"

His father shook his head. "There's something strangely wrong with him, Joel, and I reck'n we can't do anything 'bout it. Maybe 'twill only fetch more trouble on us to try. It do seem mighty strange to me."

"You're not meaning piskies have got hold of him? Or witchcraft? Do 'ee think 'tis witchcraft?"

"What else can it be? I've never seen the like of it afore. 'Tisn't a natural sickness that would be driving the creature round like he was mad. And if 'tisn't natural, then it must be witchcraft, and that's an end to it. And an end to Davy too, I reck'n."

Sure enough, the horse was showing signs of acute distress, eyes bulging from his head and his whole chest lathered in foam. Several times he plunged and stumbled in his mad rush, and at length failed to recover himself, rolled over, kicked madly and lay still. They both ran to where he lay, but even before they reached him and examined his great steaming form, they knew he had fallen dead; that he had galloped himself to death.

"And Davy was the best horse we got," remarked Richard as he rose sorrowfully to his feet. " 'Tis a strange thing, and the like of it

I've never known afore. I can't figure it out; bain't natural for a horse to go on that way, and no horse of mine, or indeed of any I do know, has ever done it afore."

"Then 'tis witchcraft; I can't see what else it can be. And I don't like it; I don't like it at all."

"I reck'n we'll take t'others back along of us to stable, where they may be safer. 'Twouldn't do to have any more of this. Get back and fetch the halters and I'll bide here with 'em till 'ee come."

When Joel returned they put the halters on the three horses that had stood puzzled in the middle of the field and led them back to the farm-place, leaving the dead horse where he had fallen. As they were in their Sunday coats they did not climb up and ride on the broad backs, but walked soberly with the halters in hand. Only now were they beginning to realise what the mysterious business was costing them and the thought, coupled with the affection they had for the beast for his own sake, cast a gloom over their spirits and deepened their depression in the face of something they could not understand. It was not that they were more, or less, credulous than other folk, but there was nothing else to answer the facts; as these were, they pointed straight towards witchcraft.

"Who do 'ee think has done it, Father? And why?"

"That I couldn't say just 'zactly, not straight off. 'Tis kind of serious to give any soul the suspicion of being a witch; but someone is, and what's more, she's ill-wished us. What troubles me is, if this here's the beginning, is it a-going on? And if so, what'll be end of it?"

"I reck'n we'll ask Mother, she knows more 'bout things like that than what I do. Maybe she knows of some way to counter the stuff and take the badness out of it. What do 'ee think?"

"Oh, I reck'n if anyone do know, 'twill be your mother. Her's got a rare clever head, and what with all her reading and learning maybe she can tell us what's best to do."

So after stabling the horses they went into the house to consult

Elizabeth. They told her the whole story of Davy; she listened to it all carefully, and considered the situation well before giving any answer to their inquiries.

"How sad for the poor dear. Davy too, our best horse, poor beast. You're both sure 'twasn't a natural sickness took him? Neither of you ever heard tell of anything like it before?"

"As certain as I'm standing here."

"That's right 'nough, Mother. You should have seen him, it made me feel queer, as though something were behind him all the time. Kept galloping, so he did, as though every hound in Hell were hunting after him. Run! I should reck'n he did; I've never seen a horse his size going at it so hard."

Throughout the discussion the children had listened with startled eyes, absorbed by a sense of horror which, although it frightened them, held them in its grip. Their father and big brother were anxious, even frightened by something, and that awful something was at large, loose to threaten them round and about their own house. Salome, with full belief in witches and piskies common to her age, had her eyes large and staring with awe, and wedged herself for greater safety between Ralph and Polly. They knew already what was suspected, although so far no one had voiced the suspicion.

"Then it seems to me as though someone has ill-wished the horse. We'll have to inquire round and see if anyone has seen a likely witch about, looking at the horses, for that'll be what has happened, I'm sure of that. And if 'tisn't to happen again we'll need to find out who 'tis."

At that moment she noticed the children's faces and made a sign to her husband. He turned on them sharply.

"Get away with 'ee, and you too, Salome. This bain't no talk for children. Be off with 'ee, now."

Reluctantly they obeyed, leaving Joel and their parents to decide what was to be done.

"Till we find out," she repeated. "There's nothing we can do. Just ask a few folk round about. Suppose you ask the men, they'll tell their wives and so on; in no time we'll hear whether an old woman has been looking over the horses."

"I'll go now and see Matthew," said Joel, taking off his good coat and hanging it up behind the door, and he set off across the yard to the cow-house ready for milking. He entered the low doorway, took a sacking apron off the wall and picked up a pail and stool and went over to a stall where one of the unmilked cows stood. He returned down the gangway for a pail of clean water and the cloths, and washed the cow's udder and teats before he sat down. Pressing his forehead into her soft warm side, he made gentle coaxing noises to her; she regurgitated and commenced to chew her cud contentedly and at once gave her milk, letting it stream in two strong hard jets against the pail under the quick rhythmic pressure of his fingers.

"Davy's dead, down in Four Acres," he volunteered.

"Davy! Why, he was down there right as a trivet this morning, I seen un," Matthew exclaimed.

"Well, he's dead 'nough now, anyway."

"How's that? What took un?"

"Well see, Father and I were down that way little while agone, and Davy was pounding round that field as though Old Artful hisself were a-riding him; all of a lather, and nothing we could do would stop him. Over a while he stumbles and falls, rolls a bit, kicks out and fetches up dead. And that's all we could see, and nothing to show what drove him or what killed him. What do 'ee make of that now, Matthew?"

The old man spat fiercely into the kennel.

"I've only once heard the like afore. Mister Tredinnick up Marazion did have a horse took that way. He said 'twas witchcraft and sent up for Parson to come quick, and he did tell a prayer and the horse was hisself again in no time at all. So you mark my word, Joel, that's witchcraft, sure 'nough."

"I'm in no mind to disbelieve you. Father says he too can't

'zplain it, only by witchcraft; and Mother says 'tis certainly an ill-wishing."

The old man slapped his thigh a resounding whack.

"Now I come to mind it, 'twas this very morning when I come up along, there was old Blanchey Buckett looking at those horses. I wondered what her was up to at th' time."

Joel whistled. This was news indeed; the very thing they wanted to hear.

"Old Blanchey, you say? Now, I never reck'ned her along with witchcraft, did 'ee?"

"Well, I've heard tell how she do ill-wish those she don't like. And with all respect, I can't say her's overfond of your father."

Joel knew that was right, Blanchey had no love for his father, and he had himself been told before that those she did not like she could put the evil eye on. And if Matthew had seen her out at Four Acres looking over the horses just before the unnatural sickness had taken hold of Davy, then the case was growing strongly against her. He finished milking his cow and stripped her off, and went on to the next beast. He wondered what his mother would have to say about this piece of news, and hastened so as to be soon in with it.

"Mark my words, Joel, Blanchey Buckett ill-wished the beast. But 'tis easy to find out for sure, for if 'ee do cut out the horse's heart and burn it over a fire at midnight, then the witch, whoever it is, will be drawn to the place as sure as I'm telling 'ee. She'll be drawn there as by the devil's own chains, and nothing can keep her 'way. That's what to do, then she'll come. You see, she'll come all right."

This was something indeed; if only they did that, then they'd know for certain whether it was Blanchey or not.

"Where does it have to be done? Anywhere?"

"Bless you, my dear, no. It must be where the heart died, just 'zactly – and at stroke of midnight. Then she'll come, and no power on earth'll be able to hold her back. No, not even if she were to bind herself up with ropes and chains will she be safe, for as soon as midnight do strike, they'll slip off and away she'll be drawn right up to the burning heart. That's what I've always heard tell, and when I was young there was a deal of witches and warlocks about, and when they'd been at their wicked tricks that's how decent folk used to catch them – in their wickedness as 'twere – then there's no doubt 'twas right and proper to punish them."

When the pails were filled with milk, Joel carried them across to the dairy, and as his mother and Betsy poured it into the cream bowls for the scalding and skimming he told what he had learned. His father stood in the doorway and listened, seeming to think there was something in what Matthew had said.

"It seems a strange thing to do," remarked Elizabeth. "And I shan't enjoy it myself, but if 'tis the only way to find out then we must do it. For whether 'tis Blanchey or someone else, she can't be allowed to go about doing evil to good horses just out of spite. You and Father'll have to go down to the field tomorrow night and do it; and you're not going by yourselves, for, scared as I am at anything strange and evil as witchcraft, I'd be a deal more scared to be left behind and not know what was befalling down there."

"As you say, Elizabeth; then tomorrow night we'll do it. I'd set about it tonight if 'tweren't Sunday, and anyway I reck'n I've had 'nough of witches for today. 'Deed and 'tis a bellyful we'll be getting afore we've done, seems to me."

At that the household settled down to its usual Sunday evening's rest and talked no more of the plans, at least not in front of the children, for their father said it was not for them to learn of the workings of a witch. The next morning Joel and his father went down to Four Acres and set to work at the unpleasant task of removing the horse's heart. The body they hoisted into a cart lined with straw, ready to take to Marazion where the dealers would buy it.

In the middle of the field, just where the horse had died, they built a fire ready to kindle that night, and a strong green thorn branch was cut and pointed to use as a spit. The heart was wrapped up carefully and taken back to the farm until the time came for the burning. They spread sacks over the firewood to keep off the light driving rain that fell almost all day.

The night was fine, but with a high ragged cloud rushing across the sky, bringing the light in watery patches hurrying across the field from a moon just off the full. When the cloud obscured her the edges showed white and feathery against the clearer sky behind, the wind tore at them and changed their shape as they passed; wild hurrying shapes that seemed so anxious to get away from the rite that was going to take place down below. Thin, lean witches fled across the face of that moon; fat ugly hags, fierce warlocks and racked shapes writhing in agony, while all the time she seemed to be flying away and away from them, yet still doomed to be held to her slow ordered path.

"I don't like this business; I do tell 'ee, I don't like it at all," grumbled Richard, as the three of them hurried down the lane towards the field.

"No more do I," agreed Joel. "But there's nothing else for it, if we're to put a stop to this witchcraft. We've need to find out who's done it, so we can keep her off the farm-place and tell the neighbours, or what mischief she may yet do the Lord only knows."

Elizabeth, hurrying along between them, touched something at her throat; it was a small gilt cross on a chain.

"I've no mind for it myself. I've a cross here, for I've heard tell how it will keep off the evil eye."

Joel grinned and put his free hand in his pocket – it was he who was carrying the heart in its shroud – and pulled out a holed pebble.

"See, I've brought this 'long for the same reason, but if it comes to being face to face with the witch, I reck'n I'll be using my legs more readily."

"And if 'ee west to ask me what I do reck'n, 'tis that we are on a wild goose chase and would be better and a deal more comfortable in our beds, like other Christian folk. Anyone prowling about this time of the night bain't up to good, and 'tis my mind the only thing we'll draw will be the preventive men to see what the fire's about. But 'tis too late now to turn back."

"Oh, I haven't took fear; after all, I'm no horse," exclaimed Elizabeth.

Down in the field they got busy kindling the fire and persuading it to burn. In the fresh wind it was not easy but at last a good start was made and the leaping flames lit them up brightly in the ruddy light and cast the surroundings into far deeper darkness. Joel unwrapped the heart and held it firmly while his father impaled it on the green thorn they had prepared and at a few minutes to midnight he held it in the centre of the fire while the others piled the wood around and kept up the blaze.

As the heat seized on it and the flames curled about, it hissed and bubbled on its spit. A dark thick fluid began to fall drop by drop into the centre of the fire, a smell of burning flesh reached their nostrils. The thing became hotter and drier, it scorched and blackened, shrivelled and writhed as though in pain, so that the stick twisted in his hands. All three had their eyes fixed steadily on the horrid sight.

None of them spoke, and the night was all quiet around them, apart from the sighing of the wind and the sounds coming from the fire. As the flames took hold of their strange fuel, another sound reached their ears, coming down wind from inland, the strokes of St. Breaca's clock up at Breage Churchtown beating out midnight. Each stroke came after a seeming endless silence, and the three watchers counted them against the beating of their hearts as they stood around the fire, with its light splashed about and on their strained white faces. The flames burned lower about the black heart lying in the glowing wood ash.

Just as the hour and circumstances, and their own fears and imagined horrors were straining their nerves to a thrumming tautness, an awful yell echoed over the field from the direction of the lane; a yell that was repeated and echoed and re-echoed nearer and nearer, as at an incredible speed wild, mad footsteps were rushing down the lane. Into the field and firelight dashed Blanchey Buckett, hair streaming, shawl and garments torn and flying, her eyes fiercely bright with anger and her face all contorted and strange by rage.

Straight up to the fire she rushed, and with her foot kicking frantically at the ashes, she lifted the burned heart and heaved it away into the darkness in a shower of sparks.

That was enough for them; the experiment had worked with astounding and terrifying success.

"Run, Mother, run," gasped Joel and seized her hand in his, while his father grabbed her other and away they ran at their fastest, out of the field, up the lane, panting and gasping, stumbling and even cursing softly, with never a thought of stopping until they had fallen inside the good solid door of Kenneggy, and slammed and bolted it securely behind them.

Elizabeth staggered over to a chair by the fire and sank into it; her husband dropped down in one by the table and rested his head on his hands, while Joel leaned against the wall and looked around him, glad indeed to see strong stone and a bolted door instead of the darkness and the presence of evil that lurked outside.

"That was terrible," exclaimed Elizabeth, between sobbing breaths.

"Lord, 'twas indeed."

Richard lifted his head and turned around to them. "Thank Heaven none of the children were with us, 'twould have been no sight for them."

"So old Blanchey is a witch. I should never have believed she was so steeped in the black art that she would have been drawn out by that burning. She must be a real bad witch, sold her soul to the devil and all, to be mastered by such a thing. And what are you two doing about it now? Something will have to be done, for I'm not

going to live here now with a wicked old witch as good as sitting on
my doorstep. You surely can't expect it of me, Rich? What do you
reckon to do about it?"

He hitched his chair up to the fire and kicked a log on to it.

"I don't reck'n to do anything 'bout it just now," he grunted.
"I've had 'nough of witches and witchcraft this night – 'es indeed,
and for many a night to come, I do swear. No, no, Elizabeth, if you
want to do more than we've done tonight – and I say we've done
more'n we ought to – thee cust do it without me. They be queer,
those witch-women, and I'm having no more to do with them. Joel
can do what he's a mind to, and thee cust too, but I'll do no more. I
do tell 'ee both, I'll do no more of it."

He glared defiantly at his son, for Joel standing there had a very
different appearance from the big fellow who, a very short while ago,
was pelting up the lane as fast as his powerful legs would carry him.
He felt different too, for now safely inside with the candlelight and in
the surroundings of their own house, he was beginning to regret
leaving the field to Blanchey's undisputed possession. Witch as she
was – had they not proved it – what power could she have over him?

"I tell 'ee what," he said. "If I'd only kept my wits about me and
heaped up more wood on that fire, so as to have it mighty hot, then
when the old body came rushing up a-looking for Davy's heart maybe
she'd have gone right into it and burned herself up. 'Twould be the
right end for a witch anyway, they do say, and 'twas up St. Austell
not very many years agone they burned one, on Menage Stone, there
where three parishes meet. And if Blanchey's a-going 'bout making
trouble as she's done for us these past two days, then something'll
have to be done here, for I won't stand for it."

"And I won't stand for such barbarous talk, Joel my son, for 'tis
today we're living in, thank God, and not those cruel times,"
exclaimed Elizabeth. "Not that I don't think something should be
done, but it can be done decently. We want no burnings down here
whatever they may have done up St. Austell."

With his foot, Joel prodded the fire thoughtfully, and made the flames leap up the chimney. He gazed into them and seemed to see shapes writhing and twisting in an agony of fiery death.

"Why don't 'ee go up to her place tomorrow, Father, and tell her we'll have no more of it? Tell her 'twill go hard with her if folk get to hear talk of Sunday's work, and she proved to be a witch-woman by being drawn to the fire tonight. Then I reck'n she'll be glad 'nough to swear to leave us and our beasts 'lone. Why not do that, Father?"

Richard looked up in astonishment at the suggestion.

"What, me go up and talk to her that way? No, I'll not; no, never. No word of this night'll ever pass my lips towards Blanchey Buckett."

He spoke as though there was something indecent about their discovery, as though in exposing a witch they had in some way laid her soul bare in its wickedness before their eyes and they, having seen so much, needed for shame's sake to keep it unmentioned.

"Well, Rich!" exclaimed Elizabeth. "You were always one for peace and easy-going with your neighbours, and I don't say 'tisn't a virtue exactly, but there are times when you can sit too quiet under things; for then folk just reckon you're dull. It makes me vexed with you when you're so soft. You'll have to think what you're going to do."

He looked up at her solemnly. "Maybe thee'st right, Elizabeth. Shall I tell 'ee both what I'm a-going to do? 'Es, I'll tell 'ee 'zactly what I'm a-going to do. I'm a-going to my bed."

How the story got about the district they never found out for certain, although as Matthew was the only person outside the family who knew of the project, they later guessed he had something to do with it. But get about it certainly did. The strange death of the horse Davy was common talk within the next few days, and the way Blanchey Buckett had been drawn from her cottage at midnight and right up to the fire in Four Acres was discussed at every cottage

90

about the cove and among the mines. Very soon further evidence of Blanchey's ill-wishing came to light. First it was remembered that when Henry Wheeler's cow had sickened away and died the old woman had been seen passing near the meadow just before the sickness began. And Jimmy Polglaze was reminded by someone that the time when he had gone out for three days in succession and lifted nothing but catfish was just about when he had mentioned that Blanchey had been watching him launch his boat on most days that week. Tom Cobbler too, had taken the measles the day after he had brushed past her in the lane and she had called to him to go more carefully. There was no end of it, and once the trail had been touched it blazed back for months, revealing every misfortune in the parish to be directly connected with some action or word of the witch.

Popular opinion ran strongly and ever more strongly against her. A growing tide of resentment rose about, for it was felt they were all suffering from the crabbed spite of one old woman, who because she was a familiar of the darker spirits had power to ill-wish them and their stock. An unpleasant thing had neighboured them too long; the blight on their prosperity had continued for long enough. Something would have to be done about it.

Up at the "Falmouth Packet" it was the chief subject of discussion and argument; every time men gathered there, Blanchey's case grew blacker, under the influence of good brandy and rum, loosened tongues told lively stories based on infinitesimal facts. The men from the cove and Wheal Speed were particularly hard on her, for the weather had been bad for a long time and the fishing poor even when they could get out, and several promising pitches had turned out tin-stuff of lower value than had been expected. It was as easy to have a scapegoat for their ill fortune as not, and far more interesting.

One night, after it had been monthly pay-day at the mines, the inn was full, and every man having a glass more than he usually allowed himself, they were trying to get Richard to tell how he had practised witch-finding so successfully.

"I've heard tell how you had to run for your lives with her a-riding her besom up the lane after 'ee like the wind. Bain't that so, 'Drewartha?"

"Well now, I can't say we didn't run, 'cause we did, but 'twere more the surprise of it all than the fright she give us as set us off. It doesn't sound mighty fearful sitting round here in the light and company and telling of it, but out there in the middle of a field and at dead of night, with wind howling and the cloud rushing 'cross the moon, 'twas all mighty queer. We were kind of 'zpecting her, and yet we weren't, if you get my meaning; 'twas the suddenness of her coming, and just as clock struck, what upset us. Or maybe 'twas the yell she let out when she saw what was afoot. Anyway, there 'twas, and I wouldn't do it again, not for the finest horse."

There was a general murmur of approbation.

"Tell us how it came 'bout, right from the start."

Andrewartha shook his head. "No, maybe I've said more'n I should; leave her be now. Why not disremember it? 'Twont do any good to keep raking it over and over."

So saying, he drained his glass and rose to go.

"Good night, all."

A chorus of growls was his return for disappointing them, and he left them to turn the talk into any channel they chose. But they chose to continue on the same theme, and when Joel looked in a few minutes later to see if his father was there, he was given a cheery, boisterous welcome.

"Ha, Joel boy, come in with 'ee and take a glass. No, he's left long while agone. There's no hurry boy, what's to do this hour of a Saturday night? Save wenching. Ha, ha, that's hurry is it? Well away with 'ee, and give her a smacker from me."

The taunt worked, for Joel came in and closed the door. His baiter was standing in front of the fire with his glass resting on the shelf near to hand, a thin wiry man with a tongue that would chip granite, it was so quick and sharp, a weapon he used on the others with telling effect whenever he chose. Joel looked at him for a moment and then winked at the others.

"I mind now she sent 'ee a message, Bob Cornish," he said quietly, as he crossed the room. "She said she always had a warm spot in her heart for you. And . . ."

With a quick movement he had hold of the fellow, and in a second had whirled him over and gripped his head, face up, between his knees, with his legs in the air held firmly in strong hands. A slight shifting of the hold and Bob's knees were doubled down on his chest, his body projecting forwards across the hearth.

"And just to show 'ee how warm her heart is, I'm a-going to heat your sit-down for you, Bob Cornish."

He shuffled forward, ignoring the impotent struggles of his victim and the cramped blows showered around his thighs and shins, until the seat of the man's trousers was over the fire. And there he held him until a strong smell of scorching cloth filled the room. Swinging around he dropped the imprisoned head to the floor and, reaching out, seized the half-consumed drink and emptied it over the smoking seat. A howl of laughter went up as the discomfited wretch struggled up and plucked the wet cloth away from his skin. Joel brushed away the dirt left on his jacket by the boots and signed to the innkeeper to give him a couple of glasses. He handed the second across to Bob.

The appreciation of his rough fun put him in a cheerful mood, and with judicious prompting, and a second glass which someone gave out to help him on, they managed to get the story of the other night.

" 'Tis a terrible thing," one of them declared. "That witchcraft should lift its ugly head among us."

And with this there was general agreement.

"Why not teach her she can't go 'bout ill-wishing us this way?"

" 'Es, give her a lesson, the besom."

"Let's go down along and dip her in pond."

" 'Es, if she floats, her's a witch sure 'nough, and if she sinks there bain't nothing 'gainst her, so I've heard tell."

"And what arc we to do if she does float?" asked Henry Wheeler.

"They used to fish 'em out and burn 'em, while agone," explained Bob Cornish. "And if they did sink, then they bain't witches, though 'twas mostly too late to do much but give 'em decent burial," he added dryly.

"Anyway, we could go down 'n' try it, just to learn her, as it were. And then we could light a fire up, like as though we were a-going to chuck her on it, if she floats. Just to fright her, mind."

The idea was discussed with growing enthusiasm and rapidly gained favour. The resentment that had been brewing against Blanchey began to pour out and, added to the pay-night spirits which would have welcomed a spree readily enough without the extra relish, soon had them all eager to put a stop once and for all to the witch's practices. The innkeeper, seeing the way they were heading, made a last effort to get their custom before they all left.

"Take a glass all round to keep off chill and the evil-eye afore 'ee go," he cried above the uproar.

" 'Es, fill 'em up," cried Joel. He had taken little part in the discussion, for he was torn between the memory of his fright from Blanchey and his certain knowledge that his father would disapprove of any such expedition. Grown man as he was, he had a strong respect for his father's opinion and judgment, which in this case he was certain would be supported by his mother's, and he was uneasy about the consequences. For he could see rather further ahead than the other fellows, and his knowledge of human nature – which he certainly possessed in some degree even if he was not conscious of it – warned him that semi-drunken men on a spree like this promised to be, often went further than they intended at the start. He decided that he must be in with them and be there to see no real harm came to the old woman.

Someone opened the door and ran out, baying in imitation of a hound on the scent.

"Witches and warlocks," yelled Bob Cornish, and added, "I'll not be the only one roasted this night."

They were off down the turnpike, a pack in full cry. All decent enough fellows individually, together they made a pack, hungry to hunt and hurt something, the original object already more or less forgotten in the excitement, and reverting to the old witch-finding of not so many years before. Their blood was heating and their cries and shouts became more threatening as they ran along towards the old woman's cottage where she lived with her daughter. Joel hastened along with them and, in spite of his resolve to restrain the pack, found himself being carried away, to some extent, by the hunting instinct roused so strongly by the general excitement and the fear of Blanchey's powers.

The cottage, a simple cob, two-roomed affair with a linney wood store at the back, was out near the turnpike by Kenneggy Lane. Rough wooden shutters were over the windows, which had several of their few panes of glass cracked or broken and depended more on the wood than the glazing to keep out the cold. The knot of witch hunters gathered in front of the little hovel and seemed irresolute now the action was about to begin, uncertain whether they were going to meet something they could not deal with, or whether in their very numbers and each other's company they were safe from the power of evil.

A large stone hurtled past the foremost of them and crashed against the cottage door.

"Witch, witch." The shrill voice of Bob Cornish led the outcry.

"Come out, Blanchey Buckett, and we'll learn 'ee to ill-wish us."

"Who put the evil eye on 'Drewartha's horse?"

" 'Es, and put a curse on the fishing, you old witch."

A shower of stones rattled on the door and shutters. The collection of hunters took an uglier and more aggressive attitude on finding they were not met with brimstone fumes or attacked by legions of black cats. One of them, a fisherman from the cove, advanced and beat on the door, and after failing to get it opened, used his stick as a lever and tried unsuccessfully to force away the hasp of the bolt inside. Several scattered in search of a more effective tool, and in a short while a heavy log was brought from somewhere with room on it for three of four to grasp, and with this they at once set to work.

The heavy rhythmic blows on the splintering wood roused them still further, while the cries for help coming from the two frightened women inside goaded them on. With a rending of the woodwork, the bolt within gave way, and the door crashed inwards, and a rush of excited men tumbled into the cottage. As they entered, two cats streaked out, running, had they known it, for their lives; and seeming as though they did know it. A shouted curse or two followed them, together with hastily aimed stones, wooden billets or anything coming to hand, but the hunt was out for the witch herself and in the haste to be in at the kill her familiars were allowed to escape. Through the miserable little kitchen and meagrely furnished bedroom, they poured, crashing over the table, kicking aside chairs and stools, anything in their way, but there was no sign of Blanchey or her daughter.

Had they made themselves invisible or whisked away up the chimney? Both were common tricks known to witches, and extremely probable. Disappointment maddened the sportsmen and enraged them further against their quarry. The door of the linney was flung open a dozen times, eager eyes searched in vain for someone inside but saw only a pile of furze and wreck wood, a few peats and rubbish; a dozen times the door slammed back in disgust. One, perhaps more sceptical of the reputed powers of witches, pulled aside the furze, and in the next second frightened screams told too plainly that they had been run to earth.

Back into the cottage and through the broken door old Blanchey was dragged, and not only her but the younger woman too, who if not a witch would very soon prove herself innocent when flung into the pond. Down towards the horse-pond by Kenneggy gate they went, shouting triumphantly, and, so strongly did the pack madness get a grip on some men, they were now dragging bundles of her own kindling along with them, and savage cries were heard of, "Burn the witch!"

The altering tone of the party frightened Joel back to his senses, and realising that single-handed he could not hope to check them in their crazy plan, he dashed off down the lane to reach Kenneggy ahead of them.

Elizabeth and his father were sitting by the fire, he dozing and taking the relaxation he allowed himself on a pay-day, she knitting, when the door of the house burst open and in a second Joel rushed into the room, and paused with one hand on the door ready to dash out again.

"Father, I reck'n 'ee'd best come quick. They're for burning Blanchey as a witch. Up the lane, outside our gate."

They sprang up, Elizabeth white very suddenly, his father, dazed at the startling end to his nap, stared at Joel in horror.

"Come, we'll have to be sharp. We can't let 'em do it. 'Tisn't only 'cause of the old woman, we've got to stop them from going mad. Come on, Father, hurry I do beg 'ee."

"All right, Joel my son, don't get worried. I'm a-coming. No, you stay here, Elizabeth; I reck'n you can't help in this."

Stooping, he thrust his feet into his heavy boots and whirled the laces around several times, without threading the eyelets, and knotted them firmly. He reached for his thorn stick, looked at it and set it down again, then followed Joel.

"Best not to take a stick; if 'tis a fight, fists are best – and safer. Come on with 'ee, Joel, don't loiter, now."

They hurried out of the house and up the lane; they were soon within close range of the shouting and yelling that was growing each minute.

e

"Ease up, Joel boy, 'tis no use getting blown. Be fresher – if we take it easy."

The hubbub contained no really agonised shrieks, from which they judged the real business had not started yet and they would be in time, so they slackened the pace.

Apparently the witch-proving had been carried out by the time they reached the pond, for the pack was dragging out two wretched figures into the light of a big fire rapidly blazing up in the field beside the lane. Blanchey and her daughter had been securely lashed to a couple of their own besoms, the very ones no doubt they had used on their nefarious rides to the witches' Sabbaths, which local sayings had it were held on Tregonning Hill, where they danced mother-naked around the Devil himself. There they were, drenched and foul with mud, being pulled out of the cold water and carried up the bank to the road. The old woman was shouting imprecations on all around, but her daughter, perhaps because she had fallen face downwards in the pond, was silent, and appeared unconscious.

"She floated, she floated! Burn the old witch; burn her!"

The other woman was dropped on the ground while excited interest centred on Blanchey. Eager hands gripped the broom handle and began to drag her towards the fire.

"Cowardly murderers! Murder a poor old woman!" she was screaming. "Do what 'ee like with me you'll die yourselves over a while. And afore long, my pretty men. You, Jimmy Polglaze, who drowns women, you'll drown one day. Thee'st to know what 'tis to drown. And you too – and you Bob Cornish. You, Joel 'Drewartha, thee'st to struggle in mud and water same as me. I do tell 'ee, God Almighty'll make 'ee suffer for this night." She had evidently taken the two Andrewarthas for fresh enemies, as she must have recognised in them the probable cause of her troubles, so her curses fell equally on them. Fortunately for her they ignored them in their rush, not so much to save her, perhaps, as their neighbours from their own folly.

Wait for the Wagon

Like two bulls they charged up alongside the men drawing the besom and brushed them violently aside, so that their burden dropped to the ground.

"Hast 'ee gone mad?" shouted Andrewartha in a terrible voice. "Thee'st took mad, a-killing a wretched old woman."

There was a pause in the hubbub, while surprised attention was turned on them, like two powerful giants in the firelight, with the helpless old soul moaning on the ground between them. Then it broke out afresh, with a new and angry note in it, threatening the interferers.

"Leave us be, 'Drewartha. Us've had 'nough of the old hag, a-killing the beasts and sickening the children. Get 'long with 'ee, and leave us to finish her."

Andrewartha half turned his head and looked at Joel over his shoulder.

"Ready, boy?"

Joel nodded. He was ready for the fight he knew was coming, and as his father had given the word, prepared to enjoy it. Like most powerful men he was tardy of using his strength against his fellows in hot blood, but when occasion demanded a fight in a good cause, he was the first to welcome it. The men around gathered to recover their victim and get on with the burning they had planned, for the fire was now a fierce blaze and just ready to receive the old witch. With a rush they closed in; the two defenders moved out to keep Blanchey from being trampled to death under the milling of heavy boots.

Andrewartha's fists crashed out and met two objectives with violent force, and continued to batter furiously at the men pressing in on him. Joel preferred to get a grip on an opponent and, as they were so many, clutched at the first that came within range to use as a weapon against the rest. It happened to be Bob Cornish – eager to avenge the insult he had suffered earlier in the evening – and, grasping him firmly by the waist, he lifted him high above his head.

For a second the kicking, struggling figure stayed there poised, and then like a baulk of living timber he was crashed down on those pressing in to attack his captor. A tangled heap of men surged about under the impact, and Joel lunged forward to tackle them as they picked themselves out of it. The weight and strength of his arms beat off clutches that would have held an ordinary man, and first one and then another was wrenched off his feet and cast away out of reach. The fight was on in earnest, but it was a fight among men who knew and had a friendly feeling towards each other, even if for the moment they were contesting a difference of opinion. For this reason no evidence of savagery stole in, knives were not drawn, or even thought of; it was wit and quickness, combined with strength of arm and skill in punch and throw which were used. Weight of numbers, however, pressed in upon the two Andrewarthas and threatened to drive them from their stand, until Joel, stooping, in one movement hurled a man away by striking his legs from the ground and clutched the prostrate woman lashed to the besom.

Gripping her limp body he charged in towards the fire. His father covered the retreat and prevented attack on him as he dropped her and seized two stout pieces of brushwood from the fire, their ends a foot or more of glowing, burning wood, and waved them before him. The check gave Richard a chance to do the same, and in a moment he too had cleared his side of attackers as they fell back out of range.

There was an instant lull as they drew back beyond the waving firebrands, none wishing to have one in his face.

"Listen, boys," Andrewartha seized the moment to shout at them. "Ease off now and listen to me. The fun's over. You can't murder an old woman in cold blood, and I'll see you don't do it in hot. 'Tis today we're living, and not back along in the times of witch burning. I've lost a good beast myself, and I'm vexed 'bout it, but not mad 'nough to get our parish to be a laughing-stock in Cornwall. Leave the old body be, leave her alone, and get 'long home afore the wives get to hear what thee'st been up to. Anyone who reck'ns he can give 'ee better advice can come out two-three at a time and we'll argue with them, but I do warn 'ee that you can't go on with this without being mighty sorry for it in the morning. Her's had enough, leave her be now, and get 'long with 'ee. Don't 'ee make us a laughing stock from Helston to Penzance by foolish doings."

There was a moment's hesitation, and it seemed as though the line of reasoning would tell. And then a shrill voice of derision came from the rear, and Bob's piercing cry broke the spell.

"Yah! Rush 'em. Thee'st took fear, boys. Thee'st been easy scared. Burn the old witch afore she does 'ee more mischief. Haven't 'ee had 'nough of her? Come 'long with 'ee, are you so easy put off that two men only can turn 'ee 'side? Burn her! Burn the old bitch of a witch!"

There was a moment of indecision; some were for taking Richard's advice and others for completing their purpose. Things swayed this way and that; at one moment it seemed the Andrewarthas had won their way, at others they were in imminent danger of being beaten up. In fact, the more hot-headed were drawing together for a concerted rush when a new and unexpected sound reached the group.

Up from the cove, borne in on the sea breeze, came the clamorous ringing of a bell. Fading and falling, then rising loud and strong, it beat up to them, the notes of the alarm bell down by the boat slip. A wreck, a ship in distress, perhaps a fishing-boat needing help with a mighty catch? There was immediately a babel of speculative voices, arguing, asserting, questioning; but one thing was clear in every man's mind. His first intention was to get as quickly as possible down to the cove or the cliff above it to find out the cause of the signal.

With the fading footsteps sounding in their ears, Joel turned to his father, pulling out his knife as he spoke.

"Now what, Father? Get 'em home, I reck'n, where we can look to 'em and see what's damage. Poor old Blanchey, her's had a rough passage."

He cut the bond tying her to the besom and hoisted her limp body over his shoulders, starting off for Kenneggy. His father ran across to the pond to get the younger woman; he found she was breathing feebly, and to his relief groaned as he rolled her over, cut the cords and hoisted her up. He hastened after Joel, thanking Heaven for what was a merciful intervention, and wondering what it was had caused the bell to be rung and what was going on down in the cove.

Neither had any fear of the attack recurring; once the pack and the spirit of the witch-hunt had been broken up and attention diverted there was little chance of it being renewed. Good neighbours as were all who had fought against them that night, not one would have dreamed of an onslaught on his house. The fact that they were sheltering Blanchey, even if it became known, would not make any difference; indeed, it was unlikely any further attack would be made even on her.

He caught up with Joel at the farm-place and they entered the house together, each with his burden. Salome was in the living-room, stirring broth over the fire; she was in her nightgown with Joel's jacket over her for extra warmth. Though her eyes were heavy and sleepy, the sight of the two wretched women dropped on the floor before her started her broad awake.

"Where's your mother, my dear?"

"She went out, Father; I don't know where. She woke me up and told me to get the broth hot for you against the time you came in."

Joel flung wood and furze on the hearth until the flames leaped up the chimney; the sight made him think of that other fire the old body had so narrowly escaped. He remembered her prayers that a curse should fall on her tormentors, how she had sworn, as they pulled her from the pond, that this man and that would himself be drowned. What truth was there behind her ravings? Well, he had fallen in a pond before now and survived, none the worse. He was awakened from his thoughts by his father's voice.

102

"Come, Joel my son, get their boots off, can't 'ee? Bain't time yet to go to sleep."

He set to and pulled off the worn boots and held their feet towards the heat of the big fire. At Salome's request he went with her for blankets from the chest, and just as they were wondering how to get on with the stripping off of the wet clothes, Elizabeth returned.

"Just in time, Elizabeth. They've both had rough handling, but I reck'n they'll be all right over a while, if we take care of them. We brought 'em down 'cause the cottage up there is in a mighty litter. I thought 'ee'd agree to that."

"Of course, Rich; you're quite right. I heard a deal of shouting; was there a fight?"

"Oh, little 'nough," exclaimed Joel. "The fun stopped just as they were getting heated up to it. The bell went down in the cove; and away they all trooped."

"And a good thing for us too, I reck'n, though 'tis easy to talk lightly of it now," said his father. "I saw they were just getting ready to get dirty. They were for burning her all right, Elizabeth."

"The poor soul," cried Elizabeth. "Now, Joel, do you go and get in some soft sacks of straw, for we've to make up beds for them tonight. And, Father, you help with these wet rags they've got dripping about the place. Salome, help your father with old Blanchey."

They worked hard to get circulation restored in the two women, Betsy and Polly being called in to help; and succeeded at last, after wrapping them up in every article of warmth the house possessed, so it seemed. Hot broth and brandy were forced between their clenched teeth, and gradually life began to return to them. Their bruises and cuts were washed and dressed, though actually they had little real damage done to them. The partly filled bags of straw were laid out by the fire, the patients lifted on and settled for the night.

The next morning, Jimmy Polglaze overtook Henry Wheeler coming up the lane towards Kenneggy. Both paused at the door and waited for the other to go on. Seeing a deadlock had occurred, Jimmy declared himself on the point of going in to see how they were doing after the night.

"Well, I declare, I came up for the very same thing myself," exclaimed Henry, so they went in together.

In the living-room the two Bucketts were sitting up pale and bruised in the big chairs. Salome and Elizabeth were repairing garments that had already been washed and dried. Andrewartha, sitting by the window with his pipe, was enjoying the morning and watching for folk in the lane.

"Come in, both of 'ee," he called as they approached the door. "How are you this morning?"

The two entered and stood awkwardly, with their hats in hands, looking at the various persons in the room.

"I reck'n there's something I want to say," began Henry Wheeler. "First, Blanchey Buckett, I'm real sorry for the part I took in last night's business. In broad daylight, and on God's day at that, I do feel proper 'shamed of myself. And to you, 'Drewartha, I got to give thanks for trying to knock sense into my thick head, for if 'ee'd let us get on with what we'd a mind to do, I should have been a sorrier man today. I do hope thee cust all find it in your hearts to hear my 'pologies, though I know 'twould be real hard to forgive."

As he was speaking, Jimmy was nodding hearty agreement with all he said.

"The same goes for me, Mother Buckett, and all of us in cove are mighty vexed for hurting 'ee. It do seem each man by hisself would wish 'ee no great harm, but come the whole mob of us got together, after a glass or two, we just took leave of our senses, as 'twere. I'm mighty sorry, ma'am, and Mr Andrewartha, I'm glad for the trouble you took to knock me 'bout last night, when I was a-making a beast of myself."

Listening to them, Andrewartha himself looked as uncomfortable as they did; he waved aside their attempts to thank him.

"There was no great harm done, and they'll both be right as trivets by the time we've all got the cottage straight for 'em. Don't 'ee think any more 'bout it. 'Twill be best for us all to forget it just as soon as we can."

The callers looked most happily relieved and their eyes sought Blanchey for some expression of understanding.

" 'Twas a bad time you gave us, and I hope 'ee won't do it no more. Then I do reck'n we'll let bygones be bygones; my life is too short now to be holding grievances 'gainst 'ee," she said generously.

"Tell me, what was to-do in the cove for the bell to be rung?" asked Richard.

The men shuffled their feet and looked confused. "That do puzzle us all; see, there weren't nothing for to ring the bell, and no one to ring it. It do seem 'sthough it rung itself by unnatural means. 'Twas a good thing as it happened, but 'tain't very pleasant to think on."

Elizabeth looked up from her mending.

"Don't you vex yourselves, it was rung naturally enough, for I did ring it myself. I did reckon 'twas the only thing to bring 'ee all to your senses, so I just slipped down to the cove. On the way back I just stepped over the hedge and waited till you'd all passed, and then came on home. But I'm mighty sorry if you think I am no pleasant thing to visit the cove, Henry and Jimmy; I am indeed."

Chapter Five

A NDREWARTHA carried through his determination to make young Chris a tinner, and at six years old he was going across to Wheal Speed each day to do boy's work about the surface. If Elizabeth's three sons were to be farmers in accordance with her wishes, his youngest was going to be a miner like his father. Together they went across with the teams to the whims and worked under the shadow of the bob of the Cornish engine, rising and falling as it lifted the rods running many fathoms down the shaft to the pumps at the bottom that drained the levels. From the mouth of the shaft trailed a thin smudge of steamy smoke from the blasting, rising up slowly with the hot, stale air from the workings below.

In the past few years, Joel's skill as a wrestler had grown with his strength and experience, and being nimble in his head as well as on his feet, he possessed a tremendous advantage over the big opponent who was just muscle. One throw particularly he had brought to a deadly perfection; his Flying Mare was reputed to send his man from Marazion to Helston, and by his trick of dropping on his right knee as he made the turn it was very difficult to check the hoist which followed, over his shoulder, by the extended arm. It was a difficult move to bring off successfully and the average wrestler could not get a throw from it as surely as from a Cross Buttock, but Joel had the speed and strength to play it, and played it most successfully against the rushing type of man.

His father did not give him much encouragement in his love of the sport, for he was all for hard work, and with his teams he set an example to his sons which was hard to live up to. It was only at the end of the month he let himself relax; then it was payday at the mine, and to celebrate he walked up to the "Falmouth Packet" and took a glass or two in its congenial atmosphere, charged with smoke from strong plug tobacco and good brandy.

As the evening wore on he would return to Kenneggy and take his chair by the fire and doze, sleepy and weary, before the big pans of rich, creamy milk scalding for the butter-making – now happily fuller and more numerous than ever before. The long, stone-walled room was lit by candles in the brass holders with the slides inside to raise the ends, and its warm quietness filled with the friendly clicking of knitting-needles plied by Elizabeth and the girls. Even then, the fact that he was doing nothing seemed to lie uneasily on his mind, for often with a sigh he would raise his head and ask, "Are the cattle all in? And the sheep all tended?"

And Elizabeth would answer him quietly, without looking up from her needles.

"Take 'n' rest, Rich; everything's all right."

In the care of her big son Joel she knew it would be, for he was never the one to give himself food or rest until the beasts had theirs, or to allow anyone less responsible to see to their needs without his supervision – although both his brothers were capable by now of seeing to things as well as he could, and used on occasions to do so, especially if he had promised himself a visit to a wrestling match.

There was wrestling at a fair going on in Helston; it was Charles who brought the news back from Breage. They were in the cow-house at the milking, he, Joel and their father, when he was telling them.

"Oh, and Joel, there's a wrestler called the Tiger, a Greek, who they do say, has never been beaten, and he'll try a hitch with someone every night, and a guinea for the man who can beat him. And on Fair Day they're going to make it two guineas. But I've heard tell he's mighty rough, and a dirty wrestler."

"Has any man at Helston worsted him?"

"I haven't heard of it."

Richard snorted. " 'Twould be a mighty surprise to me if any man ever does. These furriners are proper twisters and no decent clean wrestler can get at 'em; they've a dozen dirty tricks they can pull out and beat a chap afore he do know where he is. 'Tis the way they make a living, I suppose, but none but a fool will go into ring with 'em."

Joel stripped the teats of his beast down to the last drop and emptied the pail into the churn. "When's Fair Night, tomorrow? I've a mind to go over Helston and see him. Maybe I could give him a run for his money, anyway."

" 'Twill be you more likely who'll have the run, and no money. Thee cust please 'self, only don't say I didn't warn 'ee 'twould be a dirty fight."

"Dirty!" exclaimed Charles from the warm flank of his cow. "They do say 'tis difficult to keep the crowd off him at times. They've got a small ring roped off, like they use for prize-fighting in the north, so I've heard tell, and all the folk can gather round and watch by paying a bit."

" 'Es, and don't see too much I'll wager," added their father.

"Maybe thee'st right," acknowledged Joel. "But I can't bide here with someone a-calling hisself a champion without being all of an itch to see him, and have a throw with him. Just for the fun of it, I reck'n I must go over Helston."

The next evening, Joel pushed his way through the crowds on the fairground to the enclosure where the Champion Wrestler of Greece was proclaimed on great banners, that had once been bright and

108

arrogant, but were now tattered and considerably faded. He read the posters and bills stuck all about and gathered that "The Tiger" was willing and eager to meet any comer for the extravagantly large purse of two guineas, the offer being open for that night only. Indeed, it seemed likely to be closed forever within the next few minutes; crowds were already paying their way into the enclosure, and Joel passed in with them.

His eyes turned at once to the centre where was the roped-off ring Charles had spoken of. It was a raised square platform covered with sawdust and looked to him uncomfortably small for wrestling, and within the space marked off by ropes stretched between the four corner-posts a powerful man, thick-set and ugly, was strutting slowly up and down with an exaggerated swagger. He held his bare shoulders so that a great deep cleft showed between the blades on his brown back; his chest was inflated until the ribs threatened to burst through the greasy skin that covered them. He carried a considerable paunch on him, and two massive long arms.

A second man, a sharp, rat-faced little fellow, was shouting at the people gathered about the platform; his voice was so raucous and penetrating that it scarcely seemed possible for it all to come from the one small creature. Joel stepped in behind the crowd and listened.

" . . . And, ladies and gentlemen, tonight I mean to double that offer. I will give two guineas to any gentleman who can worst the Tiger in five rounds of five minutes each, and one guinea if he can only remain unbeaten. As you know, Greece is the home of wrestling, and I am presenting to you tonight, for the last and final appearance in this town, the Grecian Tiger, the world's finest exponent of the Art of Wrestling."

Loud derisive cheers rang from the crowd, and the Tiger puffed his chest and strutted about in his red tights with a peculiar straddled gait, as though his legs were too muscular to pass each other easily, or, as Joel thought, looking for all the world as though he had wet them. There followed some preliminary bouts between professional wrestlers, in a style quite new to him, for they took hold of each other anywhere they could get a grip, and even when on the floor continued in a regular dog-fight until one or other had his shoulders forced down, or called submission under a cruel lock. He watched carefully, knowing this was what was expected of the challenger.

"And now, gentlemen, for the purse of two guineas; let me call on one of you to challenge our champion."

Joel had taken good stock of the fighter and guessed that what his father had said and Charles had heard, would be right. Such a swaggerer coming into their midst, however, should not be allowed to get everything his own way, and he determined at once to have a try at equalising the local score.

"I do challenge him!" he called, and as the folk around turned to see who had called out, and made way for him, he worked his way down to the side of the ring.

"You sir? I thank you. Ladies and gentlemen, a challenger has come forward in the person of this handsome young man. Come up into the ring, sir. What's your name?"

"Joel Andrewartha."

"Joel Andrewartha challenges the Grecian Tiger to five rounds of wrestling, catch-hold style," shouted the showman, and turning to Joel added in what was evidently his conversational tone, "The changing room's up that gangway, sir."

Joel slipped out of the ring and hurried to the little screened section he had indicated; he had his stockings rolled in his pocket with his canvas jerkin, and it did not take him a minute to slip off his shirt and don them, and return to the ring.

"Pardon me, sir, but we don't use these here coats in our style. Do you mind playing without it?"

"Just as 'ee please," replied Joel, and slipped it off.

The showman ran dirty hands over his arms and chest, examined his finger-nails and, turning him round, did the same across his

110

back, looking for grease. Passed, Joel leaned on the ropes in the corner and flexed his muscles. Standing there semi-nude he showed his fine figure to perfection. His legs tapered down from narrow hips, firm and muscular, but without one ounce of superfluous flesh on them; every roll and bulge of his fustian breeches was brawn and sinew. From the waist he broadened to his immense shoulders and powerful neck, his finely featured head well balanced and handsome with his black hair and side whiskers.

"Ladies and gentlemen, on my right the Grecian Tiger, on my left Joel Andrewartha." He turned and made the introduction to the other side of the ring. The two of them stepped to the centre and shook hands.

"Everything allowed except fist blows, kicking, gouging and biting. Agreed?"

Joel hid his surprise at the necessity to forbid such unpardonable offences; although kicking was allowed by Devon rules. "As 'ee please," he answered.

"The gong will start and finish each round; when it goes, let go your holds at once and separate."

They parted and returned each to his corner, facing outwards and leaning on the ropes. At the sound of the gong they faced about and approached each other cautiously, Joel in his favourite left-guarded manner, the Tiger with his hands raised a bit and curved like claws, moving in little circles. Joel reached up and gripped them, straining to bring them down.

Immediately the other stamped with his foot heavily on his instep. The surprise of the attack hurt more than the blow, for it was the Cornish rule to strike with the side of the foot only, but it taught him more of his opponent than had all his father's warnings, and as he released his grip and sprang back he determined to profit by it. He retreated across the sawdust, limping; the crowd laughed at the hurt expression on his face – it was there to be amused and see some fun and not in the mood to stipulate true sport. The Tiger

111

followed him up, a self-satisfied grin on his face, as he returned to grapple him.

He backed away as Tiger advanced, their hands locked up shoulder high, but this time he took his feet away and appeared concentrating on avoiding that painful stamp. So it came as a surprise when he suddenly planted a foot square on Tiger's diaphragm and pulled him right over to crash on the sawdust. Joel released his grip, leaped up and in a twinkling had jumped lightly on the fellow's stomach and bounded across the ring out of reach. The Champion staggered to his feet, feigning having had the wind kicked out of him, and pointed an accusing finger at Joel's feet.

The crowd hooted; here and there someone shouted, "Did 'ee not stamp first?" and "Sauce for the gander." The showman, knowing the crowd as well as he knew his man, waved the two together again. Tiger dashed in madly and caught Joel unprepared against a hard forearm smash to the neck which staggered him, but his neck was as strong as a horse's and, quick on his feet, the backward movement he made was more to lessen the blow than the effect of it. What it also did was to convince the Champion that he had his young local on the run and he followed his first smash with another, and yet again, each time wilder, less guarded. At the fourth jab his wrist was caught in a vice and forced down, a fierce straight-arm lock spun him round back to Joel and in the next instant his arms were pinioned with Joel's hands locked under the shoulder blades and he was pulled off his balance, held behind and unable to stamp or move.

For a moment or two Joel waited, gaining his breath after the smashes, and then he leaned back, carrying his man outstretched in the air; his arms strained, the muscles of his shoulders rippled and swelled as he lifted him up and up. For a second the champion was held poised, and then with all his force Joel dashed him to the boards, smashing his bottom down heavily under the falling weight of the man's own body. He rolled over painfully, and, showmanlike, exaggerated the agony on his face. The crowd roared its delight as Joel skipped back out of reach of the lunging arms, looking just like a fine black devil. Tiger scrambled up and they closed in again: some arm locks, followed by heavy work on the sawdust brought no advantage to either, until Joel found himself uppermost with a strong arm-behind-shoulder-blade lock on his man, face down. However, he humped himself up and threw Joel off, grabbing at his legs, but Joel already had them tightly crossed at the ankles, and by folding his arms and keeping himself rigid avoided a hold. Thwarted, his man gambolled around him like a playful puppy, tugging ineffectually at the smooth surfaces offering no grip. At the right moment, Joel bounded up and clear; Tiger, thinking perhaps he had thrown his bolt, closed in, only once again to be tossed lightly over by Joel somersaulting backwards.

A bit more hugging and the gong called them to their corners. In this first round Joel had sized up his man – a tricky devil, strong and determined to get the better of his challenger by any means, fair if possible, but foul if it seemed the quickest. He guessed it was a quick victory he wanted because, running to a paunch as he was, every minute passing gave an advantage to the younger, leaner man. The gong struck and they resumed the bout.

From the rushing approach Joel could see more forearm smashes were coming, and as the first whipped out he caught the wrist and drew the arm fully extended to hand him out the Flying Mare as skilfully as he had ever done. It was a piece of clean, spectacular wrestling, coming suddenly after the mix-up of the first round, and the crowd roared excited appreciation as they both retired to their corners after that brief meeting. The showman took the centre of the ring and made his announcement.

"Point to Joel Andrewartha by a fall. Ladies and gentlemen, the third round."

Tiger rushed in madly, eager to finish this antagonist right off, but Joel adopted the tactics used against him, and met his chin with a smash from the forearm which sent him staggering. As Joel followed up, the Champion retreated, pointing accusingly at the threatening forearm; he even climbed outside the ropes to impress his refusal to wrestle if Joel used the attack he himself had introduced. The crowd booed and roared for them to carry on, and the showman waved them together. Tiger went wild; he just dashed in with a full weight blind rush and, seizing Joel by the side-whiskers, slung him right across the ring to fetch up against the ropes, pained and disgusted by such play. The crowd booed and hissed; a certain amount of crudeness they were willing to see in this rough and tumble at the fair, more than they would have tolerated in any contest on their own turf, but a sudden attack like this infuriated them. All eyes were on Joel leaning against the ropes, looking across at Tiger, who expanded his chest and swaggered about not in the least abashed by the disapproval of the crowd. That violent tug on the whiskers had been sore, it had hurt his dignity too; he rubbed his cheeks thoughtfully.

But the Greek gave him no more time, coming down on him again to press home the advantage of the attack. Over-confident, he was deceived by Joel's feint and found himself gripped by the ears and hoisted in the air.

"Get rough, would 'ee, old cockie? I'll learn 'ee to control your temper."

Joel roared at him as he hurled him across the ring; before he could recover he had grabbed him by the hair and slung him back to the other side. The discomfited champion landed heavily against the top rope, his arms behind it and holding to the middle one, a sorry figure. Joel stooped and, lifting his heels, tipped him over the ropes so that they plaited around his arms. Over again and he had him properly tied up, his arms spread and twisted in the ropes.

"That'll teach 'ee to fight fair, you jelly bellied bastard," he said, standing off.

From down below him, right beside the platform, a girl laughed.

Joel heard her, and the ripples of it woke something in his memory. In Marazion, in Penzance, at every village fair and sports meeting girls must have laughed and Joel would have heard them, had he ever listened, but at this moment it seemed no girl had ever laughed with him since this had last come to his ears. Wondering, he stepped to the ropes and searched along the front ranks of spectators; his eyes were drawn at once by a girl smiling up at him. It was the same mischievous, elfin face of years ago: an elf more mature, more restrained than when he had last seen her, slim and lithesome in blue trousers and guernsey, on the Sunday afternoons before his father had belted him for wasting time with a girl.

All around the crowd was hooting and yelling with joy at seeing the foreigner put in such an uncomfortable position, a real piece of justice after the uncalled for attack on Joel's handsome whiskers. Under cover of the noise the showman was toppling his man back through the ropes, untwisting him roughly and speaking sharply in his ear. Taking advantage of the pause Joel leaned over the ropes.

"Caroline, I must see you afterwards. Will 'ee wait for me?"

"See what you can do first to your paunchy friend," she answered. "Watch!"

Her warning came none too soon; Tiger, released, and raving from the indignity that had been put on him, was determined to finish him off at once. He made a running dive which caught him against the chest, hurling him back into a corner, and seized his throat. At once Joel felt a panic attempting to cloud his mind; the throttling startled him, and when he saw the showman was going to allow it he was dismayed. The powerful hands were squeezing his throat, he felt thumbs pressing on his wind-pipe. And then suddenly he remembered Caroline and the tricks she had taught him years ago, the counters for just such holds as this which was choking the strength out of him at every moment. His right arm slipped between the Tiger's, and linking fingers with his left, passed over the strangling forearm; he bore down with his left and up with his right.

115

At once the grip on his throat was broken, and by the suddenness of the movement Tiger was thrown off his balance; Joel gripped the crossed arms and threw his weight forward, crashing him to the ground and bringing his strength to bear on the scissors, forcing the arms over one knee. Tiger used his legs in an attempt to work free, but the pressure was too hard; his arms were in Joel's power and he was threatening to break them.

" 'Ave a heart, mister," he panted. "I've got to get my living by this and I'll starve if you smash me."

"Then why don't 'ee play fair?"

"The boss made me, 'struth he did. Said you'd grab the money if I didn't do something quick. Give me a chance and I'll keep clean, honest I will."

He was in Joel's power at the moment and both knew it. If he wished he could smash at least one arm as easily as not, and, toying with that idea, he had not forced him down for the point. But the showman had known exactly what the position was and before his man touched down the gong was struck, closing the round and calling Joel off with the point in his grasp.

A sound of disappointment escaped the crowd, hushed almost at once as it saw Joel rise and hold out his right hand to help Tiger to his feet. He took it and pressed it warmly for a moment, then both retired to their corners to get the most out of the few minutes' rest.

The next round brought them on the sawdust giving as fine a display of clean ground work as the crowd had seen in the booth. Each found the other could give him as much as he could manage, the greater strength of the young Cornishman being counteracted by Tiger's experience in the style and ringcraft, but as the minutes passed without a deciding grip being gained by either, Joel's strength told more and more. At last he broke away and leapt to his feet; as Tiger swayed at him he did some quick work and the crowd roared excitedly to see their challenger with his man trussed across his shoulders, held tightly by an arm and a leg. At once Joel put him into a shoulder spin, turning round so his man's head travelled in swift wide circles, making him dizzy. It looked like an easy point coming, for when he was dropped it would be easy to touch him down; but something went wrong. A slight chance came off and even as he fell Tiger managed a hold on him and pulled him over too, and as it happened it was Joel whose shoulders hit the floor. Amid genuine applause for some good work, Tiger received the equalising point.

As the final and decisive round commenced, Joel could see the other was spent. He was a tired man, suddenly looking old, and to young eyes strangely pathetic; striving to keep his bread and butter safe against youth in all its strength, against which even his experience was no longer equal. At the first bit of ground work Joel put his mouth close to Tiger's ear.

"I do reck'n thee'st taken enough. I can worst 'ee now whenever I do want it."

"You're right."

Joel's face assumed an expression of intense concentrated effort; as he bent over he spoke softly. "Suppose 'twere a draw 'tween us, how'd that do?"

"It'd save me a cursing and me money cut."

They broke away and leaped to their feet, closing to do some showy work without damage and followed by some light throws, Joel, in particular, taking several tosses, which he had a knack of accepting without punishment, for he could always land on his bottom or his hands and feet, taking the weight off any angular part of his body that might suffer. He held himself off from forcing any deciding point and the gong went in what seemed a very short five minutes. The showman burst between them and roared the result to the crowd, now well pleased by having its money's worth, and willing to suffer a certain disappointment at Joel's not wiping the floor with the Grecian Tiger.

"I have great pleasure in announcing the result of the magnificent contest to be a draw between Joel Andrewartha and our unbeatable Tiger." Loud and derisive applause. "And now it is my privilege and pleasure to hand over the guinea purse for having stood up to five rounds and remained unbeaten . . . to Joel Andrewartha."

He took the prize and shook the donor's hand. Turning, he held out his hand to Tiger, gripped his and hurried out of the ring to change. After a brisk towelling he arranged his clothes and came out to look for Caroline.

She was outside the enclosure waiting for him; as he approached and walked away with her, several inquiring glances followed them as he was recognised. For a few minutes they were silent, Joel finding it harder to wrestle with shyness than with any man.

"I'm glad you remembered something, Mr Andrewartha; you remembered me pretty quick, once you really looked at me."

"I'd have a head like a colander if I didn't."

She left the subject and came around it to the bout he had just fought. The tone of her voice was very matter of fact, quite impersonal; it implied that there was no intention on her part to resume their friendship where it had been so suddenly broken.

"You could have worsted that Cockney Greek had you wanted to, in the end he was mighty tired. Why didn't you?"

He looked at her inquiringly; she had not missed much with those lively eyes of hers.

"I don't reck'n he'd have been as easy as all that. But it did seem mean to worst him when he was there to earn his living by besting others who challenged him. When he was a bit younger I reck'n he'd have taken a lot to worst. That rat-faced little chap too, he had him proper scared to death; threatening to stop his pay and all that."

"He took fear of that pippet? Well, maybe you're right; 'tis strange how all you big chaps are led by the nose by someone you could snap between your fingers."

The statement was a trifle too sweeping for his fancy; it seemed to include him.

Wait for the Wagon

"Led by the nose, are we? And who d'ee reck'n leads me? I'd be mighty glad to know."

She searched his face, trying to read the truth there.

"Your girl, I should reckon."

"Any particular one?" he laughed, and flushed a little. "I'd surely like to know."

"How do I know who your best girl is?" she parried. "Or are you going to tell me the girls have left 'ee 'lone all this time?"

Joel stopped; she stopped too and faced him. The crowd surged by, parting for them and closing in again like an easy tide flowing around a rock.

"You're chipping me because I let 'ee down when we were kids – at least, when I was a kid," he said reproachfully. "I'll tell 'ee how 'twas. My young brother found out 'twas with 'ee I did spend my Sunday afternoons, and he, kid-like, blurted it out. Father was mad and talked a mighty lot 'bout the farm a-going downhill if I had my head full of ideas about girls, and he belted me till I was proper sore. And I hadn't the heart to 'splain how you'd been helping me with the wrestling. And afterwards he as good as held me by the cuff all Sunday."

"So, young Joel wasn't to have a girlfriend? Well, I'm mighty sorry you were belted 'cause of me. But I reckon your father must have thought he was saving 'ee from worse, though he should have known a girl would get his handsome son sooner or later."

This time he did not refute the suggestion; he did not want to stress the fact that he had no girl of his own, neither did he want to disturb shadows that had settled across any little amours in the past. They had stopped in front of a hoopla stand and the owner was loudly advertising the beautiful things offered there to be taken by the rings. They moved across and Joel bought a supply for both of them, changing his guinea to do so.

Looking over the prizes offered there, Caroline picked out a small blue pitcher among them, a daintily shaped little thing in a fine grey-blue, with a long delicate lip in white pressed well down to flow into the slender waist.

"See, Joel, I want that handsome little pitcher. If I miss you must get your ring over it and win it for me."

Her first shot went wide; her second fell short. The third and last ring landed on the lip, hovered there spinning for a moment and fell away. She sighed with disappointment.

"Now see what you can do. 'Tis a proper handsome little pitcher, and no mistake."

His first ring fell short. The next swung spinning through the air as though it were hanging from a long thread and stopped for a fraction of a second over the jug, hung there and settled around it, as neat as ever.

Caroline clasped her hands in joy. "Oh, Joel, that was clever of 'ee. We've won it."

He aimed his last hoop, attempting to ring an orange for Salome, but it went far off, proving he had won the other more by chance than skill.

"I reck'n these hoops are weighted to make them fly off the straight," he grumbled, but she was too pleased accepting the prize to worry about that. She held it up in her hand, appraising it from all angles. Around the top edge was a white line, and at the foot a band of white, as though it had stood in milk; it certainly was as dainty a little pitcher as either of them had seen.

"I can keep it, can't I, Joel? Although you did win it, 'twas for me you tried, wasn't it?"

" 'Es, I did try for it 'cause you asked me to."

He was rewarded by a smile, just such a smile as he had loved to see when they had first known each other; now he realised that he had known through all the years he had been parted from her no one had smiled quite like Caroline.

"I do love to see you smile. I reck'n 'tis 'cause your eyes smile too; mostly with girls 'tis just a crease across their face they call a smile."

"Why, Joel! You do remember me when I laugh; you do like me when I smile. Now I've a mind to cry, or sing, to see what that can make 'ee do!"

He touched her arm gently, just laying the tips of his fingers on it.

"What would 'ee like it to make me do?"

"I would like it to make 'ee take me home, Joel. 'Tis time I was getting back home."

Together they left the fairground. Because of the jostling of the crowds she took his arm, and at the touch of her fingers on his sleeve he felt his heart pounding against his ribs in a manner that surprised him. He wondered if she would hear it and the very thought sent a furious blush into his cheek, tingling up under his whiskers. This was an entirely new experience, to have a young woman walking by his side; he glanced at her, so neat and slim, like a well-bred filly. There was something of the lady about her, just the same quality, he guessed, which had made Elizabeth seem so different when compared by his father with the other more ordinary girls.

"Are you still living with your aunt and uncle? They didn't come up here with 'ee this evening?"

"Yes, at Tremearne. They don't hold with fairs and such like. But they let me come up with the folk from Trequean – they're neighbours. They left the gig down at the "Angel"; we'd best leave word there for them that I'm 'way back . . . because I left their company to get into the wrestling and couldn't find them after."

He led the horse and gig out of the many tied at the edge of the fairground, and wrapped the little pitcher in his wrestling jerkin and laid it in the back. They left the message with the hostler at the "Angel" and took the road for Breage. At the top of the hill before the village he turned the horse to the left past the vicarage and chapel. The road climbed up over the higher ground until it finally dipped towards the coast.

121

f

Wait for the Wagon

On the seat of the gig Caroline sat by his side. Sometimes the lurching sent her against him; once, bumping down a slope, she held on to his arm to steady herself. He kept the horse at a good pace so the pleasure of it would continue, until it suddenly seemed they were very near her home, and he drew up to a walk so as to prolong the trip as much as possible. Neither had spoken for some time; Joel felt he had so much to say there was no possible way of beginning. His sisters were too young to have been much help in accustoming him to girls' company, and now he felt sadly at a loss to take advantage of his good fortune in discovering Caroline again. He was burning with a desire to find out if she had a beau of her own; alternately he reasoned that if she had he surely would have been with her at the fair, and yet how could so smart a girl be without many admirers?

"To left here, Joel," she said as they entered the Porthleven road.

A little further on, a lane went to the right down a hill, and she asked him to take it. He stopped the horse a few yards on, where they overlooked the sheltered valley running up from the low cliffs down which Tremearne faced.

" 'Tis a proper lovely little place," he remarked.

"Yes, but lonely; lying off the road the way we do 'tis few 'nough folk we see of all that go by up along. It has taken you a mighty long time to find it."

"Do 'ee be fair, now. How was I to know where 'ee did live? For if you did ever tell me I didn't heed it. I reck'ned I'd be seeing you most Sundays, 'twas a settled thing and I was not to know how 'twould all be spoilt by Father. Then even if I had dared to get 'way to look for 'ee, how was I to start? The two years between us did seem more'n they do now. I was only a boy; you were 'most a young lady."

"Even in trousers?" she laughed.

"Now I reck'n I've caught up with 'ee."

"And will be going right past, I don't doubt." There was a challenge in her voice.

122

"Not if I have my way. If thee west to crook your little finger, I reck'n I'd be mighty glad to go 'long with 'ee, all the road."

She looked at him for a moment, and for the first time he saw a blush tinge her cheek.

"Reckon I'll get down here; 'twill save question when a strange young man brings me home."

Joel leaped down and came around to help her; for a moment she left her hand in his strong grasp before she drew it away.

"Thank you for bringing me back; 'twas good of you. And 'twas nice to see you 'gain, Joel." Her fingers played on the shaft of the gig, tracing out the polished grain of the wood. Her eyes were lowered, screened by her bonnet and their own long lashes. "And you're a pretty wrestler. I'm glad you were kind to that man, though he was cruelly rough with 'ee."

Quite suddenly she stepped back and held her right hand in front of her.

"My little finger's proper stiff," she exclaimed. "But see, it do just bend a very little."

She looked up at him and laughed, the same mischievous laugh he had enjoyed with the girl in trousers and guernsey, who could bring him to the grass at her feet with a flick of her wrist. Now it seemed she could do it with a smile, or a glance of her eyes, or even a crook of her finger.

"Good-bye," she called.

Already, with him still trying to believe his eyes and ears, she was away down the lane, only turning at the corner to wave back to him. He turned the horse and climbed back into the gig; he guided it out into the lane and towards Rinsey Croft, but after that his thoughts had all his attention and the horse set his own pace for Kenneggy. It was not until he had him stabled and tended, and had wheeled the gig in under the shelter of the cart-shed and reached up for his jerkin and socks, that he remembered the blue pitcher.

For a moment he stood there cursing himself as an absent-minded fool. Caroline had been so set on winning it and had so enjoyed handling it when he had been able to get it for her, and then he had driven off with it still in the back of the gig. What a fool she would think him; just a scatter-brained fool. How was he to get it to her now? The question answered itself almost as soon as it had formed in his mind, and at once his spirits rose with his opinion of himself returning to normal. Here was a Heaven-sent excuse for calling at Tremearne at the first opportunity, and one which relieved him of the embarrassment of going there with the purpose of seeing Caroline too glaringly apparent.

He was whistling as he went towards the house; already he had been heard and Salome was coming out to meet him. She must have been waiting up, for by now it was dusky and long past her bedtime.

He halted, struck by a second misgiving.

"Joel! Oh, Joel, did you wrestle? And what have you got for me with the prize?"

To Salome it seemed impossible for her darling big brother to wrestle without getting the prize; in her mind the idea of his being beaten simply did not exist. If there was wrestling then Joel won; and when he won there was always something in his pocket for her. And now for the first time, he had forgotten her.

Her eyes fell on the bundle made by his jerkin around the pitcher and curiosity devoured her.

"Oh, Joel, what have 'ee got for me? Let me see, quick."

" 'Tisn't anything in there for you, Salome. I dis-remembered to bring 'ee anything tonight, my dear."

The disappointment and astonished unbelief in her face made him feel guilty of the grossest selfishness. To lessen it he decided to trust her with his secret.

"But I've a secret to tell 'ee. Can 'ee keep a secret on solemn oath not to tell a living soul?"

"On my solemnest oath, I can."

"Swear to it, then."

She held her right hand to her heart and stood straight before him.

"I do swear not to tell a living soul of Joel's secret, and if I do break my solemn oath may the black bogle have my heart. Now tell me."

He picked her up on his arm and carried her just away from the house and set her on the top bar of the meadow gate, so he could talk to her at nearer his own height. Leaning over the gate he pulled grasses one by one out of their green sheaths and nibbled the tender tips. The meadow before them whispered and sighed softly in the evening air, grieving because it would be cut down in its prime.

"I do reck'n we could start mowing tomorrow; if we leave it longer 'twill not make better feed."

"Is that the secret?" she asked in disgust.

"The secret's just 'tween you and me . . . and someone else."

"Who else? I thought 'twas 'tween us two only?"

"Us two here. But . . . Well, see, she is the secret. She's my sweetheart, I reck'n."

Salome gasped. This indeed was terrific; she was not at all sure whether she liked the idea or not. It would mean sharing Joel, probably losing most of him; hadn't it already started tonight, the first time he had ever forgotten to bring her something out of his prize? But on top of all that was the tremendous importance of sharing the secret, she alone out of all of them at Kenneggy.

"What's she like, Joel? Unless she's lovely I shan't even begin to like her, 'cause she'll not be good 'nough for 'ee."

"Well, she is lovely." He turned to her, trying to make her feel how Caroline looked to him. "You know how 'tis in the house wintertime; one day you look out at the sky all dark with rain, and showers do keep lashing down on the wet trees in the orchard and on the grass there all flat and old. Everything seems cold and most dead. And then you cross to t'other side of the house and open the door, and at once the sunlight streams into the room and you see the rain-clouds are being chased 'way behind 'ee by clean-washed blue sky. The sun seems to touch 'ee with warm fingers, friendly and gentle, and everything do smell sweet and new, 'cause 'tis spring come all of a sudden and winter's running away behind 'ee as fast as he can. You know how 'tis like that sometimes. And I reck'n that's just what 'tis like to be with my sweetheart."

"Perhaps I shall like her when I see her too. What's her name, Joel?"

Before he answered he picked her up again on his arm and started towards the house; she put her hand around his neck to steady herself.

"I'll not tell 'ee her name just now. 'Tis dear to me tonight and I'm jealous of it. I reck'n I don't want anyone else to say it, or even think of it, but only me tonight."

Inside, their father was sitting with his pipe near the stove where the cream pans were heating, for the sight and smell of it more than the warmth, as the windows and doors were wide open. He looked up as they entered, and Joel set her down on the floor.

"Everything all right, Father?"

" 'Es, my son, there's nothing for 'ee to do tonight. Did'ee see the wrestling?"

"I had a bout with him in his own style; 'twas rough, but the folk expect that. I reck'n 'twas a dog-fight they wanted."

"I reck'ned 'twould be. Did he worst 'ee?"

Joel kicked his boots off before he answered. "We drawed. 'Twas a proper fight. Time you were to bed, Salome. I've just seen that hay afore I come in; I could take the scythe to it tomorrow, eh Father?"

Andrewartha pulled at his clay, apparently considering the suggestion with all the weight of his experience.

"You'll know, son," he decided.

The next morning the sun had hardly risen over Tregonning Hill before Joel was out in the harness-room fingering the edge of his scythe; he stroked it gently with the hone, coaxing the final keenness out of the steel until satisfied it was razor-sharp. Out in the

126

meadow it was still cool almost to coldness, although the sun promised soon to change it to a fine heat; cuckoos called incessantly and swallows skimmed about ready for the first insects to rise under the growing warmth of the sun. The first stroke of the scythe slipped the steel in among the crowded stalks and sliced them away to leave a neat little green wall waiting for the full swing. As each rhythmic pull levelled a thick swath, meadow browns fluttered up sleepily from the disturbed grass and the swallows dipped and dived about his very feet to catch them on the wing.

For the remainder of the week, Joel was mowing from dawn to dusk, his broad shoulders bent under the hot sun, the loose shirt showing a dark patch where the sweat damped it between the blades and down his spine. For hours at a time he only straightened his back to whet the scythe or drink from the pitchers brought out to him by Salome; otherwise the steady swing went on apparently untiring. Unhurried it seemed, and yet when the other farm work permitted Charles and Ralph to come out to follow him it was as much as they could do to keep pace, fresh as they were and Joel at it for hours. By Saturday night the first cut had been turned and should be ready for carting on Monday, several acres of good hay lying in even swaths.

Salome had come out to call Joel in to supper, knowing well he would continue until he was fetched. He wiped his scythe carefully on a handful of grass and gave it a whetting to have it in readiness for next week, and they walked off together towards the stable. As he hung it up out of harm's way he touched the edge of Ralph's with his forefinger.

"That boy's for ever putting his 'way dirty. Look at that edge. 'Tis so blunt thee cust ride it from here to Helston. And that's what we'll do tomorrow evening, Salome; we'll go to Helston, just the two of us."

"Not on Ralph's scythe, I do hope."

"Would 'ee rather we took the gig? Well, don't tell anyone; keep it under your curls."

127

Wait for the Wagon

The next evening, washed and brushed, and in a clean white shirt
and his good jacket, he handed his sister into the gig.

"Here, take this little parcel and put it somewhere safe."

It contained the precious excuse, the blue pitcher.

"Where are you two going?" Polly asked as he swung himself up.

"I reck'n we'll try to get there and back."

"Why are you taking Salome?"

He shook the reins and the cob started off. "Because she doesn't
ask questions," he called back over his shoulder.

They went steadily along the slope of Kenneggy Downs and
bowled past Angove's smithy to the dip near St. Aubyn's mines.
After that there was a long pull up to much higher ground, past the
clay works and Hendra Croft to the top of the hill at Ashton where
they turned right and sped down to Rinsey Croft, and downhill more
after that, a long fine stretch right to the lane above Tremearne. He
pulled up where the road formed the fourth side of an open square of
fine grey house and buildings, the stone for which had obviously
been quarried out of the hill by the side of the Porthleven road, back
a little from where the lane joined it. The square was filled with a
colourful garden, big masses of herbaceous flowers growing as they
wished, and had a view down the valley to the sea and onwards
without interruption down the coast past Loe Bar towards Mullion.

A young man strolled out to them, smoking a pipe and evidently
enjoying the evening, jacketless and with no work to do. He was
rather older then Joel, twenty-seven or more, but neither so dark nor
so broad. He leaned on the wall at the foot of the garden in the gap
where a gate might have been, and looked at the visitors.

" 'Evening," said Joel, as he climbed down from the gig.

" 'Evening."

There was a pause; conversation seemed already exhausted.

"My sister, Salome. Our name's Andrewartha."

The young man heaved himself towards the gig and held a brown
hand out to the child.

128

"I'm proud to know 'ee, Miss Salome. And so you're Joel Andrewartha? I reckn'd thee west."

He ran an interested eye over him, as though checking up on catalogued details.

"Joel Andrewartha, the wrestler; so that's who 'tis."

"Well, I do wrestle a bit, come I've the time," he admitted.

"And I don't. I reck'n God gave me my sit-down to rest on – though He disremembered to give me 'nough time to use it – and not to be thrown down on, boomp. What do 'ee say, young lady?"

Salome giggled. "Mother does think 'tis only for spanking."

"Maybe she's right. My name's John Trounsen. This here's my uncle's place." After a long pause. "Well, how's haymaking? On cutting yet? I reck'n we'll start tomorrow."

"We've close on five acres down and ready to cart. You're damper here, maybe; up Kenneggy the goodness goes out of it quick if 'tis left standing a day after 'tis ready."

"Come down see ours."

Joel turned to the gig and helped Salome to jump out; they were just moving away from the house when she stopped.

"Why, Joel, you did forget the parcel."

"So I did." He returned and picked out the wrapped jug. "Is Miss Caroline about, for I did bring this 'long of hers, she did win it at the fair t'other night, and I took it home with me by mistake."

"Caroline? Why, 'es, her's 'bout somewhere. Caroline," he called towards the open door of the house. "Caroline, here's Joel Andrewartha asking for 'ee, and if 'ee bain't quick belike he'll not wait."

Trounsen turned to Salome and winked gravely. Joel was too anxiously waiting for a glimpse of Caroline to notice the fun, and in a moment she appeared at the door and ran down the path to join them.

"Could you not have kept him a few moments talking and given me time to see to my curls and make myself pretty," she said, laughing.

"My tongue would have worn out first," replied John. "This is Miss Salome Andrewartha, and her brother Joel. Maybe you know him?"

Caroline tossed her corkscrew curls at him, and turned to the visitors.

"Do you get teased like that?" she asked Salome. "He said that 'cause I've talked of nothing but your brother since the night I did see him wrestle at the fair. But he was fine, and did handsomely in that queer style they use in the north, and 'twould be mighty strange to him."

Salome was won immediately by anyone praising her big brother.

"Joel's a great wrestler," she agreed. "I've heard tell that when he throws his man with the Flying Mare, he'd go from Marazion to Helston."

Joel laughed at her. "Give Miss Caroline the parcel and stop your fairy tales now. We did bring your pitcher over, for I went off with it t'other night, and 'twasn't till I was putting the gig in shed that I did mind it."

She held out her hands for the parcel and, after unwrapping it, showed it to Trounsen.

"See, John, 'tis a proper handsome little pitcher. 'Twas good of 'ee to bring it over, but I did hope you would. 'Tis a pretty thing."

" 'Tis a pretty shape. Come now, we'll go down and see hay. Andrewartha did tell me they're on cutting up Kenneggy. I reck'n we'll be starting tomorrow."

The four went off towards the lower meadows, Caroline between the two men with Salome on Joel's other side. Both of them were greatly interested by the line of white foam stretching away down Loe Bar Sands.

"You mind what they do say 'bout those sands? At one time ships did sail right up the Pool to Helston, but the wicked Tregeagle was set to carry bags of sand across the harbour mouth, and each time when he got halfway, the devil did trip him so the sand ran out and filled it right across," John told Salome.

"Do you think 'tis true?" she asked.

"Not wholly. Maybe there's a bit of truth and a lot of story."

"That would be long while agone," Caroline remarked.

They reached the gate of a meadow and leaned over it, the three and Salome, who climbed a bar or two to get nearer level with them.

"Good bit of stuff," was Joel's comment. "Good bit of trefoil with it too. That's the stuff, when you're turning, catch the prong under the end of the swath and over it goes, right 'long."

"No trouble at all," agreed Caroline. "That's our work, Salome; they take the scythe and the interesting part, while we have to turn the old dry stuff."

"This harvest Joel's promised me a sickle," said Salome. "He always leads the line of mowers up Kenneggy; one day I'm going to lead the women binding, but I'd dearly love to mow like he does."

Caroline glanced at her; the resemblance to her brother was very noticeable in profile – the same straight nose, the promise of the same determined set of the chin.

"Maybe you will, for you're very like him and will grow up strong."

"What do 'ee like best on the farm-place, Salome?" asked Trounsen.

"Horses; I do love riding them, though I reckon I'll have to grow to the saddle a bit yet. Next to them, puppies."

"Let's see the puppies, then," said Caroline. "We'll see 'nough of hay afore we've finished with it."

The puppies were over by the stables, a litter of brown spaniels, very plump with large soft eyes. The girls picked them up and cuddled them to their breasts, laughing at the little quivering muzzles. Salome picked out one she liked the best and asked its name.

"Why, we've not given them names yet," said Caroline. "Have you a puppy at home?"

"Not now. We had a dog but one of the horses scat him down the shaft. Charles went down after him but he was dead."

131

"What a pity. Could she have one of these later, John? When they leave their mother?"

"Gladly; have whichever one you fancy. Now let's go and see my horse, shall we, young lady?"

They left Caroline and Joel playing with the pups and went across to the stables.

For a moment there was a silence between them; then both looked up at the same instant and met the other's gaze. She lowered hers at once.

"Who is John Trounsen?" he asked, a question that had been burning his tongue since he had first set eyes on him.

"He's my uncle's nephew, a sort of cousin of mine. My aunt married his uncle. That's how we're related, if you could call it that."

He was silent for a moment, thinking how best to ask what he was determined to find out.

"Is that all?"

"How d'you mean?"

"Is he your intended husband?" He flushed at the directness of his question. "I do hope you'll not be vexed at me asking. 'Twas not just curiosity; I do want to know."

She stroked the puppy she was holding and did not lift her eyes. A faint blush crept under the delicate skin on her cheek.

"They do hope so, yet I've never said he was. I like him well enough, but not that way. Maybe I know him too well. Let's go 'n' see the horses."

She rose to her feet and brushed and smoothed her dress, swishing the full skirt into place and good hanging. Looking up she met his earnest gaze and returned it encouragingly.

" 'Twas good of 'ee to come over with my pitcher."

"I was glad to have it, for I did want to see you 'gain. 'Twas the thought of it made me work all week as though I could never tire. Caroline, next Sunday, after tea, would 'ee. . . Would 'ee meet me out there where we used to, years agone?"

The pause before she answered was beautifully timed. It was not too short, as though the request had been anticipated and the answer thought out; neither was it long enough to carry the impression that it needed careful and serious consideration.

"Of course I would, Joel. 'Twould be grand and no mistake; like old times."

He felt his heart pound at his throat; as they walked side by side towards the stable to join the others his hands and feet seemed suddenly to be a great distance away and it took a big effort to move them as he wished. He let her pass into the building first, and as she did so she turned her head and smiled at him, a sweet friendly smile the more precious because it was seen by no third person.

They dawdled about chatting for a little longer and then the two climbed up on their gig and drove away, waving goodbye until the bend in the lane hid them and the pleasure of seeing Caroline was over for the week.

"Joel, was she your sweetheart?"

"I do hope so," he said fervently.

She was silent for a while. Inside her mind was a struggle between her generosity and her natural desire to keep his affections centred around herself and their home.

"I do hope so too."

The week's work of hay-making sped the time until Sunday came again, the one day that mattered to Joel. The three brothers went with their father for the stroll around the farm as usual; at the rush times, when work was taking every minute of the daylight to get through with it, the look over was more necessary than ever. The amount of things that can happen on a farm in six days can only be believed by those who have worked for the land. If the movement is detrimental the rate of falling off can be appalling. The face of the land can change more often than the wind itself, and it must be studied as carefully if trouble is to be avoided. The prime of a crop can steal on him in a night, and if the harvester is not ready it will pass him by and the labour of months, even of the years that have gone into bringing the soil into good heart, will miss its just reward. Drought or rains can move the ordered calendar this way and that; only by keeping a receptive eye on every corner of the land, every beast among the stock, and knowing from experience the probable effect on them of every vagary of weather, and checking up at the first opportunity, can a farmer hope to get the better of the struggle. Joel knew this, and even the longing to be with Caroline would not have kept him from his duty to the soil.

On these Sunday evenings in midsummer he met Caroline at the well above Legereath Zawn and together they wandered along the cliffs of Trequean and Trewavas, past the Bishop and the ancient cromlech on Trewavas Head. At first they had walked side by side; later rough ground had given him the excuse to offer his arm, and so by easy stages they had fallen into strolling arm in arm in enjoyment of each other's company. It was her suggestion that they should go to Carn Clodgy by the footpath on Rinsey East Cliff and watch the sun set over Mount's Bay, and this they did, returning later by the very path along which she had been coming when they had met as boy and girl.

They had talked mostly about those afternoons together.

"And were you sorry you did ever meet me, when your father took his belt to 'ee, Joel?"

"No, I was 'most glad he was a-going to do it; it did seem so romantic to suffer for you – though 'twasn't so good once he did get started for he could lay it on proper hard. But I reck'ned 'twas worth it, and had I known 'twas a-coming to me, I should have done the same again."

"How sweet of you to think of me like that. But then you were a proper fine boy, and no mistake. I was mighty proud to be friendly with 'ee."

An encouraging glow crept through him; it was good to be assured that he had not seemed just an awkward boy to her, and gave him hopes that she might be thinking kindly of him even yet.

"I reck'n I wasn't quite old 'nough to know just what a fine girl you were. When I look back and mind you and how pretty you were, I'm fair mazed that I didn't take my tanning and come back for more every Sunday. It do beat me how I didn't fall clean in love with 'ee then."

The words had been spoken before he realised the implication, and from the glance she gave him he had little doubt she had picked it up. They had let the path go by itself inland while they continued over the rougher ground. For a while they were both silent, both conscious every step was bringing them nearer Tremearne, and shyly anxious to prolong the time when they were together in the quietness and peace of the evening.

" 'Tis a lovely night," she said, tempting him. "Let's not go home too soon."

They sat on a grey lichened stone, looking over towards the restless line of surf ever churning across Loe Bar Sands, and showing through the gathering dusk.

"I do hate the sea," she said. "The sea and the tin, it gives most everything to us, but it takes it back a hundred times over in one angry mood."

"I'm feared of the sea; 'tis not much I'm feared of, but I am of drowning. The fishermen, now, they do reck'n 'tis terrible to be 'way underground; they do say they couldn't bide still a minute for thinking of all the great weight of rock and earth over their head lest it should fall and crush them. But if I had to earn my living on the sea I'd be proper scared just to think of all the water that was 'tween me and good solid ground. 'Tis each man what's he's been used to."

After a moment she took his hand in hers.

"Maybe, Joel; but I'm glad you're not a fisherman, for I'd hate to think of 'ee always fighting with that cruel water."

He looked at her keenly, saw her head bent showing her smooth suntanned neck under the knot of soft hair; the long curls hung beside her cheeks and hid them from him at the moment. His arm stole around her waist.

"You care that much?"

She turned to him and raised her eyes to him, and smiled.

"Of course I do care."

Her hand sought his and pressed his palm to her side; through her bodice he could feel the warmth and firmness of her. She lifted up her face to him and nestled in the crook of his arm, against his strong shoulder.

"Joel!"

He barely caught the sound as she breathed his name, but he saw her lips move so near, so irresistible that he bent his head and touched them lightly with his own. The contact seemed to dispel the last of their shyness towards each other, both knew then that those dreamed-of feelings were shared and that the other understood. Her hands clasped about his neck and she pressed her lips to his in frank, hungry eagerness, while he clasped her to him in his realisation of how beautiful she was to love.

"Joel, my handsome man," she whispered.

"I do love 'ee, Caroline; how much I do love 'ee!"

Dusk was falling and they dared not delay too long; she was grateful to her guardians that they had always allowed her freedom and she was careful not to abuse her privilege or refute their trust.

"I'll come back with 'ee," said Joel. " I reck'n I'll ask them right now to let me court you for my wife. For you will be, Caroline?"

She pressed his arm as they walked on homewards.

"Of course I'll be your wife, Joel; I reckon I'm the luckiest girl 'tween Lizard and Land's End. Won't the girls be mad, but they're not going to get away with 'ee now," she laughed.

"The men will be worse, but I'll wrestle with any who dispute my right to 'ee now, and throw them where they'll not be back in a hurry. So you'll need to warn all your old sweethearts that you're Joel Andrewartha's now."

"Not all of them; 'twould take too long."

Laughing, they entered the fields of Tremearne. The joy and happiness of the old days were mixed now with stronger, more disturbing emotions, but there remained the same good companionship; they could laugh with each other as though it had been yesterday they were rolling on the turf, boy and blue-trousered girl.

Her uncle William Drenocoe, farmer of Tremearne, had let the good cooking of his wife Sibella run him to fat around the waistline, so that his stomach sank comfortably into the pouch formed by the flap of his trousers and gave them the appearance of being glued to him. He farmed well on a soil kinder than many places around, warmer and less hungry than some, but although he worked hard he claimed that things went better if he directed operations from under the lee of a hedge or haystack than if he went into action himself. After losing both their children while they were still infants, they had taken in the orphaned nephew and niece, children of their sisters, and brought them up with as much love as, and perhaps more leniency than, they would have given their own.

"Come in," said Caroline as they reached the gap in the wall at the end of the flower-garden. "And have a bite with us. Why don't you ride over next time, 'twill be so much easier than the walk?"

"I reck'n I will. Truth was I did like the walk to give me time to think of things a bit."

Inside the living-room her uncle was sitting by the fire with his pipe and glass; the table had been set for the meal but evidently three people had eaten theirs and the dishes were stacked aside. One place was waiting, and Caroline went to the dresser for things for Joel so as not to disturb her aunt, who was sitting by the window after reading the Bible until the light had failed. He had met them for the first time on the previous Sunday.

"Ah, Joel, pull thyself up a chair and sit 'ee down by the fire. Have a glass? Caroline, bring a glass for the young man."

"Thank 'ee, sir."

"I was just going to, Uncle, but he's having something to eat, too."

The stout farmer spat into the heart of the fire and took a pull at his glass.

"That's right, give him something to eat and drink; and don't let the sight of me warn 'ee off your victuals, 'cause it took a mighty lot to get me in this state, and I enjoyed every mouthful."

He laughed softly at his joke against his own girth, and the lines on his heavy face creased deeper, while his chins quivered into the loose collar of his jacket.

"You're back late, aren't you, Caroline?"

Her aunt spoke for the first time, and, although she had acknowledged him kindly when he bowed to her on entering, Joel shifted his feet uneasily at her question. Caroline never faltered in her preparations for the supper, she just looked at her aunt and patted her hand as she passed her.

" 'Twas a lovely evening, so I didn't hurry; you don't mind, Aunt Sibella?"

For a moment or two she did not answer.

"I was thinking of Mr Andrewartha; he has a tidy way to go, hasn't he?"

"Now don't you hurry him, Aunt dear, for he must have something afore he goes. Come now, Joel, sit here and we'll have supper."

He got to his feet and gave his jacket a hitch to settle it; he felt he must say his piece before he ate or the food would choke him. Not only that but Trounsen was likely to appear at any moment, he supposed, and he did not want the audience increased.

"Afore I take your hospitality I reck'n there's something I'd better ask you, sir, and you, Mistress Drenocoe; for maybe you'd not welcome me so warmly afterwards."

138

Wait for the Wagon

"Then drink up, boy, and make sure of it. Give yourself time to think and don't say anything rash," William advised him cheerily.

Joel smiled; he was tuned up now and went on to what he had to say.

"I want your leave to come over here to court Caroline for my wife."

He sighed with relief at getting it spoken, and leaned on the back of his chair, looking from one to the other to see the effect of his words. Caroline had remained in the shadowy part of the room while he had been speaking for her, and now kept very still, waiting too for the answer. Her uncle looked across at his wife, and then up at Joel; he seemed to find nothing about him to which he could nail an objection, and his eyes returned to Sibella, who had not looked their way.

"Now, Sibella, what d'you think of that?"

" 'Tis for you to say, William; I'll bide by what you say."

Again the master of the house spat into the fire; apparently he disliked the responsibility shelved on him.

"Well see, I don't reckon 'tis. Caroline's your sister's girl, not mine. Anyway, what does she have to say? Do you want this young man to come a-courting you, Caroline?"

She came forward and stood beside Joel.

"I do, Uncle; 'deed I do."

"Very well, Joel boy, make thyself at home. Good luck to 'ee, and God bless 'ee both." He held out his hand and, taking Joel's, shook it heartily.

"I hope you'll be happy," said Mrs Drenocoe, but her face did not carry the same doubt about it as her words, which perhaps were merely ill-chosen. "I think you're a fortunate young man."

"Thank 'ee, ma'am; I know I'm in luck, and 'tis kind of you both to wish us well."

William lifted his glass towards the young pair. "The best to 'ee. And come over to see her when you can, Joel. You'll be welcome."

Joel took up the glass that had been filled for him.

139

"Sir," he acknowledged, and drank, his eyes smiling at Caroline over the rim of his glass. They sat down to supper and the talk rattled on in merry bursts. Before long John Trounsen joined them, exchanging a friendly nod with the guest.

"Hullo, 'Drewartha; d'you like Tremearne?"

"Why, it suits me well 'nough," Joel laughed. John dropped down in a chair drawn near the table and leaned his elbow on it, looking at Caroline. She met his gaze and an affectionate smile showed on her face and in her eyes.

"I've got a beau, John."

For a moment he gave no sign of having heard, and then he turned to Joel.

"You have? Joel here?"

She nodded; her manner towards him was very gentle, as though he were easily hurt. He reached out his hand and gripped Joel's warmly, holding it for a moment as though he too had an affection for him because she had chosen him as her own.

"You two are the finest men in Cornwall," she said quietly.

John smiled at her. "God bless 'ee, Caroline; God bless 'ee both."

He cleared his throat, for his voice had gone husky; it had very nearly broken. And suddenly tears were in her eyes; with a little sob she left the table and ran out of the room.

Later, saying goodbye to Joel, she said it was silly to cry just because she was so happy.

Chapter Six

SINCE he had come in for supper Joel had not spoken a word, the harness he worked at was only an excuse for not giving his interest to the family. When the others had gone to bed and only his parents remained in the living-room, he looked up from the leather.

"Father, I'm going to marry a girl from down Porthleven way."

His eyes had been on them both as he spoke; as soon as he saw the effect of his words he lowered them again, examining the harness. If he had cracked a whip in their faces the surprise there could not have been more clearly shown. Neither said a word, nor moved, but just looked at him as though horns were growing out of his head.

"Joel!" his mother was able to gasp at length.

In her voice was the knowledge of all the disaster in the world. Joel her son, her first-born, the child of their early and sweetest love-making in the glamorous days of young romance, wanted to marry. After all she had done for his comfort and his welfare, after all her pride and admiration for his fine strength and grand physique due entirely to their care and attention, he wanted to marry. Was her care not enough for him, was her study of his every comfort, the love and devotion she had lavished so generously on him not sufficient, but he must marry some chit of a girl? And a girl from down Porthleven way; of all the far-off, unget-at-able places to choose to go to find a girl. To marry a bit of a thing from down Porthleven way! Nearly twenty-five years of her life's work crashed to earth in that one anguished cry of "Joel!"

His father had taken the parental stand, back to the hearth, and stared at this rebel in his demesne.

"How long have 'ee had that idea in your head?" he asked, keeping his voice mild.

Joel continued to regard his work, searching for further bits to repair.

"A month, not much more."

Richard looked across at Elizabeth, his glance charged with a great deal to the effect that here was a situation requiring very careful handling, and she should watch him to see how tactfully he was about to do it.

"When did 'ee reck'n to get married? Sometime next spring?"

Joel rose and slung the harness over his shoulder, preparing to go out with it.

"Bless 'ee, no, Father! Why, most as soon as banns have been called, I did reck'n."

This was an unexpected blow and Richard took it hard, but retained his ground and returned to diplomatic attack.

"But, Joel my son, you can't marry a girl I haven't even seen!"

"Surely you didn't want me to ask 'ee to go over Porthleven and see her afore I asked if she'd take me, did 'ee, Father? Now 'tis settled I'll bring her over to Kenneggy sometime so you can get to know her."

"But listen, son," broke in Elizabeth. "Suppose we don't approve of her?"

This thought had never entered Joel's head. If he loved her then that had seemed sufficient to him – and could anyone help loving Caroline? In a second his mother's supposition was dismissed as too

142

absurd; most folk liked his parents and she probably would, and on their part they would take to her either for her own sake or his.

"Why, 'course you'll like her, Mother. She's. . . Oh, there's no one quite like her round here."

Elizabeth appeared resigned. "Well, son, I only hope you've chosen wisely; I must say I'd feel happier over it all if I knew the girl."

"Never you worry, Mother," he said and went over to kiss her, but she turned her cheek to him and did not take it on her lips.

In her heart she felt the first little stab of pain – she would not admit it was jealousy – because now she was no longer the only woman he loved, nor was she the one he most liked to kiss. He gave no sign of having noticed it, and left them to go outside. As soon as he had gone she turned to her husband, a look of inquiry on her face.

"Why is he wanting to get married so soon, Rich? You don't think. . . ?"

He kicked nervously at the wood on the hearth, distressed by the same thought himself, but not wanting to express it. A loyal belief in his son struggled with his knowledge of the world and his own experience of the weakness of human nature.

"Of course not," he said sharply. "There's nothing like that 'bout Joel. He's Andrewartha. No, I wouldn't say anything like that 'bout Joel."

She did not seem to find so much comfort in that fact; kneeling down by the hearth she began sweeping it tidy and safe for the night.

"Oh, Rich, I do hope 'tis all right. Folk talk so over a hasty marriage. I do hope he hasn't got in tow of some fast hussy."

"He's all right. Why, you and I didn't take so long over getting married ourselves, and what you saw in me to make 'ee do it I can never tell. And we've been happy, haven't we, Elizabeth?"

"We have indeed, Rich. You were a fine man and enough to please any girl, and our son is worth the best girl in Cornwall. I can't but think he's foolish to rush into this without a second thought. 'Tis so unlike him. And so inconsiderate too, for she'll have to come here to live with us, as we can't manage to give him a place of his own. I really do think he might have talked to us first, don't you, Rich?"

Andrewartha knew he had consulted no one when he had fallen in love with pretty Elizabeth Nancurvis. He had not forgotten all the sweet hopes and desperate disappointments of that time, and supposed now his son was living in his turn in the springtime warmth and coolness of young romance. For all his solid, straightforward nature he was not without imagination or understanding, and would have enjoyed, if he were allowed, looking on at Joel's courting.

"We mustn't be too hasty, my dear. Young folk are very taken up with theirselves and don't reck'n a great deal of others; when we were young we had more thought perhaps, but these days we older folk are not counted in their plans. 'Tis a sign of the times and we must put up with it. Same as we mustn't let ourselves take a dislike to the girl afore we've seen her; maybe she's all right. After all, his father had very good taste, now didn't he?"

Elizabeth was not so easily jollied into a different mood. She had already cast herself in the role of slighted mother and was playing in her imagination as a devoted slave to the family, who did her duty towards them and was cast off when she was no longer needed. This time of learning that her boy's eye had roved to another woman was a glorious opportunity to indulge in a little self-pity, and without trying to discover whether she had just cause she allowed herself a really good wallow.

"I know I shan't take to her, Rich, I know it. I can feel in the very way he told me about her that she has set him against me. He never used to hide anything from me; Joel never had any secrets from his mother. Now he is so changed; I haven't been able to think what had come over him lately. All the time he's been hiding this from us! Oh, how could he?"

She fumbled about until she found her handkerchief and began to sob quietly into it. By this time she was convinced that she was the mother of a cruelly unnatural son, that she alone of all women had given so much and received so little in return. It was wrong; it was cruelly wrong, but she could bear it. Yes, with God's help she could bear the hardest slurs and slights he could put upon her, and do her duty towards them until the end. And the end could not be very far off now; she was no longer young.

"There now, Elizabeth, come. 'Tis not as bad as all that. Why see, Joel's a quiet boy and keeps his thoughts to hisself 'most always, and this matter of courting is one he's not likely to be anything but shy over. Eh, Mother? We must be fair to the boy. We just have to talk it all over together and find the best way out. When he's in again I'll ask him what he plans."

Drying her eyes and contenting herself with an occasional sniff she turned her attention to the preparations for bed. While she was away Joel returned. Father and son both felt it was an awkward moment, with a strain about it which was almost unknown before. Joel was on the defensive, and his father realised it without seeing any reason for it; he was not contemplating any attack, nor even frustration of the boy's hopes. Both waited in silence for Elizabeth's return. Whether she knew he had come in and delayed on purpose, or not, she took her time.

At length she came into the living-room with the jug of herby beer and poured them a glass apiece.

Richard cleared his throat.

"Now, my son, tell us what you've a mind to do; your mother and I both want to make things as easy for 'ee as we can. We've had a very happy life together, all of us, at Chywoon and here at Kenneggy. We've had a very happy married life, in spite of troubles and hard times, and we want 'ee to have the same. Tell us just 'zactly what you've in mind."

Joel had perched himself on the edge of the table; his mother had taken a glass of milk for herself and was sipping it down on the stool before the remains of the fire.

"Well see, most of it boils down to this – I want to marry Caroline Rowe; she's the girl Charles met out Rinsey way years agone, when I used to go out to see her Sunday afternoons till he told on me and you had me in on the door and belted my back for having truck with girls. Do 'ee mind the day? I was fond of her those days, and that was long while agone, but after that tantarra I did see no more of her till t'other day, and then she took my fancy more'n any girl I ever come across. It pleases me just to look at her; and after no time I reck'ned 'twould be the grandest thing to have her 'bout the place all time. So over I did go and ask her if she'll have me, and bless you, she didn't make any bones 'bout it at all. Looked just like she'd been expecting me. Then I began to figure out just how 'twould be at home here if I did bring back a wife, and the more I thought 'bout it the better it seemed. If Betsy gets married things'll be much harder on you, Mother, what with dairying and housework and baking, errands to Marazion and so on and she'd surely help 'ee a lot. Be company, too, Mother. In that way we'd not feel the extra one to keep. And I'm not asking 'ee to pay me more, Father; I figure out we'll manage all right."

He looked from one to the other hopefully. His mother continued to sip her milk in a silence that was charged with suggestion of coming storm. His father seemed to find the way he had put the proposition agreeable and was ready to see it had certain advantages for them all; his cue, however, would come from Elizabeth and his reply was non-committing until she had expressed herself.

" 'Es, Joel, maybe there's a lot in what you say; that is, if she can do all that in the way your Mother likes it done."

"Oh, take no fear of that, there's none can do better," said Joel confidently. "And what d'you say, Mother?"

"Well, Joel, I don't want to say much till I've seen her. 'Twill not be easy for me to grow used to a strange girl in my house, and if she's contrary and difficult I'll not put up with it. I'm prepared to make big sacrifices for you, my son, but I'm not going to commit myself to anything till you've brought her over here to meet your mother. I'll not have you throw yourself away on a girl who is unworthy of you, Joel."

"More likely to be t'other way 'bout," replied Joel. "I'm not such a great catch and I reck'n she is. She'll not have far to go to find many men willing and glad to win her."

The wonder of her accepting him after so brief a courtship was continually with him and made him ponder on it many times a day, as he was doing now, leaning forward and gazing at the low fire, trying to find some substantial reason to explain the mystery.

"Who is the girl, anyway?"

His father's question brought him back to reality.

"She lives with her uncle and aunt down Tremearne, 'tween Breage and Porthleven. They've a big farm there."

"Is she an orphan?" his mother asked.

" 'Es. I mind she told me her father was from the north, and she must be like him, for she's quite different from most girls in these parts. She's fair and small, not like Betsy, nor May Eade, nor Mary."

Richard sniffed; he saw no necessity for naming Mary.

"Has she money of her own?"

"Bless you, how do I know?"

"Haven't you asked her, Joel?"

"Why no, Mother, I never thought of it. 'Course I never thought of it."

"Well, you're a smart fellow to choose himself a wife. Not finding out whether she had any money afore you asked for her! What's the use of a penniless wife to a man like you? Where would your father have been today if I hadn't brought him money? How d'you think he could have managed without that help?"

Richard fidgetted about, none too pleased to be reminded of his obligations. In his opinion her money had indeed helped him, and yet it had equally benefited her by improving his position, and the implication that it had all gone on his own personal aims never failed to rattle him. And Elizabeth, sweet as she was, never let him forget it, nor failed to inform others of his debt to her.

"Well see, I don't know, and what's more, I'm not caring. What have I to need money for, anyway? I'm glad 'nough to have the girl herself."

"Yes, but all this will be yours one day," she answered, her glance taking in the living-room and converting it into a mansion, and their fields outside into many broad acres. "And you'll have to keep it up. But still, 'tis too late now, I suppose."

" 'Es, I'm not changing my mind, if there's money or no money."

He tossed off his beer and picked up the other empty glasses.

"Then 'tis settled I bring her over one day. You'll lend me the gig, Father?"

" 'Es, son, you know you can take the gig any time."

He took the glasses out to the back kitchen and put them in a bowl, pouring water over them and leaving them to soak. He returned to the fire and kissed his mother on the forehead.

"Good night, Mother; good night, Father. I'll be off to bed now; sleep well."

He left them and climbed the steep ladder stair to his room.

Joel's courtship, going on at the busiest time in the farming calendar, during hay-making and harvest, was of necessity limited to Sundays. All the weekdays there was work enough to keep everyone busy from dawn to dusk. When they were on carting, the big wagon was pulled out by a team borrowed from the whims; on the tailboard was painted in scrolled characters:

Richard Andrewartha
Breage

The place name was newer and done over a sweep of brighter red paint which showed up against the rest of the wagon, and under could still be traced faintly the name of Germoe, with Chywoon above it. Now Higher Kenneggy had been done in the panels on either side, a word in each. The framing had been at one time a royal blue, but the years had dusted and faded it down to a whitish colour. Immense hanks of rope hung about it from convenient hooks. The heavy iron skid and the chocking roller were suspended underneath.

As soon as the hay was in, harvest took their attention and kept white the margin on the black blade of Joel's scythe. Only on Sundays did they leave the work on the fields, and even on that day Richard had been known to turn them out to save a crop threatened by a change in the weather. His belief was that if the Lord had sent them a good crop it would be base ingratitude to allow it to spoil if human hands could save it, and he preferred to break the commandment and give thanks rather than to keep it and grumble.

Busy as they were at Kenneggy, Joel knew the same work was going on at Tremearne; so that even if the thought of taking time off to see Caroline entered his head at all, it never received consideration for he knew well enough that during the week he would not be welcome there in any capacity but as a worker. As Sunday was their only evening together, it was all the sweeter and naturally enough brought them to planning how soon they could get married.

"I can't leave Uncle while harvest is on, that's certain."

"He wouldn't thank me for asking it. But when 'tis over, is there any need to wait longer?"

"None that I know of; 'twill be easier then for a bit, and I reck'n we've nothing to make us wait. Dairy work will be getting lighter, and they'll have to get a girl in to do it with Aunt sooner or later, so it makes little odds when."

Making plans for their marriage brought it right out of the future into the very near weeks ahead; with the work going on at high speed the days passed fast enough. Penzance market on Thursday

149

cut the week in two, and each half had passed almost before the days could be counted.

"Name a day, Caroline, and we'll let them know."

"I've thought of the Saturday before Harvest Festival. 'Tis the last in September and 'twould be lovely to go to church when 'twas all dressed up with flowers and offerings. And 'tis right for us, being farm people."

She pressed his hand warmly at the thought of their approaching life together, and smiled up at him. He felt a thrill of excitement; the rarity of the occasions when they could meet had galled him and he was eager to take her home to Kenneggy and have done with the bondage the farms held over them where their companionship was concerned.

"Then it's the last Saturday in September for us, God willing," he said, and kissed her lovingly to clinch the matter. "And I'll count the days till then."

"And so shall I."

Her eyes promised him that she meant it.

The arrangements went forward during the few remaining weeks. Caroline had her linen in order and what trousseau she was able to collect, and it was little enough that really had to be done. Their banns were called thrice in St. Breaca's church. Her aunt was giving her the handsome big bed that had been in her room for years, together with the chest that already contained her linen and clothes. These Joel fetched over to Kenneggy a day or two before the Saturday, together with a few things they had bought on an exciting afternoon in Penzance one market day, and installed them in his room to make it look more comfortable and friendly.

John Trounsen had promised to be his best man, a service which fell on him quite naturally as a result of the friendship that had grown between them since the day they had first met outside the garden at Tremearne. Charles had not expected to be asked, as Joel knew his brothers would take over his farm duties for that day to leave him free, which of course they were willing enough to do.

On the wedding day, Richard drove the bridegroom, Elizabeth and Salome over to Breage, where they waited for John to bring along Caroline and the Drenocoes. When she entered the church on her uncle's arm, and Joel turned to her, his heart nearly missed a beat; she looked so lovely in his eyes. Her gown was of palest violet, long and full enough to hide her feet entirely, so she seemed to glide towards him. As she took her place by his side at the chancel step, she gave him the flicker of a smile, because she knew how nervous he was feeling and would reassure him, and then her picture hat drooped shyly, countered as it was by the roguish way the black ribbons tied among the long curls at one side. On either side of the chancel was a big sheaf of wheat, one from Kenneggy and the other from Tremearne; loaves of fine crusty bread, piles of fruit and countless flowers, arranged with long stalks of corn, were used in the decoration of the church.

The Curate opened his book. "Dearly beloved, we are gathered together here in the sight of God and in the face of this congregation, to join this Man and this Woman in Holy Matrimony. . ."

At once Joel felt a strange solemnity come over him and the church; it seemed that the old grey stones around him, hard and impervious as they were, had really absorbed the faith of an ageless congregation which by its very sincerity invited into it the Presence of the Good Lord Himself. His mind wandered from the parson's words, so that he heard them while he was thinking of how they had met as children, and parted only to find each other again at exactly the right moment in their lives. A deep gratitude swelled up in his heart; he glanced sideways at her and saw her breast rise and fall under the tight bodice, cut so wide he found himself wondering how she kept it from slipping off her shoulders.

" 'Therefore if any man can show any just cause, why they may not lawfully be joined together, let him now speak, or else hereafter forever hold his peace.' "

The curate paused and in that moment's silence the words found their dramatic quality. The church remained quiet, no voice spoke; all around seemed the promise of peace held forever. But, he, speaking for the Church, must ask them too before being satisfied.

Caroline's hand lay in Joel's; it seemed just then very small, yet firm and friendly as it had always been to him. He was being taught his vows to her, pledging himself to her for life.

"I, Joel Andrewartha, take thee, Caroline Rowe, to love and to cherish, till death us do part."

"I take thee, Joel Andrewartha, to be my wedded husband . . . for richer, for poorer, to love, cherish and to obey . . . and thereto I give thee my troth."

John laid the golden ring on the Book, and with that ring Joel wedded his Caroline in the Name of the Trinity.

At Tremearne later there was a merry gathering; his brothers and sisters had managed to get through with the work and find time to drive over in Henry Wheeler's gig for the breakfast, and both the boys took an early opportunity of giving the bride a hearty kiss. John caused a great roar of laughter by suggesting that the wrestler had most certainly met his match this time and it would take more than a Flying Mare to loosen Caroline's hold on him.

At length the couple managed to get away and climb up on the gig to drive into Penzance, where they were spending the weekend. Aunt Sibella dropped Caroline's carpet bag into the gig and some last words of earnest advice into her ear.

"Bring her over to see us whenever 'ee can, Joel," called Trounsen as they moved off.

They all waved; Caroline waved back, but she waved mostly to her cousin, who stood watching until they turned the bend of the lane.

"Poor John, I wish he'd get married too," she said.

"He'll get married soon 'nough now; 'twouldn't be likely he'd look afield while you were round to make all the girls seem geese beside your swan."

In Penzance they wandered arm in arm through the Saturday-night crowds, looking into shop windows, buying sweetmeats at the market-stalls, watching the gulls on the ships and luggers down at the quay. The Mount with its fairy castle showed itself floating beautifully over a slight haze across the bay, a castle of dreams, the loveliest home in England.

"Joel, have 'ee ever thought 'tis more'n' likely Jesus Himself did come to the Mount with his uncle, Joseph of Arimathea, when he was on tin-trading afore he went on to Glastonbury?"

"No? 'Tisn't in the Bible so I don't reck'n I had."

" 'Tisn't in the Bible, I know, but I've heard tell He did come here as a boy and, Joel, maybe He walked in those fields up there, over by Rose Hill and Trevenner, or over that side by Henvor and Tolvadden."

He followed her gaze.

" 'Tis a proud thing for Cornwall if He did, and I hope 'tis true."

"Maybe He saw the castle, same as we see it now, as though 'twere built on a cloud."

He shook his head.

"No, that was a long while agone and the castle's changed since then, though in parts 'tis half as old as Cornwall." He gazed at it for a few moments in silence. "If I were Lord of the Mount now, I'd call my liveried boatmen and they'd row us over in a fine barge. And you'd be Queen of the Mount."

She nestled against his side as they leaned on the wall looking out across the bay. The evening was drawing in; her cloak was held around her by her husband's arm about her waist.

"If you were Lord of the Mount, with his men and barge, or any other nobleman with any castle in the world, I'd love 'ee no more than I do love Joel Andrewartha."

And looking at her, he knew he would not change places with any man on earth that night, if by doing so he were taken from her side.

" 'Tis getting late," he said quietly.

"Yes," she answered, pressing his arm. "Shall we go?"

Passing through the streets towards their lodging, people turned more than once to look at them, the handsome tall fellow and his wife; the two moving among a crowd and yet alone together, their thoughts on each other, their eyes looking around them and yet seeing nothing but their own happiness. Several people recognised him, and laughed as he passed without noticing them, not for a moment blaming him for his preoccupation. Once Caroline heard a voice say quite loudly, "There's Joel," and knew from its tone it would be one of his ringside admirers. She felt proud of her man.

"Not just Joel now," she said, as though he too had heard. "Caroline's Joel. . . till death do us part."

"And that'll not be for many, many years, God willing."

Chapter Seven

ELIZABETH had not often gone over to Tregonebris to her home in all the years she had been married. Her people had asked her, but she was happy in the life she had chosen and content with her husband, still convinced that he was far more precious than any of the fine gentlemen she had known in her girlhood. For poor as he was in this world's measurement of wealth, he was infinitely richer than many others in his good nature; his gentleness and love towards her compensated for the hard work and thrift which were such integrant parts of her life. She knew, and never attempted to disguise the fact from herself, that she was a mining farmer's wife; the days of family gatherings at Tregonebris were done. There was no combining the two; the severance was clean and sharp, and if she was to remain happy it was useless to hope the two would overlap in the smallest degree.

Now Salome was older, frequent messages had come from her home begging Elizabeth to send her over on a visit.

"Would 'ee like to go?"

Her father's question seemed to imply that he half hoped she would not, though he would do nothing to prevent her from going.

Salome looked across the table to Joel; his smallest wish or opinion was Law and Truth to her. She was getting a tidy sized girl now and was a great pet of his, while in her turn she idolised him and hung on every word he said.

" 'Es, you'll have little 'nough chance to get 'way from home when you're older. 'Twill be good for 'ee too, seeing Mother's fine folk and how they live in the big houses. Go, and have a good time."

"I reckon I'd like to go well enough. I needn't stay very long, need I? Just a day or two?"

Their father showed little enthusiasm and took no pains to simulate pleasure now she had consented to go. He knew his daughter was his daughter, and knew where she belonged. It would have been simple for him to have vetoed the suggestion, but that was not his way of ruling the family.

"Do just 'zactly what 'ee please, my girl. There's no making 'ee go if 'ee'd rather not. And there's none can make 'ee stay if 'ee want to come home."

Joel saddled a horse for her after dinner on the following day; Elizabeth had put a few things in a neat bundle and he fixed it on the pommel. He gave her a leg up into the saddle, where she seemed to change immediately from an ordinary growing girl into the competent young horsewoman she had recently become. Once she had been permitted to ride she had soon been at home in the saddle and knew no fear of a fall.

"Keep your eyes and ears open," said Joel. "Remember all 'ee can and tell us all 'bout it when you come home."

"Give them all my love." Elizabeth could not help a touch of sadness getting into her voice. "And we'll be expecting you when we see you back."

Her father ran his fingers over the girths, although he knew all would be correct if Joel had seen to it. He looked up and spoke to her quietly.

"There's nothing to keep 'ee 'way if 'ee want to come home, mind. Be polite and behave well; if 'ee likes it there stay as long as they'll have 'ee, if not, come straight back."

She waved her hand to them and was away in the next moment, trotting up the lane for the turnpike.

As he went about his work that afternoon, Joel thought of his sister and how she would like Tregonebris.

"I do wonder how long she'll stay," he said to Caroline that night.

"Not long."

And she was right. Salome was back next morning; long before the midday meal was ready she came riding down the lane, slid off the saddle in the farmplace and led her horse to the stable. Joel had heard the hooves and came across to meet her.

"Back already? Why, you've hardly had time to get there."

"Time enough to get there, and to get enough time there," she retorted. "More'n enough. D'you think Father'll mind?"

"No, he'll not bother." He knew his father would be more pleased then annoyed, so long as Salome had been tactful – and it was almost a certainty her behaviour had been good. "But Mother'll be hurt."

"Yes, I reckon she'll be hurt a lot, but I couldn't help it, Joel. Poor Mother, I do wonder a lot about her, what she really do think of us, and Father, and the way we live. She's had nothing but hard work since she married Father."

Joel had stalled and attended to the horse.

"Is it all so very different, then?"

She made a gesture to imply the hopelessness of ever coming to the end of the differences.

"So different! There's nothing in their life that's like ours. We work, and always have more work to do than can ever possibly be done; they have men and servants to do everything they don't like doing for themselves. We walk or ride or go in a cart when we want to get anywhere; Mother's folk have strings of fine horses and a carriage always ready for them. But I could never abide their ways. I was put to sleep in a fine room with a wooden floor, in a grand soft bed all to myself – I had the whole room to myself – and I was mighty lonely. I didn't like it."

All the while she was talking, Joel was wondering what would be said to her when she went indoors to her parents. The others were always ready to put a spoke in her wheel, and criticise her as though she were already a grown adult. On his part he could get into her mind to a certain extent and experience some of her impressions and troubles; there was a greater sympathy between these two, Elizabeth's eldest and youngest.

"I tell you, Joel, I couldn't abide their ways. I woke early and just packed up my things, slipped out and saddled the horse, and rode off home."

"Well then, come 'long in, my dear, and get it over; for Mother'll have plenty to say to 'ee, I know."

They left the stable and went across into the house. Elizabeth was evidently prepared for her, having seen or heard the horse, and was ready primed to greet her.

"Salome, what do you mean by coming back so soon, you ungrateful child? I do hope you haven't disgraced me and been sent away?"

"No, Mother, I did come of my own accord, no one sent me away. I couldn't get along with them, they're so different from us. I could never abide their ways. Don't be angry with me, Mother."

Elizabeth turned away and busied herself with something. Perhaps she had known this would happen – she must have known it. She had become a part of her husband's home, and had brought up his children much as he himself had been brought up; the only influence she had attempted to bring into the home was some smoothing of the rougher surfaces of his life. Salome was his child as much as hers, she could hardly take to the spacious gentler manner of living at Tregonebris; she was not old enough to enjoy the easy comfort of it; it could only make her feel inferior and out of place.

Their father had joined them now, and stood in the doorway, leaning against the jamb.

"Well, Salome, so you don't want to be a grand lady for very long?"

Only about her folk was he ever in the slightest way unkind to Elizabeth; as he spoke of them there was always a touch of venom in his voice, whether it was jealousy or envy caused it she never knew. Now hearing it again she bit her lip. In her heart she was bitterly disappointed that her child had not been a success over there; she had so wanted Salome to prove that she was capable of taking up a higher social level as easily as her mother had been to adapt herself to being a poor man's wife. This she knew she had done successfully; then why had Salome failed her?

"You silly child! They're my folk, so they're yours, and they were willing and glad to see you. I had hoped you'd like the change, and to see how I had lived as a girl like you."

She tried hard to check her words, to avoid showing her disappointment. It galled her to have their father standing there taunting her, almost triumphing over the fact that he, and the love she had for him, had taken her away from these fine folk and made her and her children his, and his alone.

He dropped his casual attitude at the door and strode possessively into the room.

"Leave the child be," he said. "She's more Andrewartha than Nancurvis, and she don't care for the likes of them."

Knowing it was true, Elizabeth took her defeat proudly without showing her wounded spirit. Salome was Andrewartha right enough in character, and in looks, growing tall, as dark as big Joel himself and with the same straight nose, and a chin set and determined. They went their way, these Andrewarthas, there was no driving them or crossing them; they got what and where they wanted. And she was proud of them. She loved them all, and was glad and happy to wife and mother them. They were good sound stock; the salt of the earth, and she knew it.

"Ah, but Father, you disremember you were proud and glad to

marry a Nancurvis. I reck'n 'ee could go far 'nough without seeing a finer lady than Mother, and she's a grand woman. We Andrewarthas are proud to be her children, and mark what I do tell 'ee – today we're small farmers, but our children or their children will be different. 'Tis bound to be so, for if 'ee take a slip of a fine tree and graft it on to stock with good heart, the fruit's even better than 'twere. So 'twill be with us. We'll be dead and forgotten, but they'll mind Mother for many, many years."

His father looked at Joel, considering carefully what he had said. He never gave an answer suddenly; if he was swayed by argument he shut his mouth tightly and never showed he was moved until second thoughts had come. It was one of his mannerisms that had built up his authority in the house; often they all waited, sure some profound ruling was about to be uttered, convinced the subject was being turned over in his mind and in a moment they would hear the refined truth of it. And as often as not he kept it to himself – if it was there at all.

"Your Mother was the best of the Nancurvis family; she's the only one who'd sense 'nough to become Andrewartha."

Caroline had never known a winter so wet as the one after she had been a year at Kenneggy. She wiped over the last few feet of stone flags and rose from her cold knees; this was the second time she had been over the floor in the one day, right down the full length of the living-room with scrubbing brush and cloth. If it had not been a Saturday and she wanted it clean for the weekend she would have left it after the first time, but at dinner their boots had brought in so much of the everlasting mud that she felt compelled to give it another wash. For a month it had rained, every day; if not the entire day, at least some part of it had been steadily drenching. The ground was sodden and spongy, the spring above Kenneggy cliff was fairly spouting; on those fields which had been ploughed water lay in every furrow, soaking it into a flat mass which would be impossible to work. All around the cattle-place the mud was over ankle deep, and being churned worse every day; it clung to the men's boots and penetrated to every room in the house.

The dampness all around the place seemed to have got under the house and crept through the floors; they were never dry and Caroline was weary of fighting the sticky film of mud that spread over them. She put away the washing things and brisked up the fire in the stove. Down on her knees again to tidy around the hearth, brushing up chips of wood, half-burned spills, even knockings from pipes; she wondered if they thought piskies came to tidy the house in the night, so little they seemed to bother where they left their rubbish. She lifted the hem of her skirt and held it towards the fire to dry a damp patch; the warmth touched and soothed her knees. This winter at Kenneggy she seemed to have been on her knees more than ever in her life before; it was not as though she minded that, the weather had been bad, yet if only they had tried to help a little, in some way she could not define and which she knew was lacking, it would have been easier. Somehow, here at Kenneggy, things were so different from what they might be, from what she felt they ought to be.

The door banged out in the back kitchen and she heard someone enter the room; from the way he tip-toed about in his big boots, taking two steps on the clean floor where one would have been enough, she knew without looking up that it was Charles. He seemed to be exploring the whole room, opening drawers in the dresser and banging them shut, rummaging among things on his father's desk, searching the cupboards; all the time the muddy boots tattooed the floor.

"What do you want, Charles?"

"There was a piece of twine I had here this morning, someone's tidied it away; there bain't a thing to be found in this house now everything's so durned tidy."

She went across to the dresser and took out a small twist of string from the back of a drawer.

"This was under the table after breakfast; is it what you want?"

"That's it." He took it and tried to fix a sack across his shoulders with it, but his fingers were stiff with the cold wet. "Thee'st the best of it sitting here by the fire out of all the rain."

She turned to the dresser again and picked up a large packing needle. Taking the sack almost roughly out of his hands she adjusted it across his shoulders and high up the back of his neck with a few sharp tugs, and set about fixing it in place with a properly tied string through the sacking.

"I had just this minute finished washing the floor for the second time today, and now look at it, you big looby; all your dirty boots right over it. Why don't 'ee crawl under table, 'tis the only place you've left clean. Sitting by the fire! Now get away, I. . . I hate the sight and smell of 'ee."

To his surprise she burst into tears and, flinging around to hide her face from him, she hurried through into the back kitchen. Charles made his way carefully to the door; with his hand on the latch he paused and spoke to her back, which was turned to him as she stood in the larder doorway dabbing at her eyes.

"I'm sorry, Caroline; 'twas thoughtless of me."

" 'Tis all right, Charles, don't heed me. Only this weather do make it hard indoors too, and if you'd all try a little 'twould be so much more encouraging."

"I tell 'ee what I'll do, I'll wash that floor up for 'ee after supper."

She laughed. "You'll do no such thing, after you're in you're going to take 'n' rest, you poor soul. The floor can do, 'twill be as bad as ever tomorrow, anyway. Get along with 'ee now, and be done as quick as 'ee can."

He went out. The opening door brought in the sound of falling rain and drops off a roof. She had hoped it would clear before the evening; it would have been nice if Joel could have taken her to

162

Penzance to see the Saturday-night crowds. Now it was wet again it was no use asking him. She could not remember how many weeks had passed since they had last been out together; somehow the time drifted by and she never seemed to set foot beyond the farm-place. Either it was too wet, or Joel was so tired she had not the heart to ask him. And this evening the rain was on again, and set in properly, it appeared. As she went to the dairy for the first of the heavy cream bowls, she felt all the warmth of Charles's kind words driven out by the depressing rain and the dampness of the stone floors.

Elizabeth was getting the table set as she carried in the bowl and placed it on the stove.

"What was Charles saying about the floor?"

"He was sorry he had dirtied it just after I had been over it again."

Her back was towards her mother-in-law and she did not turn around to answer. Why was it she never liked any of the men to speak kindly to her? Surely she wasn't jealous of them all? It was only Joel who counted with her; none of the others.

"The floor's all right; there's nothing wrong with it. To hear you always on at them, Caroline, anyone would think the place was a muck-yard before you came."

There it was again – before she came. It was ever before she came this was so, and that was not so. Had she made such a difference to them all by coming? Joel had asked her to come. Elizabeth was his mother, pretty.and sweet enough to love if only she would let herself be loved – and how she could have loved the woman who had given Joel birth! Was it a crime to have come because she loved him and wanted to live with him?

"I'm sorry, maybe I spoke hastily. I wanted it clean against Joel's coming in, he likes a room to be straight and tidy."

"Joel never complained when his mother had the care of him."

Elizabeth's tone cut at her like a lash across the face.

She went backwards and forwards to the dairy in silence. She was thinking, You're his mother and I'll not answer you back.

163

You're a real lady, born and bred, and yet you are letting yourself become a crabbed old bitch, just because your son wanted a love you couldn't give him. Will you ever see that you could never be more to him than his mother, just as it is in your power never to be less? I neither add nor take away from his love for you, and yet you resent so cruelly his love for me.

When she had finished the carrying of the cream bowls she ran away to her room and buried her face in the coldness of the pillow to stop the tears; she was too proud to be made to cry. By the time she had recovered control, tidied herself and returned to the living-room Joel had just come in. He was bending over his right hand, under the light of one of the newly lit candles, digging at something in the palm with his left thumb nail.

"Is there a needle anywhere, Caroline?"

She went to her work-box and found one. A great black thorn was sunk deep into the ball of his thumb.

"Let me try."

She worked at it as carefully as she could, well knowing there was no way to avoid the pain she must be giving him. It was nearly out when she stopped and, looking helplessly at him, began to slip away to the floor, and would have fallen heavily had he not grabbed forward at her just in time. For a few moments after he had lifted her to a chair and watched Betsy chafing her wrists, she was completely out; he saw the colour flow back into her white cheeks and her eyes open, looking wondering and surprised at them both.

"I'm sorry," she faltered.

"There, there," said Betsy, and he was astonished to see a half-veiled glint of triumph in her eyes as she looked at Caroline. "There, you'll be worse yet afore you're better."

Caroline pulled her wrists away and gripped the arms of the chair; for a moment he thought she was going to strike at Betsy, but she did not. Instead a look of bitter contempt showed in her eyes, while her chin and mouth set in resolution as hard as granite.

Wait for the Wagon

*   *   *   *

One March afternoon a high gig drawn by a fine stepping horse bowled down the turnpike and, slackening pace near the lane entrance, turned down to Kenneggy. Elizabeth came to the door at the sound of strange hooves and wheels outside and, seeing the visitor, was immediately striving to place his features in her memory. The handsome face she knew well enough, it was the ageing of twenty-odd years which prevented instant recognition.

He climbed down from the gig and threw the reins over the horse's back, lifted off his hat and advanced towards her, smiling.

"Elizabeth, I should have known you anywhere. Not one whit less beautiful; even more so, if that were possible," he greeted her.

At the sound of his voice she recognised him.

"Duke! Why Duke, this is a joy. However did you find your way here?"

"I smelt that delicious smell of baking out on the turnpike and it led me right to your door. I knew there was only one baker in these parishes who could produce that. 'Elizabeth lives here or hereabouts,' I said to myself, and bless my soul, I was right."

She looked at him, not as pleased by his chatter as he would have expected, and together they walked up to the house.

"I'm not asking you and Richard to stable me for the night. The fact is I'm not as young as I was, Elizabeth, and I'm suspicious of beds unless they've been prepared in advance for me. So I must get away very soon, but I wanted to see you both again."

"You should have let us know, and then we could have prepared for you," she was saying as they entered the long room.

Down on her knees before the hearth Caroline was lifting the iron pots off the last batch of loaves. With one of them in her hands, fired to perfection of crisp golden brown, she rose and faced them both. On the table before the window was the rest of the day's baking; loaves for the week, a cake yellow with saffron and another of heavy fuggan for the boys. Each was as perfect as the one in her hands, with a fine crust that would tempt any appetite, let alone a man's keen from a long drive in the fresh air. In her quiet, shy glance, she noticed there was admiration in the eyes of the handsome stranger both for herself and for her baking, and also that Elizabeth, while charming to him, was not pleased with her. Her face was flushed with the heat of the fire and tiredness, her fair hair had little dark curls pressed damp against her forehead; she wanted to get away to wash herself before preparing the meal.

"Ah," he exclaimed. "So this is the baker. Will you introduce me, Elizabeth? Surely not one of the girls, for there's no family likeness?"

"No, my daughter-in-law, Caroline. My cousin Duke Marrack from Truro. Caroline is Joel's wife. Yes, she's been baking today, and so, after all, Duke, your pretty tale had one flaw in it – the identity of the baker. You see, Caroline, he was pretending the smell of the bread brought him in to us."

"No pretence at all, Mistress Caroline," he protested. "But my mistake was that I thought the delightful tempting smell could only come from Elizabeth's baking – for I've always known her to be a grand baker – but I find now there's another in the family. 'Pon my word, the Andrewarthas can pick them out, can't they? They must have a touch of the gourmand about them."

So that was why Elizabeth was displeased. The praise for the tempting sight had been deflected from her; Caroline was glad, as glad as she was that the baking had been successful. And so she was baking today, was she? And when, dear mother-in-law, has been your day? Not since the time your son brought me to Kenneggy and you found I could do it, leaving nothing for you but to hand the titbits to your husband and let him think you had been slaving for him all day long. And the precious cousin had come just a few minutes too soon to believe the same; another ten minutes and there would have been no one around to take the laurels. On her quiet face there was no trace of these thoughts, only of the fatigue which was the chief cause of her bitterness, and as she moved about clearing up the hearth, setting things right, she appeared unconscious of the man's admiring gaze following her.

She brought Elizabeth's chair to the fire, and Joel's for Marrack, and then retired to wash and change her frock before the men came in for the meal. When she returned Elizabeth already had the cloth on the table; standing by the dresser she was talking to Duke, taking out plates and things now and then, and gradually getting them on the cloth. Caroline brought the cold joint of pork from the larder, pickled onions, mugs and a pitcher of cold water; she cut a loaf into thick, crusty slices, fetched butter, milk and cheese from the dairy, and brought the chairs up to the table. Richard was already seated in his big chair but he rose now and turned to Duke.

"Well now, we must see what Kenneggy can do for 'ee."

He crossed to the window and from the hiding-place under the seat he produced one of his precious little kegs and, fetching three mugs from the table, drew off a good measure in each. At that moment Joel entered, his broad frame seeming to dominate the room, yet quiet as usual, even as he was introduced by his father. The three men took a mug each and paused with it in hand.

"I give you a toast," said Duke, and looking across to Caroline, lifted his. "A toast to the bride. Caroline, the Rose of Kenneggy."

Joel's eyes smiled as he lifted his mug and looked over it at his pretty wife, slim and fresh-looking, with her petal skin and fair hair contrasting with the darker colour of his mother and the girls.

"The Rose," said his father, and drank.

"The Rose of Kenneggy," Joel repeated in proud tones.

She smiled with pleasure, and glanced at Elizabeth. She too was smiling, but it was on the surface only; she knew for the second time since the visit that she had displeased her.

"We can hardly call you a bride still, can we, Caroline dear? Two years very nearly, isn't it, Joel?"

"Seventeen months, Mother. And what months! Kenneggy's never been a brighter place."

"Dear boy," cooed his mother, graciously. "You're so romantic for such a big fellow."

"And where is the. . . ? Have I the opportunity of congratulating you on being a grandmother, Elizabeth?"

"You have not." Her reply was acid.

"The cause of such a disaster has made hisself 'most as unpopular by his absence as he would have been were he present," said Caroline in her quiet low voice.

"Why listen to the child, what a thing to say!" exclaimed Elizabeth, apparently horrified by such an idea. "Why, you know I'm just dying to have Joel's son on my knee."

"Oh, you are?" laughed Duke. "Then it looks as though someone is deliberately hastening your death, Cousin Elizabeth."

Joel tried to catch his wife's eye, for the turn of the conversation made him uneasy. Long ago he suspected his mother had never forgiven Caroline for not being confined within six months of their wedding-day, and when she had failed her again by not becoming a nine months' wonder, he had been convinced that to Elizabeth it had been insult upon injury. Now he sensed a tension in the atmosphere surrounding the two women and he had no wish for another storm to break, especially while Marrack was with them. Added to this he was slightly sensitive when their childless state was mentioned in his father's presence, that quiet, solid man who had sired his children as unconcernedly as he would take off his boots. But Caroline avoided his glance, seeming conscious of Duke's appreciation of her quiet thrusts, and determined to get them home while she had an audience to enjoy them.

"And 'tis proving a slow death," she said sweetly. "If the baby's much longer in coming he'll find Grannie's knee too rheumaticky for dandling."

Richard pulled his chair up to the table.

"What about the meal?" he said, to bring the talk back to less personal channels.

They all drew in and started to do the good food the honour it deserved. Elizabeth received the compliments she loved, praise for her hospitality and the excellence of the cooking, which she accepted graciously.

"Of course, I really must give all the credit to Caroline," she said. "For I don't know what I would do without her. She sees to everything for me; I have only to suggest a thing and she seems to do it for me, exactly as I like it to be done."

Afterwards Caroline seemed to vanish with the dishes, and reluctant as Duke was to take his leave while she was absent, at length he was compelled by the growing dusk to allow his horse to be brought around. Saying goodbye to them all he rattled away up the darkening lane.

Just as he was about to enter the turnpike, a figure stepped out into the way and signalled him to stop. By his lamps he could see it was a girl in a big cloak, with the hood flung back on her shoulders, and as he pulled up he recognised her.

"Mistress Caroline! What is it? Why have you come out here?"

Without answering, she flung a bag she was carrying into the gig and climbed up to the seat beside him.

"Listen, Mr Marrack, you've got to help me get away from this place. You must just give me a lift 'long towards Hendra. I can't bide here for another day."

"Why? I can't do that. I can't help you to do a thing like that."

Without further argument she leaned forward and shook the reins in his hands across the horse's back; the gig started off and down the turnpike.

"You must help me. Don't ask me many questions, just give me a lift as far as Hendra Croft. 'Tis no sudden fancy, I've had no chance to get away afore and now I've just got to go."

She pulled the hood of her cloak over her head and retired into

h

the darkness of it. Marrack knew very soon that she was sobbing; at first she made a great effort to restrain herself and dry up her tears with her handkerchief, but it was not long before she gave up the attempt and, leaning forward to rest her head on her hands, gave way to uncontrolled weeping.

"You poor child. Why not tell me about it? Perhaps it isn't so bad after all."

In a little while she quietened herself and dabbed pathetically at her eyes.

"Whatever will 'ee think of me; just a big bubbly," she said, trying to sound cheerful. "Well see, 'tis no good trying to live their life any longer. They're all so united. Joel is a darling, yet somehow the same things which in him I loved, vexed me when they are in them. And they outnumbered him by so many. His father's like him, but his mother hates me just because I married him. For that I'm damned for ever in her eyes and she makes me a buffer between them, a target to aim at when she wants to hurt Joel."

"I guessed there was something like that at the bottom of it." After a long silence he continued, "And so you're leaving them. And Joel? Have you thought much about leaving him?"

She began to sob again, this time more quietly.

" 'Tis 'cause I can do nothing but think about leaving him I'm so miserable. But he was married to his land and his beasts, his mother and father and all his family afore he was married to me. I reckon he can do without me; he can never do without them. His father has brought them up to make work their god, and the most important thing in their creed. He'll be so busy now at this very moment that he won't know yet where I am, whether I'm on the farm or in the house, and when he does begin to wonder he'll be too busy to find out. By bedtime he'll be so tired, like as not, he'll not even know I'm away from his side. In the morning he'll be in too much of a hurry to start his precious work to miss me."

Marrack pondered over the situation for some time. At length he gave his conclusion.

"All very distressing when you're so much in love with him."

"In love with him? Who's in love with him?"

"You are; as you very well know."

"Time was when I did love him; I loved him more'n anything else in my life. Now I reckon I don't love him any more. No, I can't love him any more, or I'd not be wanting to leave him so. And maybe that's why I'm so unhappy, 'cause I don't love him any more."

He patted her kindly on the shoulder, and left her to herself for a while.

"I expect you've done the best thing, getting away like this. It doesn't always do when a man's wife goes to live in his father's house; there can't be two mistresses in the same house, and peace. And a daughter-in-law isn't the same as a daughter, nor can ever learn to be, if she's worth anything. It's like throwing a stone among the pebbles on the shore; they won't rest nor let her rest until they've rubbed her as smooth as themselves. Then they'll all roll about quietly together. Some stones take a mighty lot of rubbing. Now, if you stay away from them a bit, they'll be getting to miss you, and the house'll not be going quite so well without you. Joel will then start claiming your right to a considered place in the house, and before you know what's happened he'll be over to you asking you to come back."

"You reckon he will?"

"You see if he doesn't. But then you don't love him any more, so what does it matter?"

She sighed heavily.

"No, I couldn't ever go back to Kenneggy. 'Tis true what I said 'bout not loving him. That's why 'tis so queer I'm. . . already I'm hoping he'll come."

Until they reached her destination, Marrack left her alone to her hopes and despairs.

*   *   *   *

171

Back at Kenneggy that evening, when Joel came in from the farm, his eyes searched the room in astonishment; for him it was empty.

"Where's Caroline? Hasn't she come in yet?"

"Haven't seen her, Joel. Not since afore Duke left," answered his father.

"I wonder what's been keeping her."

Salome looked up from her darning. "Maybe she's sick and in her bed."

He wheeled around on her. " 'Twould have been too much for any one of 'ee to have gone to see if she were, I suppose."

His tone was stern and bitter; unlike him to speak to his sister in that way, and she winced under it. He strode over to the dresser, brought his candle over to the fire and lit it.

"If she's up there the poor child hasn't even a light in the darkness," he growled as he left the room.

The others remained, and did not speak even after he had gone. He was away for a long time.

When at last they heard his feet on the ladderstair they broke in on the peace of the room. They stumbled and faltered as though they were treading strange ground; he came into the room as if it were unknown to him, and as though he found it distasteful and the people in it loathsome in his eyes.

Elizabeth's hands fell into her lap.

"Joel!" she gasped.

He looked at her, accusation in his gaze.

"Her's a-gone. Her's left me. You'll know – you'll know why. What have 'ee done? What have 'ee said to her now, that made her leave me? What have 'ee done, I do ask 'ee?"

Her jaw dropped as she stared fascinated at him.

"Joel," she whimpered. "Oh, Joel!"

"What have 'ee done to her now, I do ask 'ee, Mother? I know how thee'st gone on for months past, and I reck'n it has got beyond bearing for the girl. 'Tis just pin-pricking at her all while. I'd fear

172

'twould come to this; I knew 'twould come to this in the end. Well see, thee'st driven her out and got your own way. You'll be glad? 'Es, you'll be durned glad, you wicked scolding woman, you."

"Joel," his father roared. " 'Tis your mother you're speaking to; you forget 'self boy."

Joel turned on him, unabashed.

"I reck'n at this moment I do mind myself, Father. If I'd given Mother a straight word afore – or if 'ee had, and I can't 'count for why you didn't – maybe this wouldn't have happened. I do reck'n Mother's a-gone too far this time, else it has been piling up till 'twere just unbearable for the girl. Truth is Mother bain't wanting her here; she never did want her here. And no more did 'ee for that matter, but you'd put up with her if 'twould keep me here working for you all. I can toil and toil, and for little else than my food, and you say sweetly, ' 'Tis all for 'ee, Joel; 'tis all for 'ee, my son,' and that's my pay. Over a while I want a wife for myself and you say nought 'gainst the idea, but ever since she come 'tis, this bain't right and that's all wrong; nothing she could do would please 'ee. It has been nag, nag and bicker, bicker till now her's a-gone. Mighty pleased with yourselves you'll all be, now thee'st robbed me of the one thing I did ever ask of 'ee. I do reck'n I've done all God would ask me to do for 'ee, Father and Mother, but this one thing was too much for 'ee to do for me. I don't want the farm-place, I don't want the cattle nor the sheep; I've done with 'ee. Do 'ee hear me? I do say I've done with 'ee. God help 'ee now, for I'll do no more."

Andrewartha sank back in his chair; at heart he was stricken sorely by his son's grief and despair. He felt in a great measure the boy was right to blame him for letting Elizabeth's petty tongue run away with her better nature to such an extent that Caroline had reached breaking-point. One word now and again from him was indeed a little thing for him to have done, and yet it would have prevented this, but instead he had allowed Elizabeth to fall into a habit of twitting and baiting until it had become second nature with her. If Caroline had left them, as it seemed only too obvious she had, then the real blame lay in his inertia, his passive allowance of such a state in his house. Compelled to face up to the fact that she had gone he felt crushed by the difference it was going to make to them all, he realised what she had meant to them with her quiet presence in the house. There was not only her going, there was Joel's now to face.

He watched glowering as his son swung on his heel and grabbed his coat down from the hook on the door, searched around for his hat and rammed it down on his head. His footsteps resounded through the house as he stamped his way out. Then came the slam of the outer door, closing with miserable finality.

Joel crossed over to the cow-house and climbed the ladder to the hay-loft; he decided there was nothing he could do until morning, and he flung himself down on the warm hay to pass the night. He rose early, fetched his saddle from the harness-room and entered the stable. Although his hands shook with the urge for haste to get away before any of the others came out, they were gentle enough with the horse, considerate with the adjustment of the girths and placing the bit and bridle. He led him out and closed the door, across the farm place and beyond to the lane. He mounted and, on reaching the turnpike, headed towards Helston.

Once on the road he was in no hurry, all day was before him. Why and where he was going he did not at first pause to think; eventually his purpose resolved itself into a search for Caroline. The obvious place to commence that search was at Tremearne, and if Duke had helped her on her way she could easily have reached there. The more he considered the likelihood, the more reasonable a supposition it appeared to him, and his plan for the immediate future was to visit Tremearne to establish her whereabouts and ease his mind of any fear that harm had befallen her. What was to happen later he could not see for the time being, and that question had to be left to the future.

The ride was a long and lonely one; all the way he contrasted his spirits now with what they had been when he last took this road, on their wedding day. The happiness and hopes he had then were now replaced by misery and fears that his marriage had been a disaster. If she had arrived safely at her home it was unlikely she could be persuaded to return with him; the step she had taken would be premeditated, or at least the impulses to take it would have been felt before. Even if the action was the result of a momentary decision the previous contemplation of it would have robbed it of justification for being called hasty, and if so carefully considered it would need slow and careful thought before it could be overruled. With these thoughts he was occupied all the way and by the time he had reached Rinsey Croft was no nearer a conclusion.

The lane up to Tremearne became longer than ever. It had been daylight for some hours by now, and when he reached the wall surrounding the house and orchard, he dismounted and threw his bridle over a post. Advancing on foot to the opening leading through the orchard to the dairy, he paused and looked up towards the open doorway. The stream of water bubbled out through its stone chute and ran down the gutter beside the path. From within sounds of activity reached him, and a snatch of song.

It was Caroline's voice, and with the sound of it in his ears conflicting emotions struggled in his mind. Uppermost at first was relief that she was here, well and at work already, as of old. The song too told at least that she was not unhappy, not in the same melancholy state as himself. How could she sing on such a morning, and he with his heart so heavy and sore! Was it because today she was happier than for months past? Today there was peace and serenity around her; the work she did required her skill, and her skill was equal to it and would command appreciation. If she had found tranquillity by her return had he any right to disturb it by appearing on the doorstep, begging her to give it up for his sake? What had he ever given that could make up for what life at Kenneggy meant for her? Was his love, big, clumsy fellow that he was, so wonderful that it could compensate for losing peace of mind and rest? Quite obviously it was not, for by her very act the previous night she had shown that he himself was not enough.

As things were at Kenneggy he could not offer enough to call on her again to make that sacrifice. For the time being he had no right to intrude, no claim on her life at all. Quietly and reluctantly he returned to his horse, remounted and turned in the direction he had come. His thoughts were sad and bitter; the road before him seemed long and uninviting, and worthless. What was there to return to? How was he to face the dreary emptiness of the life at the end, alone?

Horse rather than rider chose the way and so it was until, his mind having been completely absorbed by his innermost thoughts, Joel realised he was on the outer grazings of Kenneggy. He called a halt and, sitting there, looked around him. Almost at once he exclaimed in annoyance, for he noticed the sheep had pushed out a gap in the hedge and through it, one by one, they had strayed from their place. Dismounting and throwing the bridle over the horse's neck he went over to the gap and by loosening a few more stones enlarged it to make a clear opening.

"Hup! hup!" he called sharply. "Hup! Hup!"

Slowly he gathered the sheep against the hedge, and with great patience shepherded them up to the gap. For a short while he had to wait, content with having them in a group; when one of the old ewes ventured back through the hedge the others followed. Roughly he replaced the stones to some extent then turned his attention to the ground about to find some better stones to make a more solid repair. These he pulled from the grip of grass, enjoying the struggle and triumph of his strong arms, and carried them over to the hedge.

For years the same process had resulted in the clearing of the nearby ground, the immediate surface having been cleaned to build the original hedge, so that many of his stones lay at some distance off and necessitated a considerable amount of carrying. The physical activity was a relief after the excitement of the past hours, and brought his thoughts back to the work he had been responsible for ever since he had been old enough to take it from his father. The hedge repaired, he leaned on it, looking at the sheep and thinking of the other stock for which he had done nothing during the day.

Over in the meadow beyond the farm-place he could see the cattle; he counted them. They were all out; for a moment he wondered why this did not seem right to him, until he remembered that Pisky, one of the favourites, was due to calve down at any time now. Pisky was always difficult; he doubted whether anyone who was not used to her could be of use when her time came. In that case there was nothing else for it; he must go across and bring her in so that she would be comfortable and he could keep an eye on her. He rode towards the meadow, but changed his mind and led the horse to the stable, brought him a pail of water and tossed some hay into the rack. He took a rope halter off the wall and went down to the meadow.

Pisky, a fine red cow heavy with her calf, was standing by herself over on the far side. As he approached she eyed him languidly, and made no move to avoid the halter he slipped over her muzzle and behind her horns. Talking quietly to her, he coaxed and cajoled her into action, until with a stilted motion she began to follow him slowly home to the cow-house. There he shook out some clean straw in her stall, filled her rack, and after gauging with an experienced eye how long he would be able to stay away, he walked out of the shed and stood for a moment in the weak sunshine.

For the first time he realised he was starved with hunger. Crossing to the house door he went in; they were at the midday meal. He hung his jacket on the usual hook, seized a pitcher and returned outside to the spring and filled it. The wash refreshed him, and he entered the living-room and took his place at the table. Neither he nor the others made any comment on his absence or his return; he took the plate of food Elizabeth offered and ate it appreciatively. He had worked for it; things they had forgotten or been ignorant of had been attended to by him. He was not vitally necessary to them but he was to the creatures of the place. A man cannot slip off the claims of his beasts; he can leave his folk, his parents, even his wife, but he cannot break away from the animals in his care. Those who have tongues to tell their needs to others are not helpless in desertion, but the beasts, with only the man who knows them to tend them, are lost without his care and have no means of making known their necessities. How can a man, if he is a man, leave them to want, to suffer pain without comfort or aid, to endanger themselves by their own poor sense?

Joel knew that whatever way out of his difficulties might open to him, Kenneggy must remain worked by him while he had strength to work. He pushed away his plate before he had finished the food, and glanced up to meet his mother's unhappy gaze, and for all he had suffered his heart melted towards her.

"Cheer up, Mother," he said quietly. "The night's its darkest an hour afore daybreak."

Chapter Eight

IF only Joel had been with her at Tremearne, life would have seemed perfect to Caroline during those first days away from Kenneggy. Uncle William Drenocoe and Aunt Sibella had been a little astonished on her arrival so suddenly that night, but after the brief explanation that she wanted a few days away from her in-laws they had accepted her without further comment. Although her aunt made it clear that in her mind a woman's place was at her husband's side and there she should stay, come wet, come dry, her presence about him again so pleased her uncle that he never spoke a word of conciliatory advice likely to hasten her return. In no time she had slipped back into her niche in their family life; the day's work, their meals together, the four of them collected around the stove after supper all seemed to fall into place with a click to leave no trace of the break from the old times before she was married, save only in Caroline's secret heart.

She was so sure Joel would come, so confident he would use her revolt as a means of forcing them to realise they had been unfair to her, the first daughter- in-law, and demanding her recognition as his wife and a member of the family, that she found herself waiting, expecting every minute to hear the sound of his horse's hooves, or to see him walking up to the door. Hope deferred, and days passing without bringing him or word from him, found her heart sick; at night she lay awake in what now seemed the strange emptiness of her unshared bed, or fell asleep to dream of him and to wake again to all the loneliness of the small hours, without the solid comfort of pressing against his sleeping body, or the sweet pleasure of having his arm around her and clasping his hand across her breast. The days were different, for they were exactly as they had always been before he had ruffled her heart; her work in the dairy went just as it had always done, the door stood open on to the orchard path, the fruit trees about to blossom just beyond. The drowsy sounds of the farm drifted in as she skimmed the scalded cream off the pans, as she churned and worked the butter. Aunt Sibella was glad enough to let her do the dairying, and to take a hand with the baking, and Caroline wanted to work, for it relieved her mind of the tension fast straining her nerves.

Why did he not come to take her back to Kenneggy, to tell her his mother was going to be more reasonable because they had all missed her as soon as she had left? How nice it would have been if his father had asked for her, and the boys persuaded their mother to like her just a little in place of that reasonless jealousy. Or why did Joel not come to tell her he had arranged for them to live apart from the rest in a cottage of their own, just the two of them? That surely would have been possible and worth the inconvenience of being further from the farm-place. Indeed, as she gave more thought to the idea, it seemed doubly good for that very reason, because once he had left for home the boys would have to see to any unexpected need and he would not be disturbed. Their life would be more their own and not, as it had been, just what part of it the farm spared them. Could it be that Joel did not love her any more? Had she, by running away from his folk, dealt him a blow which had shattered his affection for her, and now he was waiting cither for her to come crawling back or to forget her very existence?

Her cousin clattered into the dairy with the afternoon's milk pails and set them down on the floor. He looked approvingly at the butter she had patted up, and then at her, questioning.

"Joel didn't come over to see us Sunday?"

"No." After a pause, "Were you wanting him?"

He did not answer, but picking up one of the Dutch hands twirled it idly on its corner.

"There. . . there bain't nothing gone wrong 'tween 'ee? That is, unless you don't want to talk to me?"

She was silent for a few moments. It was not because she resented the question; she was thinking where loyalty to her husband should place her. To have told John everything would have been a relief beyond realisation, he was so level headed, tranquil and reliable. And above all he was fond of her. Just now she felt she had to count and re-count those who were fond of her; her heart craved for slight signs of affection to ease the sharper yearning.

"No, there's nothing wrong 'tween Joel and me; least, nothing you could point to. 'Tis his folk – they're queer. And his mother, I've never seen her like afore. There's nothing I can do right for that woman, and after a while it did get me so low I just couldn't bide there with her for another day. That's how 'tis."

John strolled over and leaned against the doorway, his thumbs stuck in his leather belt.

"And a proper tantarra there was over Kenneggy when they found you'd gone, I'll warrant. So neither one of 'ee will go to t'other and say, 'What about it?' "

He jerked himself upright and stood there, his back towards her as she poured the milk out into the scalding pans. She thought he was going away without saying more: suddenly he swung around on her.

"Why don't 'ee go tell him thee'st come back? Because you're nothing but a miserable little sinner without him."

She flushed at the accuracy with which he had touched the place that hurt; it angered her to find he read her heart so plainly.

181

Wait for the Wagon

"Because she'd never let me hear the end of it. Joel's got to choose 'tween his mother and me; I'm not sharing him with her any more. And I reckon I don't care much whether he comes to ask for me or not," she lied.

For a moment he watched her trying to be bravely defiant in the face of her boast, trying to look as though she really did not care. Her face was sad and the long lashes drooped over eyes which, he guessed, were wet with tears.

"Don't 'ee fret, Caroline, he'll come. Maybe 'twill be some time afore he does, but in the end he'll come. It bain't natural for him to be able to stay 'way from 'ee."

And with that he left her. From then on he was gentle and very kind towards her, although he never once spoke a word against Joel, or expressed disapproval of him in a word or gesture. Because of this the affection she had for him grew deeper and filled part of the emptiness left in her daily life by the separation.

The fine weather broke; one night it became almost stormy, while a cold wind made it worse. A young heifer chose to start some trouble over her first calf. John had gone out with a lantern about the time the others had gone to bed and for a long time Caroline, lying awake with her thoughts, listened to the wind howling and heard no sound of his return. It was after midnight when he came in and bolted the door; he would be tired and cold after so long in the sheds on such a night, so she pulled on her cloak and ran down to the living-room to mix him a hot drink.

She threw some wood on the fire and with the bellows soon had it blazing, and sank back on her heels before it waiting for the kettle to heat up. He took off his jacket and hung it across a chair back to dry; untied his boots and kicked them off.

" 'Tis good of you to trouble over me, Caroline. You should be asleep by this time."

"I seem to have forgotten how to sleep for a whole night. Often enough 'tis just the few hours afore morning that I sleep at all."

"What keeps 'ee wake?"

She held out her hands to the fire and gazed through her spread fingers.

"Thoughts."

The kettle started to sing; came up to the boil. She fetched a glass, sugar and brandy, and mixed him a night-cap. As he sipped it she dropped back again on the hearth rug at his feet, leaning against his knees. His hand touched her hair lightly; caressed it tenderly.

For the first time in many weeks she felt almost happy.

"You do think too much."

"What else is there to do? Can I help it?"

"Forget. There bain't no man, nor woman alive, that's worth too much thinking on if thinking makes 'ee unhappy. Forget, I say, and start afresh. Can't you love me a little, Caroline? For there's never been a woman in the world for me, save only you. With all my heart I do love 'ee, my dear, and I've never loved another, just you."

She was very still, scarcely seeming to breathe; her face was towards the fire and away from him; her hands were clasped over her knee.

"You knew it, Caroline?"

In the silence only the kettle simmered, an ember settled in the fire.

"Yes, John, I knew. It seems I've known it for years and years; I never reckoned 'twould be as hard for both of us as this. Back then I didn't want to believe it, 'cause I'd set my heart on Joel Andrewartha. There's never been anyone quite like him in my eyes – belike there never will be. Now I'm vowed to him in church, for better, for worse till death do part us, and 'twouldn't be seemly to let 'ee make love to me just 'cause 'tisn't all smooth at the moment 'tween him and me."

She rose to her feet, and standing before the fire with him just behind her, she felt his hands on her shoulders, drawing her against him.

183

"How long are you going on like this, Caroline. Are you going to waste all your life on him, even if he doesn't want 'ee? Hasn't he had time 'nough to make up his mind whether you're more to him than his mother?"

She did not answer. As these were the very questions that she had put to herself for the past weeks, how could she answer? He turned her around gently to look into her face.

"Caroline, can 'ee tell me you don't love me?"

Her hands clasped behind his neck and, drawing herself close to him, she laid her cheek against his.

"You almost 'suade me that I do. I'm mighty fond of 'ee, John, but you're only second best. If I was to tell 'ee that I did love 'ee 'twould be just because having you near while I'm so hungry to be loved do put me all in a mizmaze of doubt as to what I want."

He half turned his head and nuzzled against her hair, pressing kisses on her temple, her ear and then her cheek.

"Don't, John, don't. You do make me all weak inside, so I'm feared I misbehave myself. Oh, let me go, John; do let me go. For pity's sake, if 'ee do really love me, let me go."

He let her break away from him, and he dropped back on his chair, leaning towards the fire with his hands clasped, elbows on his knees. Looking up at her where she stood in the firelight his eyes met hers. For a moment it was as though each had seen the other naked and yet was not ashamed of the discovery; now the danger of it was past they admitted frankly that desire had thrilled along their veins.

With Caroline leaving, Kenneggy began the only spell of real trouble Joel could remember in later years. The stone flags were often damp and cold, the solid walls soaked up the rains and mists of wet weather, and without much light and ventilation the house was often in a poor state for children. Betsy, even grown up, had

184

never seemed strong like the others and these conditions told on her health more; for a long time Elizabeth had watched with dismay her weakening and it was soon obvious that she was taking the dreaded King's Evil, a disease very prevalent among the children of the district, especially among the girls.

Betsy took it dangerously, in the cheens, as Elizabeth explained it. It was not good hearing for the men when they came into the house in the evening and they were very distressed. Real trouble had come so rarely to the family, and illness made a great impression on them; their own robustness made them feel helpless in the face of it.

The work of the place, and of the house, went on in a hushed, joyless manner; they talked in low tones and felt they had done wrong if absent-mindedly a laugh escaped them. The gloom of illness and threatened death hung about Kenneggy, an effective damper on all their spirits. Elizabeth nursed the patient and the girls helped her in the house and dairy to relieve her for the more exacting task. It was of little avail, and Betsy sank fast, the abscesses spread around the small of her back to her sides, causing her great pain. Before long the family gathered to their meals with the depressing knowledge that one of them would never join them there again.

In the dark of the morning, the sad faces of the Andrewarthas and their neighbours showing up strange and dull in the light of smoky torches struggling with the gloom of fog and drizzling rain, they bore the coffin from the house to the big wagon. At a word from Joel the four horses strained at their chains. The wheels turned slowly as it moved up the lane towards the turnpike; two lanterns, swinging on either side, lit the road under them as they went slowly towards churchtown and Betsy's grave.

Now Betsy was no longer there to help, more work fell on Elizabeth and she was busier about the farmplace and dairy than for a long while; she was often harried by the necessity of rushing from one place to another at a pace no longer easy for a woman of her years.

185

It happened while Joel was away at Penzance market, and as soon as he returned he was aware of an unusual silence about the place. Neither of his brothers were in sight, nor did his father appear to make his inquiries after sales and purchases. None of them seemed about, and even his sisters did not come out to welcome him. He stopped the gig outside the door, collected an armful of the parcels and entered the house. In the living-room Salome was humped up in a chair by herself, sobbing. He hurried across to her and bent down, comforting her with his arm.

"Salome, my dear, what's matter with 'ee?"

" 'Tis Mother," she whispered, pressing her hand to her mouth with horror. "Oh, Joel, I'm scared lest we've killed her."

It was then he heard the low groaning coming from his mother's room. He caught Salome's hand and almost dragged her from her chair and ran with her to find out what had happened. With frightened face he opened the door and stole in.

In the bed, white almost as the sheets and with pain written in every line of her face, lay Elizabeth. On either side of her sat Polly and his father; he was holding her hand between his, and on his face was a look of bitter self reproach and anguish at seeing his wife suffer, so that Joel could not bear to look at him. He dropped on his knees beside her bed and touched her forehead tenderly with his fingers.

"Mother, why Mother, whatever is the matter with 'ee?"

She lifted her free hand from the sheet and pressed his feebly.

" 'Tis my leg, Joel, it hurts so. Don't worry, there's a dear boy, for 'twill be better afore long, please God. Don't upset yourself now, and tell your father 'twill soon be all right."

He looked across the bed at his father, who shifted unhappily on his chair and tried to avoid his eyes.

"What's happened, Father? Has she broke her leg?"

"No. I don't know whether 'tisn't worse than that. She did slip out in the yard, and when we come to pick her up 'twas plain as daylight her leg had gone clean out at the hip, just like that old cow's we had couple of years agone, and her fainted with the pain of it. Well see, there was only one thing to do, I reck'ned, and that was to give it a little pull and let it slip back at the joint. So Charles and Ralph did take hold of her and two of the fellows I got to lend a bit of a hand, while I saw to the hip and tried to ease it in, if you take my meaning. But somehow 'twent wrong; how the plague those durned fools managed I don't know, but instead of getting the hip back they took her out at the knee and, I do believe, down at ankle too. So that's your poor mother's leg, all gone out, right up, and she in such pain as soon as she come out of the faint that it do make my heart bleed to watch her."

The extraordinary tale seemed scarcely believable to him; he lifted the bedclothes and felt the leg through her nightgown. There was no doubt about it, poor Elizabeth had been racked most effectively; the hip was sadly out and so was the knee, while the ankle was severely strained. Already the joints felt puffy and inflamed.

"And have 'ee done nothing for her but get her to bed?"

"We didn't know what we could do, it seemed to pain her so getting her here that we reck'ned she'd better rest awhile," explained Polly.

"I wonder what would be best, now," he mused. "I reck'n we'd best put on hot and cold poultices, turn about, to take the swelling down, eh Father? See what 'twill do, anyway. Salome, run now and get the kettle hot, and Polly, find us cloths to make the 'presses. Do it hurt 'ee much, Mother?" He bent over her. "Do'ee find the clothes heavy on it?"

"Yes, Joel, but there's nothing to do about it."

"We'll see 'bout that. We'll soon find something to do 'bout that. Now, Father, you'll help the girls put hot and cold cloths on the joints? Wring them out well and shake them, or we'll be scalding her; and I'll see to something to fix the bedding. If 'ee can bear up, Mother my dear, we'll have 'ee right as rain in a few days."

He went out to the farm and cut a number of young withies to make a cage to fit over the leg and lift the bedclothes from it. When he brought it to the room the girls fixed it up and it served admirably. The compresses took the swelling down and certainly eased the pain a little, and she was able to get some rest.

The burden of the housework and cooking fell heavily on the two girls. Salome, only just thirteen, was able to do many things, but even with help from outside coming into the dairy and sometimes to clean the house, it fell away rapidly from the clean comfortable place it had been so recently. And the succession of improvised meals, or the brave attempts to cook big dinners, soon told on their health and spirits.

It was after one dreadful failure to serve up a satisfactory meal, which had brought Polly to tears, that Charles gave expression to the thought in all their minds.

"If only Caroline were here."

Joel glared across the table at him; for long enough no one had dared to lift her name in his presence. "And what happened when she was here? Just 'cause she was willing to do any mortal thing for us all, we made a servant of her, and let her work harder than any servant would have, too. No, when Caroline was here 'twas little thanks she had from any of 'ee, and I'm not asking her to come now we need her. And let me catch any of 'ee asking."

Poorly cooked meals, the general decline in the comfort of the home and the bedridden state of its chief organiser all told heavily on the family. Tempers wore thin and cheeks grew pale; out on the farm and at the mine the men found their strength suffering.

John Trounsen found them so when he came over to Kenneggy. Salome went to the door to let him in, and politely dusted a chair for him.

"Why, Salome, you look as though you're doing a lot these days. Is Mrs Andrewartha not well?" he asked

"Well see, Mother's hurt her leg badly and will have to lie up for a bit yet. And now she's getting the screws in it, she says, I expect because she can't use it all she should. So Polly and I have to do the best we can; we have a woman comes to help, but 'tisn't the same."

"And where's Betsy, your big sister?"

"Why, didn't you know? She's dead. Died of the King's Evil, and we buried her up churchtown, seems years agone."

"You poor souls, what a bad time for 'ee. Where's Joel?"

"He's on the farm somewhere; I believe he's carting dung to the fields." Suddenly lowering her voice and coming close to John, she spoke confidentially. "Mr Trounsen, is Caroline with 'ee at Tremearne?"

He nodded.

"Give her my love when you go back. Tell her I do miss her sadly, and. . . and Joel do too. He's so solemn and sad, he scarcely ever do smile now since she left us. Will you tell her that? But don't tell Joel I asked you."

" 'Es, I will tell her, surely. Now I'll go to find him, for I've business to talk."

Out in the field he found Joel, and after a cautious greeting given in reply to his own, came to the point.

"Now, see Joel, maybe you'll not like me for telling you this but I've got it in me to let you see how things are. What's up 'tween you and Caroline?"

"That's none of your business," retorted Joel.

"Maybe, 'tisn't; but perhaps it soon will be. I do tell 'ee Caroline's over Tremearne eating her heart out for a kind word, and there's no one she wants it from more'n you. But, by gosh, if 'ee take too durned long over it her'll be listening to the next man, and small blame to anyone but yourself. That's it straight."

Savagely Joel hacked into the loaded dung with the long toothed muck rack, pulling it from the back of the tumbril in heaps evenly spaced over the ground.

"Caroline left Kenneggy of her own will; and of her own will she'll come back, or not at all. I'll never ask her."

John looked at him pityingly; it did not take a sharp eye to see he was a changed man, and an unhappy one. The bitterness in his voice showed too in his face, mingled with it was anger against his own crass obstinacy in holding out against a reunion he would have given an eye-tooth for if only he would admit it.

"Listen, Joel, if you don't let her see you want her, there'll be someone who will. Caroline's not a girl who'll go unwanted for long, and she's young enough yet to listen to a man who's sweet on her. Take my advice and get her back while she's willing to come."

It seemed to Joel that Trounsen was conveying more than his words actually told. He looked at him hard, and as he did so remembered little glimpses of him and Caroline together, of the way they had looked at and spoken to each other. He remembered the night he had been tokened to her, how he had spoken in a voice that very nearly broke, and her tears in the next minute. He thought again of the way she had spoken so tenderly of him on her wedding day, as though she knew he had a deep affection for her.

"John Trounsen, are you sweet on my wife?"

He asked the question fairly and sharply, it cut across the air between them.

"Joel, my boy, I do love her more'n life, and 'tis no new thing. If 'ee don't help yourself while she's yours, I'll not be responsible for myself longer. That's you told, now."

With the muck rake planted between his feet and leaning heavily on the shaft, Joel looked at his rival. In fight he could have broken him to pulp, big fellow as he was, but there was more to it than a mere brawl could settle. Above all, he liked him, indeed had a great affection for him which had started from the day he had first seen him at Tremearne, the day Salome and he had taken over the pitcher they had won at the fair.

"So you love her too? Well, if that bain't a durned mix-up! What's she a-doing about it?"

"She'll do what you say, if you'd be quick and say it afore she grows deaf with straining to hear 'ee. Let me ask her for 'ee, say you want her to come back?"

In his mind Joel fought with this very great temptation; if he said that, she would come back. And what a difference that would make to his own, to all their happiness. Now it was being threatened by a definite break, a rival affection claiming her in the face of his silence.

"No," he roared. "No Andrewartha has ever begged from a woman yet, and I'm not being the one to start. Caroline walked out without a word to me, and she can walk back if she's so minded. I'll not ask her."

The heavy rake was plunged into the muck and pulled violently to its job. In silence John watched the play of the strong muscles in his arms, the ripple of them across his shoulders under the soiled shirt.

"Thee'st nothing to tell to her?"

He did not answer at once, and John turned to walk away.

"John Trounsen," the call came after him. He paused. "Give her my love. She'll always have that. There's no more I can bring myself to say."

He walked back over the fields towards the house and his horse. In the gathering gloom of the evening Joel continued his work, until the ground began to blend into the murk not many yards from him on every side. Then slowly he turned the cart homewards for the last time that night, and tended the horse, petting him and talking to him. Out among the animals he found a balm to the need for comfort that was a constant ache in his heart; in the family only Salome seemed in tune with him, always with the others he felt they had helped to drive Caroline away from him. As he crossed over to the house he paused for a moment to listen to the sound of the mines. The increasing activity had brought a new and harsher sound on the air; chains were being used to take the place of the great ropes on the whims, which were such an expense to keep renewing, and the

191

clatter of the iron links came day and night intermingled with the thunder of the stamps. It was the voice of progress and prosperity, clamorous in its day yet doomed to fade and leave Kenneggy and all the land about silent before the end of the century.

It was the day after he had admitted his love to Caroline that John Trounsen had gone over to try to bring about a reunion between the two and discovered the sad times the family had fallen on. As soon as he returned he told her of all he had seen.

"That leaves Polly and young Salome to do everything for the four men and little Chris, their sick mother and the dairy work too, save for the little help they can get from outside."

"The poor dears! And how's Joel? Did 'ee see him? Was he well?"

"Joel's missing 'ee sadly, there's no doubt; Salome asked me to tell 'ee he has 'most forgotten how to smile. But he sent you his love; he said, 'She'll always have that.' "

" 'She'll always have that.' He said I'd always have his love, did he?"

"He said that."

Her eagerness to learn how Joel was faring had, for the moment, driven out of her mind the accident to Elizabeth. Almost immediately she remembered and at once a wave of compassion for the poor soul swept into her heart.

"But I did forget the poor woman; how she must have been pained. And there's no one over Kenneggy to tend her properly. There's only one thing for it, John; I'll have to go back to see they're fed and cared for, every one of them, the poor dears."

"I'll take 'ee 'long first thing tomorrow. There bain't nothing to keep you any more 'long of us. I was reckoning as I came back that's what you'd want to do."

In the morning she collected her things and John drove her over the turnpike to the top of Kenneggy Lane.

"Put me down here, John. I'd like to walk down the lane and slip in quietly."

He climbed down to hand her to the ground, took out her bag and the bowl of jellied broth she had boiled out of an old hen of Sibella's the night before and brought along for Elizabeth.

"Thank 'ee, John. And goodbye for a little while; we'll be over to Tremearne soon, and you come along to us when you've the time."

She pressed his hand affectionately, knowing well how he had done everything in his power to make her happy again, and never once taken the opportunity to force a break between Joel and her.

"Goodbye, Caroline, and come as soon as 'ee can get things straight again. I reck'n they'll be pleased to see you when they come in crib time."

"I do hope so."

She waved, watching him turn and start back along the turnpike. Picking up the bag she went down the lane, her heart beating with eagerness and trembling at the near prospect of seeing them all again.

The place was empty and no one in sight as she reached the door; pushing it open she walked in and looked about the familiar long room, now so badly needing a woman's hand to restore it to clean comfort. There was a sound behind her, and turning she was just in time to catch Salome as she flung herself into her arms, tears already streaming down her cheeks.

"Caroline! Oh, Caroline, I did tell a prayer for you to come. Don't ever leave us again, promise you won't," she sobbed quietly.

"I'll not leave you; and I'd have been back long ago if only I'd known."

They clasped each other tightly for a moment, each perhaps thinking how in the past they might have been more understanding towards each other, glad now to look into a future promising to be so different.

j

"Come, Salome, over a while Joel and the others will be in for crowst; we'll need to work. Where's Polly?"

"In dairy. Leave her be just now, let me have you all to myself for a little while."

She laughed, and after hanging her bonnet and cloak on the door began to brisk up the fire. Soon the chicken broth was hot and she carried it, unannounced, to Elizabeth's room. She knocked at the door and entered.

Elizabeth was drawn up, resting on cushions in her bed. Everything in the room had the appearance of having been hastily tidied for so long that it had lost all trace of comfort and order. The bed was roughly and unevenly made, Elizabeth herself looked as though no one had found time to attend to her that morning. At the sight of Caroline standing in the doorway with the streaming broth her eyes filled with tears of joy and she held out her arms to her as though she were her own daughter.

"Caroline! I had almost given up hope of ever seeing you again. And 'twas all my fault; Joel has let me see plain enough I drove you away."

Setting the bowl down on the window ledge, Caroline came to the bedside and put an arm around the thin shoulders.

"We're not thinking of that any more, dear, only of being together and being happy. If I'd only known how 'twas with 'ee I'd have been over long while ago. Come now, don't 'ee ever cry another tear, for I'm caring for 'ee now, and we're going to have 'ee up and about with us in no time at all. Aunt Sibella sent the chicken broth over for 'ee, 'twas so strong when cold you could stand on it, and 'twill do 'ee a mighty lot of good. Take it while 'tis hot."

With the bowl on her knees, she supported Elizabeth with one arm as she sat on the edge of the bed, and fed her a spoonful at a time. The tears of happiness trickled now and then down the thin cheek, turned every few minutes towards Caroline and smiling half-timidly.

" 'Tis my leg, dear; most times 'tis bad, but sometimes 'tis more'n I can properly bear. D'you think 'twill ever be right again?"

"Please God, yes," she reassured her. "And anyhow, as soon as you get strong again we'll have 'ee about, even if 'tis with a crutch or stick, but you'll be down among us."

Soon she had remade the bed, brushed hard little dry crumbs from it and settled her higher up on the cushions, and by pulling the bedstead sideways a bit had given her a view out of the window over Wheal Speed, with the smoke curling from the chimney and the balance bob rising skywards and falling again from the Cornish engine. Then she hastened back to the kitchen and set about the dinner.

As it happened Joel was the first to come home at midday. As soon as he entered the house he stopped, seeing at once the signs of a touch that had not been felt for so long. And when Caroline ran through from the kitchen to greet him, he held up his hand to stop her just a little way off.

"Let me look at 'ee just for a moment; you're what my eyes have been longing to see all this while. Caroline, have 'ee come back to me at last?"

She threw her arms around his neck and nestled against him.

"Joel, my handsome! Oh, Joel, my handsome man," was all she could trust herself to say.

He kissed her heartily and, swinging her up in his arms, carried her outside the door. His father, Charles and Ralph were coming down the footpath from the mine and fields where they had been working; Chris was running along in front. Joel held her high above his head and shouted to them. For a moment they paused, until the boys, seeing who it was, let out a mighty roar of welcome.

Caroline took her place at the head of the table opposite Richard; wife of his eldest son and in Elizabeth's illness, mistress of Kenneggy, with them all ready and eager to acclaim her.

Chapter Nine

L ATE on a Friday afternoon Joel was coming in from the fields to attend to the usual jobs about the farm-place before the meal when he met Jimmy Polglaze on the path above Prussia Cove, and they sat down on a rock to touch off a pipe of tobacco.

From his pocket Joel drew a twist of black plug and offered it.

"I got this off a man in Penzance t'other night; seems good to me, though I'll not pretend to be a judge. I don't get 'nough to be too particular."

Jimmy sniffed at it appreciatively, and in his pocket discovered the relics of a clay, a blackened chipped bowl with a short growth of stem, which he filled with great care, letting not the slightest particle get lost. He put the stem in his mouth with the bowl upside down, for it was too short to be used the right way without getting into difficulties with his moustache.

"Joel, I'm glad I met 'ee, 'cause something queer happened to me just here this morning, and I've a mind to tell 'ee 'bout it. Maybe you'll laugh at me or tell me to keep further from the 'Packet', but there 'tis."

"Get along with 'ee, Jim, I'll not make game of 'ee."

Jim spat out a flake of tobacco he had been nibbling and handed back the precious twist. He rose to his feet and peered down over the cliff, just below them where the sea made big pools at low tide near Great Iddy's Rock. It was getting too dark to see any object below distinctly and he returned to where Joel sat, and stood over him, preparing to talk.

"Sea been clear and calm all day, quiet 'most like summer. I was working down in cove on the pots, getting a batch tarred, and when I come up for dinner I just happened to glance over cliff on account of it being such a pretty day. Any other time I wouldn't bother my eye, as 'ee well do know. But today I happened to look over just 'zactly at this here spot."

He returned to the edge and Joel went to stand beside him. Together they looked to where Jim indicated a place right below and gazed down as though something were to be seen there in the dusk if only they looked hard enough.

"I looked over and straight down there, just where I'm pointing now, in a pool beside the rock, floating about ever so quietly 'mong the weed was a dead 'un. The water was clear, there wasn't a doubt about it, there he was a-floating face down in the pool and if he'd been t'other way up I could have seen his features. He lay there quiet-like with the weed drifting about him as the water moved it up and down. Well, I think same as anyone else would, dinner or no dinner, I'll just get him out and then fetch one of t'others to help me pop him in a decent grave where he can rest 'stead of bumping about aimless 'mong rocks, and down I went and scrambled out till I come to the pool where I seen him. Of course, I'd reck'ned to get him out quick, but there weren't no body there at all.

"I pulled all the weed this way and that, and poked all round in pool but there weren't no sign of him at all. Nothing at all. So I looked up at the cliff and tried to make out if I was at the wrong spot, but so far as I could see there was no other place I could have mistaken for it, and sure 'nough there was nothing there. At that I hurries up the path and gets to this here bit again, when I just look

197

see if maybe I was at the wrong spot. And there, blast me eyes, right below in the very same spot he was a-floating about as large as life, as 'ee might say, just 'zactly where I seen him afore. This time I made certain where he was, for late as I was for my dinner I didn't feel I could eat with the poor dear so near shore and no one bothering to land him.

"Out over the rocks again I went, taking my bearings as I'd figured them from above, and sure 'nough 'twas to the same spot as I'd searched afore. And I searched again, all 'mong the weed, all through the pool, but I couldn't find him. If he were there he weren't no bigger 'n a shrimp, for he couldn't have hid better. So I give it up and hurries along home, mighty vexed for wasting so much time, and nothing to tell the missus for why. And I do tell 'ee, Joel, when I passed this here bit I didn't look over edge, not a third time. Now, what 'ee make of that?"

Joel turned away from the cliff and looked inland. He did not like the sea; he did not like the nature of it, its restlessness, its moods and treachery. He neither understood it, nor wanted to.

"Make of it? What can 'ee make of it? They do tell of things like that happening, but they always seemed to happen to other folk's folk. 'Tisn't often you meet the man it happened to, and on the very day. No, Jim, I can't make out what 'twas you saw, or thought 'ee saw. 'Tis just a strange happening. Maybe 'twas the light, or a shadow, or. . . or anything."

He looked at Jim as he prepared to move off homewards.

"Maybe 'twas a shadow, Joel; maybe. But somehow I don't reck'n 'twas."

Over the evening meal he told the story to the others.

His father laughed. "What had Jim told 'ee he'd been doing, mending pots? I reck'n he'd been doing with pots right enough, but 'tweren't crab-pots."

"And what do you think of it, Mother?"

"I don't hardly know, Joel. I don't know if it does to think too

198

much of those sort of things. Maybe they're unnatural; maybe they're just a trick of the lights and shadows, as you say, or a reflection of some part of the rock. Something that way, I do expect."

"And I think you sometimes see what you expect to see," exclaimed Salome.

"Do you mean that Jimmy came up from the cove thinking how clear the water was and how if a drowned man was there, 'twould be easy to see him? And he didn't know he was thinking that way till he looked over the edge and saw a body down in the water 'mong the weed; is that it?" asked Caroline.

"Yes, that's what I mean. You see your thoughts instead of just thinking them."

"Like dreaming?"

"Yes, Joel, only you're awake and your eyes are open; 'tis the same sort of thing."

Old Richard grunted, and finished his mouthful in his careful, deliberate way, which always made him appear to be about to make a statement of tremendous importance. Sometimes it came; more often it meant nothing at all.

"Talk of dreaming, young Bill Matthews told me of a dream yesterday, I'd disremembered it till Salome started on them. He had dreamed he did want to draw water from his butt and when he went to it he found there were six dead kittens in it, drowned. He thought this was mighty queer, yet 'tweren't so queer as when he went to his neighbour's butt, for there in it were six drowned kittens too. So on he went to Jimmy Polglaze, and even in his there were six kittens in the water."

"Oh, Father, what a horrid dream; he must have been drowning kittens that day for sure."

"Don't interrupt me, child, for I haven't finished yet. He dreamed that he did go to six butts in the cove and in each there were six drowned kittens; 'twas not till he did climb the hill to Henry

Wheeler's and looked in his butt that he found clean water. There's for a dream! 'Tisn't sense, for as we did tell him, no one ever drowned kittens in the butt."

Caroline gathered up the things from the table and made a great rattle with them, implying their thoughts should be back to more cheerful things and the duties still waiting to be done.

"Stop all this talk of drownings and bodies, for upon my word you quite turn my stomach with it all," said Elizabeth from her couch. " 'Tis all a lot of foolishness from start to finish. Get along now, Salome, for there's pans of milk to be scalded yet; do you bring them in while Caroline does the dishes."

The weather broke the next day, turning rough and wet. Through Saturday night and Sunday it grew wilder and wilder. Joel had been out all day with the boys putting ropes across the ricks and making them fast, but it did not prevent a steady tearing at the hay, which was carried away wisp by wisp to festoon everything in its path. He put two plough-chains over the hen-house and anchored them with stout iron spikes, or the roof would have been off for a certainty. The wind found a loose tile in the cow-house roof and ripped it off, another on the house itself rattled and flapped until it sounded as though it must break. All the closed shutters chattered and the window-frames shivered; inside the draught was everywhere, the fire roared away at one moment and the next sparks and smoke blew out into the room, so there was no comfort to be had. Wet garments hung around the fire and empty sacks covered the floor in an attempt to absorb the tide of rain water that beat under the door.

Sunday night saw the gale at its worst. It beat on the stout walls of the house until they shook and things rattled on the tables inside. A salt spray was flung up and carried miles inland, forming a white crust on whatever it touched and withering every green thing. There was no sleep for anyone at Kenneggy for wondering what the damage outside would be, whether the cow-house and sheds were standing and how many hedges would be laid flat in the one night.

Perhaps weeks of hard work would be caused, or ruined, in those few hours of ferocity. All shared the constant anxiety for those unfortunate enough to be caught at sea out of reach of harbour or cove, perhaps on this cruel lee-shore.

Joel lay in his bed in a sweat of anxiety over the farm-place. As each gust seemed to tear and shake the buildings more furiously than the last Caroline gripped his hand, and he found himself clutching the bedclothes and praying frantically that their precious buildings and stock might be spared. There was nothing he could do now but wait for the first glimmer of dawn; the day before he had done what he could of all he had then thought necessary, now he remembered this thing and that which had slipped his mind. If only he had fixed a rope to the good apple-tree it might have been saved; if he had repaired the hedge out beyond Four Acres it might have stood the gale, now it would all be down and hours of work needed where a single one would have prevented it. In the future, if things were spared to him, he would be more attentive and not be caught out by the gales. If they were only spared this once; oh, God! If they were only spared.

At length they could stand it no longer and, getting up, they dressed and went down to the living-room. There his father, mother and Salome were already gathered and were preparing some hot drink for themselves. They welcomed them in awed whispers, they too could not rest and were going to sit up until dawn permitted going out to learn the worst. The boys seemed to be asleep and Joel tiptoed across to their room, to find them awake and willing to join the group. They sat around the stove and sipped hot milk, talking in voices drowned by the roar of the gale, which was flinging itself at the stout walls as though it must surely break through in time and devour them.

At the first sign of light Joel put on his coat and ventured out to see if the beasts were harmed and to bring in a report of the damage. With exquisite relief he saw the dark outline of the buildings standing against the greying sky; he saw the ricks, depleted here and there, but mostly standing. The beasts were safe, if uneasy and nervous, the main stacks were safe; only lesser and almost unavoidable damage, such as the gaps in the hedges, was to be reckoned with instead of the disaster which might very well have met his eye.

On his return to the house his report was received with sighs of relief, and their thoughts turned to those who might have been less fortunate. With the coming of light everyone would gather on the cliffs to see if any ship was in distress in Mount's Bay, for the gale was piling directly in and anything caught between Lizard and Lamorna could hardly hope to escape. Joel and the boys hurried out and gave the beasts hay in their racks to comfort them, and where the roofs had leaked they collected the sodden litter and put out fresh. The rain had ceased although the wind still had gale force, seeming less fierce, however, with the promise of light.

After a hurried snatch to eat they set off down the lane and joined others already standing on the cliffs, leaning against the wind and straining their eyes to see into the waste of angry water gradually being revealed by the growing light. Beyond the shelter of the cove immense seas were running, great black waves with foaming tops whipped white by the wind tearing over them as they bore in to the land, and it seemed impossible for anything to be alive and floating in that terrible bay.

As the light grew the search became keener and it was Salome's young eyes that first made out a vessel still living in the bay. At first there was general unbelief at her excited assertion, but she persisted and pointed with certainty to where she declared it lay.

"There; over there, where I'm pointing. Can't you see her? Her's all awash in the huge seas. The waves are sweeping right over her, and her mast's a-gone. A small ship, she is. . . "

" 'Es I do see her now. Her's being washed in fast. 'Es, I do see her."

Cries of confirmation echoed all around and soon every eye was following the fate of the wretched vessel. Richard moved up to where Salome was standing to get a better view; other men collected and started speculating on what was to be their course of action.

"Her's a-coming in fast, but still too far out for us to do anything."

"She is, Henry Wheeler; there's nothing we can do yet, if ever."

"Maybe a lifeboat from Penzance could make across to her and take off the crew afore her strikes."

" 'Es, she might get across, but will she get back again?"

"That's for the lifeboatmen to say, not us," said Richard. "If they see fit to put out then they'll know best how to manage her. I reck'n if they got 'em off they'd try to make the cove and not beat back into the wind."

"Then I reck'n someone ought to go into Penzance and tell 'em. Will 'ee lend me a horse, 'Drewartha, to save time, and I'll go?"

"Take him, Henry, and good luck to 'ee. No, best take the grey, she'll keep up the pace."

"Right, I'll get 'long straight 'way."

Henry Wheeler set off at a sharp run towards Kenneggy where the horses had been stabled out of the gale; those he left did not expect he could be in time, for it was obvious now that the ship was getting nearer the shore every minute. It seemed she was being carried on until she was heading for Great Iddy's Rock, that deadly, treacherous spot not far from the entrance to the cove. As soon as its direction became apparent and it was obvious that if help was to reach her it must come from the cove to be in time, men began to discount the danger to themselves and weigh up the chances of reaching her.

Jimmy Polglaze started the movement down to the cove. He ran down to the boat slide and with the help of Bill Matthews and four other fishermen got his boat down to the water. Everyone went down to join them and help with the launch.

"Here, boys," shouted Polglaze. "Into the boat with 'ee and we'll manage to get them fellows off afore she strikes."

203

At that moment, old Richard ran up and shouted a warning to the men inside, already getting their oars into the rowlocks.

"Do 'ee know what 'tis like outside the cove, Jim Polglaze? No boat can live in it. From cliff top it looks awful. Don't 'ee go out, Jimmy; 'tis madness. 'Tis madness, I do tell 'ee!"

The women, including their wives and daughters, stood around with their hands on the gunnel, knowing fully well that what he said was true, and yet fearful of adding their weight of argument to deter their men. Even Mary Polruan, whose sweetheart, Bob Prowse, was in the boat, said no word.

"What you say is true 'nough, but I daren't do anything else but put out, Mr 'Drewartha. Those fellows out there do look as though they'll be drowned for sure; there's one chance for us to get 'em, and if we do maybe we'll be spared to pull back with 'em. We're their only chance, poor souls, and we got to let 'em have it. How'd 'ee like to bring 'em back with us, boys? Or shall we stay here safe and watch 'em drown?"

There was a shout of approval and they drove off the slip into the water, their oars shot out and dipped, a few short pulls to get her set and away they went, pulling hard and strongly towards the narrow entrance. Six of them, the finest and strongest fishermen of the cove, in Jim's own boat which he had built for himself and which he knew better than a man could hope to know his own child.

The watchers on the shore and cliff saw it reach the mouth of the cove, pass through safely and come out on the open sea. No sooner than they had left its shelter, almost before it could be hoped the rowers had got the feel of the forces opposing them, it was obvious the attempt was hopeless, for a huge wave came hurtling down on them with all the force of the gale and weight of the ocean behind it. It tore on at them; they saw the bow of the boat lift, but too slowly. The whole boat disappeared in a boiling mass of water and foam, there in front of the folk's eyes, within a few yards of them. And yet not a sign of the men; not one rose out of the maelstrom, not one struck out to fight back to the cove. One moment the boat was there with the men they knew and loved and had sent out on their chancey attempt to save the wretched seamen, and the next they were gone; the boat was gone and nothing remained to mark their grave and that of their enterprise.

That crushing mass of water seemed to have fallen too on the spirits of those left on the shore and cliffs. The suddenness of the disaster stunned them, so that at first they could not believe it true, but clung to impossible hopes that the boat was hidden in a trough of the waves. As the seconds passed without bringing any sign the realisation dawned of the sea's triumph over their men. Tears ran down their faces, grown grey and haggard in those few brief minutes, but they did not forget the part they still had to play in the tragedy of the morning, and spread out along the cliffs and those stretches of shore that could be manned waiting for any man who might win through, or, as each knew in his heart, ready to dash into the water to drag a friend's body from its grasp.

The fate of the ship had become certain during the very short while these happenings had taken; already she was being drawn on to the rocks over by Great Iddy's and far out of their reach. The cliffs and rocks were absolutely unclimbable, especially with the wind tearing and grasping at men as they stood even on sure footholds. And even if, miraculously, they reached the nearest point to the rocks, against that wind no rope could be thrown, not even big Joel's strength could have done it; the wind would just have flung it back in his face. From the cliffs they watched, helpless, as she struck on that deadly spot, the mighty walls of water driving her on harder and harder, pounding down as soon as she was firmly held, smashing, crushing, beating stout wood to splinters, flinging her numbed men into the churned mass of water, slinging them like rag dolls against the barnacled rocks, spinning them about broken and helpless in racing eddies and whirlpools. The elements were feeling their mastery that day and in their fury there was no place for pity or mercy. Men there were for the killing, and they died, both those who had been in danger and those who had left friends and safety for their sake.

While there was light the shore was watched and searched but the angry sea gave up none of their bodies, and the bereaved women and saddened neighbours left the sorry place to the falling darkness.

The group around the Kenneggy hearth that night was only one of many in the cove and scattered about. Grief sat with them all, and in everyone's mind was the thought of the six chairs empty now for the first time, and of the vacant spaces where absent feet had rested on the hearth.

"I can't get the thought of those poor dears out of my head," said Joel, expressing what they had all done during the last few hours. "Poor Jimmy, he'd such trust in his boat; couldn't believe any sea could worst her."

"If he'd only listened to Father," exclaimed Charles. " 'Twould never have happened."

"Of course he wouldn't listen to me. How could he with them fellows waiting to drown afore their eyes? No, they were men enough not to listen, and I'm proud of 'em for it. I'm proud of knowing Jim and Bob, and Bill, Bob Cornish, Erny and Tom, all six of 'em."

In his chair, Joel shifted miserably. "I reck'n I ought to have gone with 'em. What's the use of me being as strong as a horse if I don't use my strength when I ought to?"

"That's foolish talk, Joel. You're no boatman, and if six of 'em that knew how to handle a boat as well as any 'tween here and Lizard could be so quickly beaten, what could 'ee have helped, knowing nothing?"

"I hope you're right, Father. But I can't get the thought of 'em from my mind; I can't help wondering if Jimmy's cold, 'way down in the dark water and weed. And I was talking to him two days agone, and he telling me how he had searched for a body down over by Great Iddy's Rock. Now he's down there somewhere hisself."

Wait for the Wagon

Salome dabbed at her eyes. "Don't Joel, don't talk that way. Jimmy's not down there; he'll be in Paradise now, won't he, Mother?"

"Of course, dear. 'Greater love hath no man. . .' Jimmy laid down his life for strangers, and I should say that's even greater."

Joel kicked at the wreck-wood on the fire.

"That's not what I mean. Don't 'ee see? 'Tis his hands and his face, his arms, the things we've seen and touched and know. 'Tisn't his soul; what have we ever had to do with his soul? 'Tis those things that meant Jimmy to me, and those are the things that are cold, and wet, and drowned. That's the way I do feel."

His father sighed. "And that's the way we all feel, my son. 'Cause we don't talk about it doesn't mean we don't feel. Most of us feel that way, Joel."

Some days later, those who had taken turns to watch the beach found the bodies of the ship's crew, but none of their own men. Seven of them came in, and Joel was among those who dug their sandy grave at the foot of the cliffs. They brought down bundles of fresh straw from the stackyard and spread it deep at the bottom for them to lie on, a good sweet bedding, for old Richard liked to make them as comfortable as he could. As the long handled shovels began to pile back the disturbed sand they worked in silence, each thinking what a price this last landing had taken from their small hamlet, their own tragedy linking with the end of the voyage of these seven strangers. Somewhere folk would be waiting for their return, and would never know how they had died, or where they had been buried. So they laid them to their rest, gently and decently in the unmentioned hope that somewhere others would do the same for them or their folk if a similar fate overtook them in the years ahead.

The unhappy week dragged itself away. It was Thursday afternoon when they had buried the seamen; on Friday Joel was mending the fallen hedges and by late afternoon found himself at just that spot where he had been talking to Jimmy Polglaze exactly

207

a week before. The coincidence led him to the cliff edge, with his mind running on the story he had been told and which had so troubled the poor fellow that day, and he looked down to the shore, his gaze wandering idly among the rocks and pools below.

A pool just down there, Jim had said, and there was the pool, clear and quiet, even as the sea had become after the gale had blown itself out. But the pool was not empty. As soon as Joel saw it he realised that there was a drowned body washed in floating among the seaweed, exactly as Jim had described. Was this the same phantom body which had appeared to warn them of the disaster overtaking them, a bad omen? He stared down at it fixedly; it seemed so real that he resolved he would have to go down to bring it in. It must surely be one of their own men washed back to them.

He ran quickly down the path to the cove and made his way along the beach and out over the rocks, even as his friend had done twice before. Was he too on a false errand, for Jimmy had been as sure as he was himself that the body had been there last Friday? He reached the pool and knew at once that this time it was not empty; and he knew too who it was that had come back. It was no other than drowned Jimmy himself, lying alone among the weed, exactly as he had seen himself when on his way home to his last Friday's dinner.

He dropped on his knees and slipped his arms into the cold water, swirling away the weed and gripping the sodden clothing. With scarcely an effort he pulled the body towards him and up, it came so easily it almost seemed to move through the water of its own accord. In a moment he had it out on the rock, the water running off and falling with a trickling sound in little streams back into the pool. After the first rush had ceased it fell back drop by drop, as though the rocks themselves were shedding tears of remorse for the share they had had in the bruising of poor Jimmy Polglaze.

"Jimmy my dear, poor Jimmy! So 'twas yourself 'ee searched for? If I had known I'd have held 'ee back, all six of 'ee."

A choke in his throat gripped for a moment; he fought it back but could not restrain the tears that ran down his cheeks. After spreading his handkerchief over the bruised face he put his arms under the limp thing the sea had given them back in place of the brave man it had taken, and lifted it up until it lay against his chest. In his arms it was no load and he set off over the rocks and shore, past the boat slide where Jimmy had last set foot on land and up the path, past where they had talked together and on towards the Polglaze cottage.

Several neighbours saw him coming and hurried out with weary sorrow-strained faces to inquire who it was had been washed up.

" 'Tis Jimmy. One of 'ee run on and tell them up there that I'm a-coming with him."

A woman separated herself from the group and ran ahead, drying her eyes on her apron as she went.

"Where did he come in, Joel Andrewartha?"

"How did 'ee come to see 'un?"

Questions were fired at him as they moved on. He told them.

"Shall I take 'un, Joel? 'Tis some way for 'ee to have brought 'un."

Joel shook his head. "Leave him be; I've carried him here and I'll carry him home. I reck'n I'm proud to carry Jim Polglaze. He's as light as a child in my arms."

Right up and into his house he took him, and laid him on a bench in the living-room, ready for the women to shroud and prepare for burial. The widow sobbing quietly into her apron, tried to thank Joel for bringing him up from the shore; he patted her kindly on the arm.

"Down by Great Iddy's, in a pool. 'Twas just as though he were resting there. We're mighty proud of him," he faltered, and hastened away before he too gave signs of the emotion everybody was feeling, and many giving way to. He hurried back to Kenncggy to tell the others the news. They had started the meal, all wondering what had been keeping him.

"I found Jimmy down in a rock pool and brought him home. He was bruised a good bit, but I knew him. None of the others have come in; it doesn't seem as though they will now. And I'll tell 'ee something queer. Do 'ee mind I told 'ee how Jimmy had said he went to find a drowned one in a pool last Friday?"

All around the table, as he looked at them they nodded.

"Yes, Joel, you told us that at supper, same night," agreed Elizabeth.

"Well see, that's where I found him, sure 'nough, just as he had said."

A little astonished cry burst from Salome. "Then he must have seen hisself as he looked drowned. Oh, how horrible!"

" 'Es, 'tis queer, but there's more'n that queer about this business. Do 'ee mind what I told 'ee about Bill Matthews's dream?" their father asked. "About the drowned kittens in the butts?"

" 'Es, Father, in all six save only Henry Wheeler's."

"In six butts there were kittens drowned; and the six men those butts belonged to were all drowned t'other morning. Henry Wheeler, he didn't have kittens in his butt, and he rode 'way in for the lifeboat and was all right."

"He had reck'ned on coming across in the lifeboat," said Joel. "Only 'twas too great a sea running to launch her. Good thing too, or it might have been worse; and too late anyway, as it happened."

They ate in silence for a while, all thinking the same thing, the only thing anyone had in mind that week.

"I mind the night we had trouble over Blanchey Buckett, Father," said Joel at length. "She said Jimmy and t'others with him would know what 'twas to be drowned afore long. There's for 'ee!"

Richard looked at him for a moment and then nodded. "She did say that, I mind it well."

Elizabeth, growing a little impatient at the mood the family had got of taking anything they could and putting a strange significance to it, broke into the conversation.

"Seeing that she was talking to fishermen, who spend most of their lives out at sea with all the dangers of their trade, 'twas a fairly safe thing to say. There's nothing strange in it happening, only in it coming so soon and all going at once. And yet when you think of it, as they were the quickest men about anything, either in burning a witch or in trying to save lives, even that isn't so strange."

Joel nodded. "I suppose it isn't, figured out that way. She did say too I'd be in the pond one day myself, but I reck'n that's not too unlikely, if I was to trip up or go sliding winter time."

"Or someone might throw 'ee in, Joel," Caroline suggested, and the idea of anyone being able to do that to her big brother so tickled Salome's sense of fun that she burst into laughter, in which the whole family joined. It was the first time for days they had laughed, and looking around and seeing themselves at it struck them as being out of tune with the events of the week, and the laugh died away as suddenly as it had risen.

The next day they got out the wagon for Jimmy's funeral, harnessing the horses before they got into their dark clothes, and started off down the lane to the cove. Joel, his father and brothers, Henry Wheeler and another neighbour carried the coffin out to the wagon. Joel led the shaft horse and the boys managed the others; the big wagon carried its sad load up the lane with all the mourners following. Although it was Jimmy alone they followed, in their hearts they mourned and grieved for all who had gone out with him, and who had not been returned by the sea that had supported them and finally taken their lives. Past Kenneggy and the head of the lane into the turnpike, and then the long walk to Breage Churchtown.

Up in a sunny corner of the churchyard they lowered the plain coffin into the grave dug that morning. The minister read the burial service and they all tried to feel like those who sorrowed but not without hope, yet in spite of every effort there were few cheeks, whiskered or smooth, of those who stood at the graveside looking down to bid Jimmy a last goodbye, that had not a tear.

Of the six who answered Jimmy's eager shout that morning no others were ever seen again by their folk in the cove, he alone were they able to bury and mark the grave; but whether grass or seaweed crept over them, they remained in local memory as six more men who had offered their lives in expiation for the inhospitable coast.

The past years, although happy enough for Joel and Caroline, had been childless, and now the first baby was eagerly awaited. When she gave birth to a son they called him William after her good Uncle Drenocoe, much to his delight. Since her return to Kenneggy Joel had resumed his beloved wrestling; both she and Salome took an interest in the sport, although none of the others thought it anything but a waste of time and strength. It was a great day when he returned from market with the news that Polkinhorne, the Cornish champion, was coming down Camborne way.

"I've a mind to go up there fair-day and try to play him. 'Tis now or never, for I'll get no better afore I'm older, and a man's past his best as a wrestler by twenty-eight, often as not."

"Camborne? 'Tis a long way."

"Only 'bout eleven mile from St. Hilary, through Praze-an-Beeble."

"Then why not? You've nothing to lose," encouraged Salome.

" 'Tis true, a tinner's got nothing to lose," remarked Richard, entering the room at that moment. "Did 'ee get my tobaccy, Joel my son? What's that thee wust saying, anyway?"

"Joel's going up Camborne to play Polkinhorne, the champion, Father."

"Oh, he is? And who's a-bringing him home with his neck broke? Answer me that."

"I'll go along with him, if you'll let us have the gig," said Caroline. "But I do hope I'll not be needing it for that."

"As you please, but you'd best take the wagon for him, a-coming home."

His father need have had no fear for the return; as the news got about there were more and more who declared they would not miss seeing such play as it promised to be. While it was admitted they might be under-estimating the skill and strength of the giant from up the country, it was difficult to allow too much credit to Joel, and his strength must surely be equal to any in the Duchy. As the day arranged for the match drew nearer, excitement grew among all the followers of wrestling and his chances were discussed and weighed wherever any of them met, up at the "Packet," in the smithy, and among the shafts.

Midsummer Day dawned, the great festival for miners in West Cornwall, and those who were not working first core by day went up the carns to drive holes for the plugs which were fired off at noon, when all work ceased. A flag was flying from a corner of Wheal Speed engine house, and from many another, from there or from the headgear in every bal. At night there would be huge bonfires of furze on all the high points for miles around and the shilling allowance made by the works to each man would be spent on merry-making.

Joel arranged to take Angove along with them in the gig, for naturally he was to be his sidesman for the match and had been taking his duties very seriously. Between them they had sketched out a plan of attack to be followed whenever opportunity offered, and he had spent a great deal of time advising Joel on effective counters for every throw he knew; neither thought little of the skill he was contesting and had given defence as much thought as attack, an unusual necessity when playing most of the local men.

They reached Camborne field in good easy time. There were several men competing for the honours of the day, most of them good enough wrestlers and as eager as Joel to win through to a bout with the champion; as Angove had thought, his man and Polkinhorne were easily the biggest and, to all appearances, the strongest to enter the ring, and the sticklers planned to have them on opposing sides, which meant that they could not meet unless each won his preliminary bouts and entered the final. While these were going on the crowd grew dense and more keenly interested in the play; Caroline had never before seen so many people gathered as there were about that roped enclosure where Joel was throwing his men with deliberate skill. As she knew well enough, he had set his heart on facing Polkinhorne and no minor man was going to be allowed to take his place; he was using strength and science to put them where he wanted, on grass, as soon as he got his hold on their jerkins.

While Polkinhorne was in the ring, Caroline watched every move he made, and was impressed; here indeed was a match for Joel, and glancing across to where he too was studying his great adversary's tactics, she wondered what thoughts were passing behind his dark quiet face. That he was pleased she had no doubt, for although he would go straight in to win, it was the sport he loved and, against a man as good as this, win or lose he would enjoy the play.

The final was to be played in the afternoon, so the men could be rested and fresh. Joel ate little and drank even less, being content to rinse his mouth with weak brandy and water and spit it out. She and Angove felt far more nervous than he appeared to be, indeed anyone would have thought it was the older man who was going to face the champion of Cornwall in the ring before hundreds of spectators.

The judges announced the two players, though no soul around but must have known their names and prowess, and that it was to be for the best of three falls, all fair backs on three points before any other part of the body touched grass. As the two faced each other Caroline could see that the man from up the country was taller and had longer arms than Joel, but broad and massive as he was she believed her husband to be closer built, the more agile of the two. They were moving about the ring, watching for a hold, eye never leaving eye but following every movement made by the other, like two experienced gamecocks about to fight. The feinting wearied her, as it always did; suddenly the crowd stirred all around, rustling with excitement. They had clutched and she had missed seeing exactly how it had come about, and the struggle proper had begun.

Like timbers on a well-sprung roof they leaned towards each other, arms locked about, feet back out of reach of an undercutting strike, forming almost a right angle together. She could see that if either had an advantage in the hold it was Polkinhorne. He had a hug around Joel, the same bear's hold that had punished the man of Devon, Abraham Cann, she learned from comments among the spectators.

Shouts of encouragement were flung out to both men, advice and caution intermixed in one hubbub.

"Hug 'un tighter! Why, man, he's breathing still, sweet as a babe!"

She saw Joel suddenly release his hold about his man and, in a flash, encircle the hugging arms and thrust up between them with one hand gripped on the collar and the other holding his own wrist. His elbows drew together like a pair of nutcrackers, while the upward thrust forced his man into a straighter position; Joel began to bend his knees, sitting back with all his weight and, as he drew off his balance, turned strongly to the left as they fell. A burst of cheering greeted the counter and the success it had achieved, for there before them was the great Polkinhorne with Joel diagonally across him, his weight forcing the second shoulder to the grass. The sidesmen ran in and pulled them apart, because, as everyone knew, the hitch was worthless as far as scoring went and ground work was not allowed. Caroline sighed with relief and breathed more freely, just as though it had been her own body crushed in that hug; now she knew for certain that Joel was no mean wrestler, come what might in later play.

They had caught again; this time it was Joel who held the advantage and was hugging with greater effect. Polkinhorne, experienced showman that he was, contorted his face in an agonised expression, gasped and heaved, but for all the effect it had on Joel he might have been made of brass. Then suddenly he broke the hold and rushed in, foolishly offering his left arm to a grip which Joel had

215

at once, above the elbow and drawing it across his breast with a sharp turning movement, continued with all his weight in the spin. As he brought his left side in, Polkinhorne should have fallen as he was swung off his feet, but he had applied a skilful counter immediately. His free arm gripped Joel's waist, held firmly and saved himself for a moment, but in the next Joel had turned in towards him on his right toe and caught the champion's advanced leg with his own, a swinging strike that came at the same time as a wrench of the clutched arm. At once they fell together, although, for all the crowd yelled its excitement and appreciation, it was again no back.

Twice Joel had taken the palms of the encounter without gaining a fall, and Polkinhorne must have felt the slight it put upon his ringcraft, for in the next bout he closed immediately, ducked quick as thought beneath Joel's arm and got back to back with him, his right arm over and his left under his body, and in a peculiar lift sent him somersaulting to fall heavily flat all across his back. It was the first throw of the match and a clear score to Polkinhorne; the crowd was delighted with the quickness and success of the movement and showed it, to his pleasure. But Caroline was watching Joel, lying there on the grass. Angove was bending over him, while his opponent turned and she could see him speaking. Then Joel put up his hand and they shook; Angove looked across at her and smiled, so she knew he was merely resting from a heavy fall and not really injured.

For fifteen minutes the players could rest after a fall, and Joel was ready by that time to resume. The success of his last attack had evidently led the other to believe he had found this to pay better than prolonged close work, and again he caught Joel's hand, his right this time, and Caroline knew even as he turned that it was the Flying Mare being handed to him, his own favourite attack, and she held her breath, waiting to see if all she and the smith had planned with him was in vain. Even as the attacker stooped to swing him up, Joel planted his free hand in the small of the offered back and thrust with all his might, so that she smiled, in spite of her anxiety knowing how dangerous such an unexpected counter would be. Almost at once the extended right arm clipped back across the holder's chest and Joel whirled his right hip into the other's buttock and threw him backwards across his loins, turning defence into an attack which scored a fall applauded with cheers that echoed and re-echoed all about.

Now it was fall for fall, and feverish excitement was everywhere. Some claimed that the belt would be changing hands very soon if this Breage farmer were to enter the ring as challenger; others swore the champion was merely biding his time and would show them something now he had got the weight of his man. Caroline heard the argument all about her during the rest, and smiled quietly to herself for all the anxiety in her heart, because she knew that Joel was the strongest man in the West Country, and was only worried lest in trying to prove himself the best wrestler he should be injured either by foul play or by accident. As they entered the ring again for the struggle to gain the deciding fall, a hush fell over the packed crowd, and all eyes were alert to catch every movement of the two powerful men.

They had caught at each other after only a little foining, held at arm's length by the left hand on the collar, and were moving round and round in the ring as though they had a deep respect for the power and skill of the free right hand which was poised ready to grasp at any offered hold. She caught a glimpse of the cautious, pleasant expression on Joel's face and then her eyes were drawn to the scheming angry look which seemed to occupy the champion's. Every move they made was a careful, guarded prelude to attack, to a good ordered retreat; nothing escaped the eyes that might give a hint of the adversary's intention. And then in a trice they had closed in the straining locks, thigh to thigh, a leg wreathed around a leg, tugging, wrenching to throw it off the ground. Caroline held her

k

breath in the tense silence about her, stretched herself as tall as she could to see how Joel was faring. As the efforts were prolonged, each man striving with every ounce of strength to put forward the extra mite which would bring him victory, cheers broke from hoarse throats, urging and encouraging them equally to hold out. Now and then, in the moments of silence, she could hear great sobbing gasps as they drew their breath, each now feeling his strength and endurance to be limited and yet forcing even harder to score before it failed.

She saw Joel had never slackened his grip behind the neck, nor loosed hold of Polkinhorne's left arm, and now he was turning in his left side towards him and brought the toes of his locking leg across the lower part of his man's shin. It was a lock that offered tremendous purchase, and now he was swinging to his right and falling backwards. They crashed down solidly together, but the instant before reaching grass that leg lock did its work and by lifting Polkinhorne's leg as he fell brought him underneath, his shoulders on the ground and Joel on top of him.

At once there was an uproar, some calling that it was no back at all, and many shouting that it was as fair a fall as any the day had seen, so that the sticklers hardly knew what to do. Angove was arguing furiously with the champion's sidesman, so neither were of any use in reaching a decision, indeed it seemed as though another and hotter tempered fight was threatening in the ring. Joel stood quietly, his thumbs thrust in his belt, and watched the scene of wrangling all about, his chest rising and falling with the breath coming quickly after the strain of the long struggle. She could tell from his manner that he was content, ready if he were asked to play again for the decision; he was neither greedy for the verdict nor afraid of taking a fall that would give it against him. The great Polkinhorne had risen slowly to his feet, hitched his breeches and jerkin to straightness and now, without a glance at the judges, walked across to Joel. He took his hand in his own and lifted it high, again and again, so that all the crowd could see that he himself awarded the fall to him.

" 'Twas as full a back as ever touched grass," he roared. "And I'm proud to have played with 'ee, Andrewartha. We'll meet again, and I hope that day I'll be equal to 'ee."

With that generous acknowledgment everyone had accepted Joel as winner of the day's honour, and now came surging into the ring around the two wrestlers. With them Caroline was forced along; Polkinhorne saw her struggling among the crush and, recognising her from seeing them together in the morning, he parted the folk as though they were stalks in a cornfield and made way for her to Joel's side.

"Over a while your man'll take the belt from me, Mistress Andrewartha; and there's no man in Cornwall fitter to wear it."

She blushed with pleasure at his praise, but Joel laughed.

"No, 'twas just my day today, I do reck'n. I've never played better, nor like to play half as well again, and even then 'twas a chancey stroke full of good luck for me that brought 'ee down, every time. No, I know a champion when I've met one and this'll be my great day, with no next time for me to show myself but a great lout in your hands, Polkinhorne. No, no, the leather can bide where 'tis; I'm happy and proud to have played 'ee at Fair, but I know when I've met a better man afore he do break my neck."

"What do 'ee say to that, ma'am? Would 'ee not want him to wear the belt?"

" 'Deed and I would not. 'Tis bad enough to see the two of you in all friendliness pitting such terrible strength 'gainst each other, and I'm left mazed as to how a man can stand it, but if 'twas a fight for the belt, I should be crazed long afore 'twas over. No, if Joel's happy now and content to bide quiet with the good sport he's had, then 'tis all I do ask."

"Maybe you're right, and maybe many of us would be happier men, and finer wrestlers, if like your husband we could bide content to enter ring only for the fun of it. There's a mighty lot too much naggling and fratching goes on today, and when it comes to the like of this" – he rolled down his stocking and showed the skin of his leg, under the temporary redness caused by the recent bout, all scarred and dented by the cruel shoes of the Devonian – "then 'tis getting beyond sport."

As she gazed fascinated at the marks, imagining the pain of the fearful kicks and how the man had suffered to make a show for Cornwall, aghast that any sportsman could allow himself to use such spiteful tactics, she resolved that Joel should mean what he had said, and having achieved what he had most wanted he should never enter the ring again.

Chapter Ten

THE passing years had brought changes at Kenneggy as well as about the countryside. Caroline had given birth to a second son and a daughter, Alfred and Bessie; Salome was away, married and mistress of Trevenner, in Marazion, while Charles was on his own at Greenbury Farm in St. Hilary Parish, leaving Ralph to carry on with Joel and young Chris. Their father was taking life more easily now; after much persuasion, he had listened to the advice of his family and, on turning sixty, had placed himself on retirement. Wandering around Wheal Speed, touching off a pipe in some sunny spot down on Kenneggy Cliff, he enjoyed a leisure not often granted to an old miner; indeed, he was well advanced in an old age that made him remarkable among men who had worked down the mines. In her own way Elizabeth took the credit for this, because it was she who had, years ago, brought him up to grass and set him going with his teams at the whims, and she claimed the change had already added twelve years to his life. Now it was Ralph who had charge of the whim horses, although his father would as often as not be around to see that all was going as it should; at times when the farm made greater claims than Joel could meet, he was still able to take over again for a spell. His son Chris had inherited his firm conviction that there was good metal in some rich lode just ahead, and for five years or more had been down the bal himself, daily expecting to strike it, just the same as any other tinner in Cornwall, or miner the world over for that matter. He was down the shaft every weekday, but Elizabeth, backed by Caroline and Polly, had decreed that he should work on the farm at busy times, and had pressed Joel to find excuses to bring him up into the fresh air and sunshine whenever he could, to keep him free of the blanched look of the underground man. As there were many jobs which Chris managed better than they could, with the knowledge of his trade and tools fresh in him, he was a handy youngster to have about; when there was a bit of stone to be dressed or rock to be blasted he was always called up.

Joel was discussing some of the immediate farm programme with them.

"And Chris, there's a piece of work I want 'ee to do, soon as ever thee'st time. Up by the horse pond the lane's getting soft and slippery; I reck'n a load or two of rock put in just right would save us trouble later on, and you can do it best. If 'tis left over a while, belike we'll have something sticking in there."

"All right, Joel, I'll get a seam along and build it up. Leave it to me."

"I'll leave it to 'ee, then. Come on, Ralph, we'll get on with threshing; I'll be needing that straw in a day or so, I'm hoping."

In the threshing barn they worked with the flails, getting a quantity of grain sacked up to take along to the mill, up by Retallack. The stoor shone where the winter sunlight hit it in thick bright bands slanting gently across the building, while the pile of good wheat straw grew. Within the next day or two a load of straw bundles was made ready to cart up to the Falmouth Packet Inn.

On the Friday in the first week of December, Joel loaded up the wagon for the afternoon; there would be just time for the trip in the failing light of the short day. Caroline had baked them herby pie for dinner that day and served it out to them, knowing well it was one of his favourites, although those made in wintertime were never as good as those with the fresh young spinach and lettuces of summer. And yet in Cornwall, down in the South, the weather is so mild that things can grow in the garden and flowers bloom early, and she had managed to find some greens, a nice handful of parsley and, of course, plenty of long white leeks. All went under a good crust and was baked, and when done this was lifted and some thick cream poured in, about a cupful beaten with two eggs. And where she had found those eggs was another puzzle, but Caroline had a way with the hens much the same as with the men, seeming to get whatever she wanted for the asking. After this the pie was popped back in the oven and browned.

While they were waiting for her to serve, Joel looked around at them all seated there in the long living-room of Kenneggy. Herby pie always brought back memories of that other one that had grown cold many years ago while he was held prisoner by the water down in the flooded mine. He thought now of all he might so easily have missed had things not come out as they did that day. There was Caroline at the end of the table, carving out good generous wedges of pie to all her family; plumper now, a little more serious as the mother of his children might be expected to be; for all that, she was still Caroline and everything to him. And his father at the head, grand old white-haired man, his dark eyes now faded to a blue-grey, his chin even a shade more set in its determined line, thrusting out under the thinner whiskers; his mother on her couch, tied to it by her stiff leg with its joints set as hard as stone, and a memorial nearly as lasting to those unhappy days when Caroline had been away at Tremearne. There was his brother Ralph, stout fellow, and young Chris, although now not so young as they were inclined to make him. Chris made him think of Mary, who unknown to them both had been the recipient of the young calf love which had been denied to him in the direction his heart had tried to wander.

"Come, Joel, eat up; what are you thinking of so hard?" the mother said.

He laughed and half turned towards her as he prepared to start his dinner.

"Just sometimes it strikes me, all of a sudden, I've been lucky in having you all for my folk. When I look at those others have got, and then at you all, at Caroline and the youngsters down here around me at Kenneggy, I reck'n I've been served a good slice out of life. And I've enjoyed it, every crumb."

"Why, Joel my son, you do talk as though you'd finished. Wait till you're an old man like me afore you get took that way."

Again Joel smiled; he looked up at Caroline and met her eyes. For a moment they held his and seemed to read in them the hint of uneasiness that had suddenly crept into his mind, and at once she smiled, just as she did only for him, giving the reassurance and love which had always been his, quietly, tenderly pledged again to him just by the slightest movement of the corners of her mouth.

After seeing to one or two things about the farmplace, he went out to the meadows for the horses, the two he usually took when the journey was short and the load light, one for the traces being sufficient. Starting out of the yard he had the bridle of the trace-horse in his hand, walking backwards to pilot them carefully around the curve, with the rear wheels cutting in on the arc they had to take a big sweep. He noticed the soft patch by the pond had not been built up, evidently young Chris had forgotten or neglected his instructions, and this took further care to bring the wagon around safely. There was no trouble, and from then on all was an easy trip; he arrived at the inn just as the light was failing, and soon finished the unloading.

Because it was already dusky he walked beside the horses the better to see all was well along the road, which was downhill with Wheal Grylls on his left after passing Rosudgeon Common. The horses knew Kenneggy lane well enough to need no guiding in and they pulled eagerly up the slope knowing their feed was waiting to be served to them as soon as stables were reached. Perhaps they were too eager, or maybe the wagon had over-run them a little as they dipped towards Kenneggy gate; whatever it was, for a moment Joel forgot the soft patch in the road. The next moment, and with a shout, he had sprung at the bridle of the shaft horse, trying to turn him out so the wheels would clear the shelving edge. The horse plunged, flustered in the dusk and not knowing quite what he was wanted to do, the front wheel slipped over the edge, the horses jerked forward and he saw the rear wheel hover for a second at the top of the bank and then start to slide down. In an angry effort to save the accident he leapt to the side of the wagon and, ankle deep in the mud, flung his weight against it, trying to prevent it from over-balancing. Under his feet there was no firm ground, nothing to get a purchase on, and the movement on the wagon was too much to be stopped easily. It slipped down into the mud, the horses pulled on the curve and for a second or two it hung there in that precarious position, then slowly turned over and settled down, pushing him under its side, down into the mud and water of the pond.

As it heeled over it had pushed him out into deeper water, and with him straining to hold its weight, had brought him to his knees and carried his head down under the surface of the pool. The whole mishap had taken a mere second or two, but the next few passed like an eternity, in them Joel lived through more anguish of mind and body than he had ever known it possible to bear. This to happen to him, a trivial slip which, had he been more careful with the horse, would have been avoided altogether; let alone his crass foolishness in springing between the wagon and the pond.

Why hadn't young Chris done as he was told and built up that bank? Curse him for a procrastinating little bastard, to cause this to happen. That he, Joel Andrewartha, should be held down like this, by his own wagon, by his horses, drowned in his own pond. Drowned, and in a ditch; after escaping the menace of water in the mine, to be drowned like this in a ditch. All the horror of his end leapt up in his mind, threatening to panic him with the same mad nightmare terror which he had fought in his boyhood, when he shrieked out against the blinding fear of the advancing wave rushing down on him through the level. In its agony his mind called out a prayer, as men do spontaneously when death is on them.

"God! Not this time. . . or not at least like this. Don't drown me like a rat; if I do have to die, let me die breathing. God give me strength this once more. Jesus, pity me, Thy strength this once. God, help me!"

His mind cried out the demand even as his muscles knotted and bulged as he put forth every mite of strength in his powerful body. He heaved upwards, his hands, his shoulders against the side of the wagon, his back distributing the weight and passing it down to loins and legs. It seemed in his struggle as though he were back down the bal, as though he were underground with all the weight of fathoms of rock holding him down in the released torrent of the dreaded house of water. He was like Atlas supporting the whole world, but drowning in all the seas beneath it.

"A tinner's never broke till his neck's broke!"

The words leapt through his brain as though they had been shouted in his ear. All his strength went into that one terrific thrust, one great heave upwards, knowing well it was his last act in life if he failed. Something above him moved, it lifted, yielding slowly and grudgingly to his desperation. The next instant and his head was above water, only just but he could draw a breath; and never had a breath drawn more sweetly than that one, full of muddy reek as it was. He struggled against the full weight of the big wagon, against the slipping soft foundation offered by the mud, pressed through the ooze to something harder beneath and strained upwards again. He knew his strength was limited at this tremendous output, knew he had neither the time nor the breath to shout, nor chance to wait until help could come in answer if he did. It was himself alone, with the strength he had been given, could save him.

It was a grim fight, yet once he had drawn that breath he knew he would win. All the strength of his body, all the life in him went into it; he knew he was tearing at the vitals within him, knew by the burning pain that the price was dear enough, though compared with the horror of stifling in mud and water it was cheap at that moment. Slowly, by degrees each measured in spasms of straining agony the wagon lifted; it rose slowly out of the pool, up until it passed the point of greatest resistance and gradually lessened its crushing power, balanced over and settled back on its four wheels. Even with its one side shelving down steeply, it was righted. Joel had done in those few moments what he never would have believed a man alone could do.

Staggering out towards the side of the sloping wagon he flung his arms up and held on to the edge, letting his head fall forward against them. Great gasps and sobs escaped from his open mouth; bloody spittle trickled down to join with dirty water from his hair. All his body had gone limp and weak, a sweat of pain crept out beneath the soaking clothes about his waist, while his heart struggled to beat itself against his bruised ribs. In his mind, even against a blazing consciousness of agony, was a great thankfulness for the strength that had saved him to breathe again.

For what seemed ages he hung there, content to rest and let his body taste the joy of inertia, just to do nothing. He was soaking wet, and in the cold of a December evening, so at length he forced himself to climb out towards the horses and guide them carefully forward until he saw the wagon pulled out safely and into the home yard. He backed it under the cart-shed and led them away to the stable. Not before they were unharnessed and fed, and made comfortable for the night did he leave them, pausing at the door to look back into the warmth within, to smell that tang of hartshorn and hay he loved. He looked about him at the outlines of the familiar buildings, at the sky darkening even over Mount's Bay westwards, at night drifting down on Kenneggy.

As he opened the door and entered the living-room they all stared at him, just as though he was back from the dead. Later they used to say it was as though he were drowned indeed and his ghost had come in through that door, not Joel himself. In the candlelight he looked pale and grey as death, with muddy water still dripping from his head and clothes, and pain struggling with weariness to line his face. In their silence he walked four paces to the table and fell into the chair beside it, slumping across the board. At last he could give way to the agony in his bowels, to the hot swimming pain that seemed to fill his belly. No longer was there any need to fight against it; nothing to do now but rest.

Caroline ran across to bend terrified over him and lift his hand away from his face.

"Joel! Oh, Joel, my poor dear, what have you done?"

With help from Ralph and Chris she got him to his bed; he felt easier lying on his back.

"The wagon turned over on me in the pond; I had to lift it or be drowned. Do 'ee mind the night Mother Buckett said I'd not drown in the pool, Father?"

They had always taken his strength for granted, knowing well that he was stronger than two men, yet at this feat they were astounded. Chris took his hand and gazed down on him, ashamed at the result of his negligence.

"If I'd mended that bit of road when 'ee asked 'twouldn't have happened," he whispered, wretchedly.

Joel pressed his fingers kindly.

"There's always so much to be done, don't blame yourself, Chris boy; 'tisn't possible to do everything. And for that matter if I had not gone with the wagon, or if I'd been on t'other side – a dozen ifs and 'twouldn't have happened. I reck'n it just had to be, and 'twas no one's fault."

Obviously he was a stricken man; from that night he could not gather strength enough to lift himself from his bed. All Caroline's efforts to provide nourishing broths only resulted in distressing vomiting, until she was compelled by the pain he suffered during the attacks to allow him only sips from the spoon, to sit by his side and feed him like a baby.

A day or two later he turned to her without preamble and said, "Will 'ee send one of the boys over to Tremearne and tell John I do want to see him?"

John Trounsen came over that evening and sat with Joel in the light of the candle Caroline had left when she showed him in.

"I'm vexed indeed to see you bad like this, Joel. Keep up heart, and you'll be 'bout with us again in no time at all."

He shook his head, lying there on the pillow.

"Maybe, but there's something gone in my belly, and that's not like a bone or a rib. A man can mend a leg, even though it makes him lame, but there's no mending of broken vitals."

"I do hope 'tis only just bruising and 'twill heal. Don't give up hope, for there's none can help a man as much as hisself, just setting on coming right."

In the silence of the room, each remained with his own thoughts for a while. Joel was the first to speak again, going suddenly back to their words together that day years ago, out where he was carting over the fields.

" 'Bout Caroline; do 'ee still love her, John? You did tell me once she was more'n the world to 'ee."

Trounsen looked at his sick friend, met the eyes that shone like black coals in the pallor of his face, so soon fallen away to thinness and lined with suffering. He saw in them that Joel was planning for a future he was unlikely to share. It was a straight question asked in that brief time when it seems remaining life is too short to hide the heart from one another.

"I do love her still."

"I'm glad of that," Joel answered, and was silent again for a while.

"If I go, then will 'ee take care of her? Not for my sake, but for her own. We've have been happy, she and I, and I'd like to know she'll be happy again. Will 'ee, John?"

"I'll do all I can, that I do promise 'ee, if 'twill ease your mind. But you'll not go, my son; there's many a good day waiting for 'ee yet."

The next days brought no change for the better; although the pain had gone he seemed to be far weaker.

"Caroline, I do thank 'ee for all your love for me; it has always been a wonderful sweet thing."

She dropped on her knees beside his bed and laid her cheek against his.

"Joel, why do you talk as though 'twas all over and past? God willing, and over a while you'll be about again."

He smiled at her and kissed her cheek.

"Tell a prayer for me, Caroline my darling."

She stroked his hair, kissed his forehead, and his mouth.

"All my life, day and night is just one prayer for you, Joel."

Tears were running down her cheeks and fell on the pillow beside him; she was ashamed to have him watch how she suffered to see him brought so low, and rose up, trying to smile through the grief blinding her eyes.

"Caroline, would 'ee tell Father I do want him with me for a while?"

"Yes, and I'll go to make something that'll give 'ee more strength."

She bent and kissed him again, and went from the room, his eyes following her lovingly until she had passed out of his sight. His hand dropped over his mouth and was pressed there for a moment, as though to keep back a cry that would have recalled her. A tear trembled on his eyelid, then ran down alone until it was wiped away by turning his face from the door.

Old Richard came quietly to his son's bedside and sat near him. He turned up his face as he heard his father breathing, smiled at the anxiety in his eyes. In silence they remained together; there was no need for either to speak to tell the other all in his heart.

Presently Joel half-turned his head, looked up towards his father and dropped back to hide his face in the pillow.

" 'Tis hard on me, Father!"

The words trembled, husky in his throat. The old man leaned across and laid a hand on his shoulder.

" 'Es, my son, 'tis very hard."

He wondered whether Joel had heard, he lay so still; gradually he began to realise why he made no move.

Richard looked at his son in dazed unbelief for a little while. The room was so quiet, with the natural sounds of the house and the outside world drifting in, the dull thudding of the stamps coming downwind from Wheal Vor, the creak and rattle of the whims and the crash of empty barrels, as though everything was the same as it had always been. And now it had no right to be, with Joel dead. Why did Elizabeth still talk to Caroline in the kitchen? Why was the pump engine still beating its slow rhythm when his heart was so still? He touched down the eyelids with his finger-tips, closing them for ever; he wandered out of the room and downstairs, stood in front of the women, wondering what to say now that there was nothing left to say.

"He's a-gone. It doesn't seem. . . quite right. . . somehow."

Caroline's hands clasped her breasts, she stared frightened at the old man and ran from the room, as though to make sure. Elizabeth, tied to her couch by her useless leg, dropped her head in her hands and wept quietly. He sat down in his chair by the fire, elbows on his knees; his hands stretched out to the warmth, he watched the flames through his spread fingers.

Very soon Caroline returned to the room and sank into a chair by the table.

"What did he say, Father?"

"He looked up at me and said, ' 'Tis hard on me, Father.' I thought he meant 'twas a bitter thing to be stricken so and I said, ' 'Es, my son, 'tis very hard.' "

231

She came over to him and put her arm across his shoulder, comforting him in order to help her own sorrow by feeling his.

"He likely meant the end was close on him. Joel was never one to complain," she said proudly.

Pensively the old man moved his fingers, counting on them against the fire. It was Tuesday, fourteenth of December, 1841, and Joel would be thirty-eight years old.

They buried him that Friday. It was a fortnight after he had righted the wagon, and now it stood again outside the door of Kenneggy bathed in the weak sunshine of the December afternoon, the full team of four stretching ahead of each other towards the lane. Even after washing down and sweeping clean inside it looked worn and old; now all at once the blue paint seemed weathered and powdery, and the red only a faint shadow of its former gaiety. The great horses had black ribbon plaited in their tails and black rosettes over their blinkers; Caroline and Elizabeth had seen to the making of these, because they knew Joel had loved to see the team well turned out. Friends and neighbours had gathered in the long room, talking in low tones just as though they were already in church; offering condolence and thinking what a very comely widow Caroline made, in her new black dress and short veil half hiding her curls, making them look fairer and her skin whiter than before.

A silence came over them as shuffling feet announced the bearers' approach with the coffin on their shoulders. Ralph and his brother-in-law, John Patten of Trevenner, at his feet, Chris and another tinner from Wheal Speed in the middle, with Charles and John Trounsen at his shoulders, they carried him from his home. For a moment they paused in the doorway of the living-room where Elizabeth was on her couch, with Salome and little Bessie standing beside her, and she looked straight towards them, her face proud and calm; at his passing she was determined to keep her sorrow to herself until all the folk had left. They moved on out through the doorway towards the wagon, and there others from the farm and mine helped lift and lay him on the trestles ready waiting, so that he could pass on this, his last ride, high up in view of the country around. Lashings were made fast to the handles to prevent shifting; the brothers and Trounsen took their places at the horses' heads. At a word from Ralph to the leader the traces jerked taut and the great wagon started off, out through the farm gate, past the pool and away up the hill.

As the last of the mourners filed out of the room, Elizabeth, Salome and the little girl were left alone with the sound of the wheels dying away from up the lane reaching them through the open door. While it could still be heard neither of the women moved; only when all was quiet outside did Salome cross the room and close the door. The action had a finality about it, a chapter in the family life had ended, and feeling this she leaned back against it, looking about her at the familiar room. She saw Elizabeth staring at something just beside her, behind the door, and turning her head she saw her cheek was almost touching the old jacket he had used to slip on when going out to hay down the cattle for the night; just where he had hooked it up as he had pulled it off, and no one had thought to remove it. Its emptiness struck at her heart and released the tears that had long been waiting to fall; she ran over and clasped her mother, and together they faced the full realisation that Joel had passed for ever from Kenneggy.

Old Richard and Caroline, with William and Alfred beside them, headed the procession immediately behind the wagon, for both had insisted that they would walk behind him on his way to Breage Churchtown. Along the turnpike thoughts ran of their own on the many times they had gone that way before, and of the time, yet unknown to them, when they would ride over it on the last journey. The wheels rolled on under their light load, just as before they had carried Betsy and Jimmy Polglaze, each in their turn, and the natural thought in the old man's mind was that next time he must be the one to ride.

"I reck'n I'll be riding next time we take the turnpike, Caroline."

"The Lord knows, Father, and 'tis a good thing we don't. Most of us go out of turn it do seem."

"I followed Betsy, and I followed Jimmy; but I never reck'ned on following Joel. 'Tis a miserable road."

For a little while they walked in silence, until she took up the talk just where he had left it.

"Let's think of all the happy times we have come over it. There was Salome's wedding, and our own; it seemed a grand road to me that day, bowling along towards Marazion with Joel beside me. And the day I came back to Kenneggy, how excited I was; and yet a good bit frightened too, lest Joel should scold me."

"I don't believe he did ever scold 'ee, Caroline."

"He never did, and that's the truth," she answered, looking firmly ahead.

"We've both been very lucky, my dear."

Arriving at Breage Church, the horses were tied up and the coffin taken again on the bearers' shoulders, carried into the church and laid at the chancel steps, where Curate John Perry read the first part of the Burial Service. Once more and for the last time, they lifted him shoulder high and bore him out to the grave already prepared on the west side of the churchyard, beside the pathway.

"Man that is born of woman hath but a short time to live," read the Parson. "He cometh up, and is cut down like a flower; he fleeth as it were a shadow. . . "

And they lowered him down into the earth, high up there on the hill in Breage churchyard, where he could lie sleeping with his face towards Kenneggy, and sprinkled over him the soil he was never to tread again.

" . . .Blessed are the dead which die in the Lord. . . for they rest from their labours."

Caroline moved away from the graveside. That was the hardest moment of it all, to leave him down there, so far down in the cold dark earth, and to know that as soon as she had gone they would throw back the soil on him, beating heavily on the wood above his dear dead face.

"I can't go back," she sobbed. "I can't go back to Kenneggy without him."

Someone put an arm around her and led her away.

"You don't have to, my darling. 'Tis all arranged, thee'st to come back to Tremearne with your aunt and me," said the comforting, solid voice of her Uncle Drenocoe.

The December sunset shone over Mount's Bay to where Joel slept, lulled by the friendly sound of the stamps coming up from the valley. Today they too are silent, Wheal Vor is dead and Wheal Speed forgotten; roofless engine-houses watch over their deserted shafts. And he sleeps on, dreaming perhaps of Caroline and Kenneggy, and of prosperity returning to the land he loved.